"We need to ta...

Abby tried to push the d... ...ck. "Go away!" She didn't qu... ...ow now it happened but he was soon striding through the house, shrinking it just by his presence. Abby followed him toward the sitting area near the fireplace, her thoughts whirling. *What can he want?*

Josh walked to the hearth then turned, propping his elbow indolently on the beautiful mantel her brother had carved. "So this is where you chose to raise my son."

"I haven't made a free choice since the night you took my virginity," Abby spat back.

Josh raised his left eyebrow. "If my memory serves, you did more than your fair share of unbuttoning."

Abby flew at him. Her fists balled, she struck wildly. Then in a heartbeat she found herself imprisoned against the hard wall of his chest.

"Stop it!" he cried.

Abby stared up at him. His eyes were like blue flames, his lips sealed in a straight line. *He still smells the same,* some stupid sentimental part of her brain remembered. His eyes changed as they held hers prisoner. His gaze was still hot and blazing, but desire replaced anger. His lips came closer to hers and Abby panicked. She wouldn't survive his kiss whole.

* * *

Questions of Honor
Harlequin® Historical #937—March 2009

KATE WELSH

QUESTIONS OF HONOR

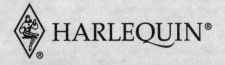

HARLEQUIN®

TORONTO • NEW YORK • LONDON
AMSTERDAM • PARIS • SYDNEY • HAMBURG
STOCKHOLM • ATHENS • TOKYO • MILAN • MADRID
PRAGUE • WARSAW • BUDAPEST • AUCKLAND

Recycling programs for this product may not exist in your area.

ISBN-13: 978-0-373-29537-1
ISBN-10:   0-373-29537-5

QUESTIONS OF HONOR

Copyright © 2009 by Kate Welsh

www.eHarlequin.com

Printed in U.S.A.

Chapter One

Wheatonburg, Pennsylvania
November—1875

Snow fell, drifting silently over Wheatonburg. Through the thickening curtain of white, Abaigeal Sullivan peered out the front window of the company store, then turned away from the lovely, flawless illusion. The soot and coal dust still tarnished everything beneath the white powder. With a heart heavy from too many burdens, she turned back to her cleaning.

Minutes later the clock chimed four. "I imagine that's it for you today, Mrs. Sullivan," Mr. Prescott said.

Abby gritted her teeth at his disdainful tone. He was the manager of the company store and as overbearing a taskmaster with her as the fire bosses were with the miners. He resented her leaving on the last stroke of four, but felt no qualm docking her an entire hour's pay if the same clock had stopped chiming twelve when she arrived.

"I don't see Daniel, so I'd better hurry along," she replied as cheerfully as she could manage.

Mr. Prescott looked up at her and their eyes met over his spectacles. "Have you decided about that dimity? You have very little on credit. You certainly need a new dress."

Abby looked down at her skirt. She could afford the lovely material, but every penny she spent kept her and Daniel in Wheatonburg longer. A new dress wasn't worth it. "I've decided not. I have three dresses. A body hardly needs more than that. Good day to you," she said, tossing her cape about her shoulders as she closed the door behind herself.

She stomped down the steps. Oh, wasn't he being sweet today after making her work on the Lord's day! And him, trying to tempt her from her goal after accusing her son of stealing. Without a drop of proof!

Abby took a deep breath and looked around, hoping the scene before her would bring her calm. Wheatonburg did look beautiful during a snowfall. Today no one would guess there was anything insidious here. Not the abject poverty of the possession houses. Not the underlying fear of armed guards at the mines or Harlan Wheaton's reason for putting them there.

At the town cemetery, Abby glanced toward the fresh graves. The deepening mantle of white hid the mud covering the resting place of the two miners who'd been killed for refusing to do the bidding of the AMU.

American Miners United had been born with the hope of forcing mining safety changes. It had sounded so promising but had quickly been co-opted by a group of thugs call Workmen who now held the whole coal region hostage—owners and miners alike.

She walked on and soon climbed the steps to the train station's boardwalk. In the distance, she heard a train whistle. She looked inside the station house and saw the stationmaster, Mr. Dodd, at his seat behind his postal counter. "I haven't heard from Amber in weeks. Is there any mail?"

Charles Dodd shook his head. "No, but I expect you'll hear from my niece soon."

"Good. I worry about her. She hasn't been the same since losing her Joseph. Have you seen your pint-sized shadow?" Abby asked, surprised not to see her son with Mr. Dodd.

"End of the platform. Likes to be the first to see it."

As the stationmaster, Mr. Dodd saw a lot of Daniel. Her son had railroading dreams and that was fine with her, but recently the railroad had become another favorite target of the AMU. "I worry about him, too, with all the trouble," Abby confided. She shook her head sadly.

Mr. Dodd looked up, caution in his eyes. "The train isn't carrying anything the AMU would care about. Try not to worry, I keep an eye out for the boy." He hesitated then asked, "You aren't worried they might try using him to get at Wheaton, are you?"

"Harlan? Everyone knows he doesn't give a hoot in Hades about Daniel. All Harlan Wheaton cares about is his coal. It wouldn't gain anyone a thing to hurt Daniel. My worry is he'll be too close if they blow a train to kingdom come now that the owners refused to pay protection money. I do thank you for all the time you take for Daniel."

"Daniel's no trouble at all." He chuckled. "The little scamp keeps me company."

Daniel was a little scamp indeed. "He isn't a nuisance, then?"

"You've done a good job with him, Abby. He's a good boy with admirable hopes and dreams."

Abby smiled. "All he talks of is going west and getting involved in railroading out there."

Mr. Dodd wiped his spectacles. "I could help him if you stay in the east."

"By summer I'll have a nice nest egg saved from my

cleaning and my brothers will have paid off our account to Wheaton Mining. We'll be headin' west. Daniel'll be much better off."

Mr. Dodd grimaced. "Neither of you will have to put up with snide remarks anymore."

"I don't let them bother me," Abby lied. She hated pity almost as much as nasty comments. "But my son will never live down the circumstances of his birth here. Now I'll just take myself along and find my railroading son. Perhaps I'll be one of the first to see the train today, too. Good day to you," she said, sketching a sassy curtsy.

Abby stepped onto the platform as the train whistle sounded again, closer, louder. She could even hear the chugging of the steam engine. "Daniel!" Abby called when she didn't see him on the platform.

Daniel popped up from behind a crate and ran to her. "Come watch the train come in, Ma!" He grabbed her hand, tugged her along the platform, and around the corner of the station house. "Here she comes!" Daniel shouted, pointing down the tracks as the clicking wheels and the puffing engine drew closer.

"I guess you'll want to stay till it pulls out, as well?" Abby shouted over the din.

"Oh, Ma, could I?" Daniel's eyes were bright. She loved seeing him like this. Happy and carefree. Not shadowed by the taunts of unkind children or the whispered condemnations of disdainful adults.

"If you promise to sweep after dinner."

Daniel shouted joyfully and ran off back down the platform. As Abby rounded the corner again, she saw he'd met up with Mr. Dodd. They consulted with each other then Daniel turned, pointing toward her. Abby waved and nodded her agreement to remaining behind, then she remembered her canvas shopping bag. Daniel and Mr. Dodd were gone when she came back around the corner again.

Abby heard a high-pitched feminine giggle as a sandy-haired man jumped off a passenger car, then swung a young woman off the stairs to the platform. They laughed as another man followed sedately. Judging from their expensive clothes, the three were guests of Harlan Wheaton. Four rough-looking men disembarked next. Though they stood a distance away, they still seemed to be a part of the wealthy group.

The younger man turned toward her and Abby's head swam. Her heart thundered as she reached out to steady herself. He'd grown taller and broader but there stood Joshua Wheaton.

Joshua.

He looked around, then turned back to the blond woman, who took a step toward him and put her hand on his forearm. Abby felt as if a knife had thrust through her chest. Then the young woman whispered in his ear and twisted the knife.

Abby wrapped her arms around her middle and gasped for breath. She didn't know what she should do. Run? Cry? Fly at him with her fists and demand to know why he'd abandoned her and how he could have ignored her last and final plea written on the day she delivered their son?

How could you condemn our son to a life of scorn?

She stepped back behind the cover of the stacked crates. She'd make him explain. But first, she had to get herself under control. First, she had to come to grips with a truth of her own. Why, after all Joshua Wheaton had done to her, after all the pain he'd caused her and their son, did it still hurt so much to see him come home with another woman on his arm?

"Surely your father sent a carriage, Joshua," Franklin Gowery said, his displeasure at being stranded evident on his face.

Joshua shrugged. "I doubt it. I was unsure when I'd arrive."

I wasn't sure I wouldn't get right back on the train. I still might.

"He knew. Why do you think we took the morning train?" Helena replied.

Joshua bristled. Had meeting Helena Conwell and her guardian been some sort of planned ruse? "I was under the impression our meeting was happenstance. It was, wasn't it?" Joshua demanded.

Gowery shot Helena a black look. "Of course it was. Isn't that right, Helena?"

Helena laid her hand on Joshua's sleeve but didn't look him in the eye. "Yes, Uncle Franklin."

Joshua let his mind wander. The town looked the same. Only *he* had changed. Emotions he couldn't analyze raced through him, making his heart lurch painfully. Memories of Abby rushed at him. *Why, Abby?* his heart cried. *How could you forget us? How could you marry Sullivan?*

Taking a deep breath, Joshua tried to relax, remembering how he'd hoped his anxiety would be lessened by arriving with a pretty young woman on his arm. He forced a smile just before Helena stepped away.

"He could have at least sent a carriage for us. He knew *we'd* be on this train," Helena groused.

"It must have slipped his mind. Apparently he hasn't been well since his injury. I'll find someone to send up to the house."

Joshua saw a boy dancing after Mr. Dodd. "Son, how would you like to earn a penny?" he shouted.

The boy turned, his blue eyes bright and intelligent. "Sure, mister, as long as it's not something against the law. My ma'd skin me alive if I got into trouble."

"Maybe you ought to head on home," Mr. Dodd interrupted.

Joshua chuckled. "I just want him to go up to Wheaton Manor and tell someone to send the carriage, Mr. Dodd."

The boy grew visibly tense, his eyes shifting to the station-master then back. "Make it a nickel," the boy demanded.

Josh arched an eyebrow. "A nickel? That's rather steep."

"Won't go *there* for no penny."

"It can't be that bad going up to the manor."

The boy's face was set. "For most folks, maybe. A nickel or walk, mister."

"Two cents," Josh offered

"Four."

"Three and that's my final offer."

"Who do I say is waitin'?" the boy wanted to know.

"Say Mr. Gowery and his ward are here and Mr. Joshua Wheaton and all his worldly goods are here, as well, so they'll need to send a wagon along, too."

The boy's face hardened. "Is that you?" he asked, his cupid's bow lip curling at the corner.

Joshua had grown unused to the hatred the name *Wheaton* evoked here. "Yes, but I'm not my father, son, and things will change now that I'm back."

"I'm *not* your son. I'll never be your son," the boy snarled, then pivoted and ran away.

Joshua stood staring after the retreating figure, wondering what he'd said and what it was about the boy that seemed so familiar. Probably the son of a boyhood friend and that stung all the more.

"Little beast!" Helena gasped.

"The boy has his reasons," Dodd grumbled and after shooting Joshua a sharp look, he turned and shuffled toward the station-house door.

Franklin Gowery spoke into the silence left by Dodd's remark. "These children grow up fast and hard, my dear. In a way, they're more dangerous than wild animals. They appear human till they turn on you."

Joshua turned away from the sight of the fleeing boy. His gaze fell on Helena. Her eyes seemed to blaze with fire as she stared at her guardian. Perhaps he'd found a kindred spirit. "It's hardly necessary to teach social niceties to children doomed to poverty if they manage to live into adulthood."

Gowery shook his head. "Still a dreamer, are you? I'd have thought working in Wales would have cured your idealism."

"I worked for a company more progressive than even the strict mining regulations Great Britain has adopted. We made a handsome profit while managing to treat the miners like human beings with hopes and dreams."

Helena stepped toward Joshua and smiled up at him. "That sounds promising. You must tell me more of your reform ideas."

The clatter and jingle of harnessed horses and wagons distracted him. "Ah. We don't need a messenger after all," he told his companions. "If you'll both excuse me, that looks like Henry."

Joshua moved toward the wagon hoping it was his father's retainer. As he walked down the steps, he saw a flash of color near the side of the station and froze. There, scurrying along, her auburn hair radiant against the backdrop of white, was Abby. His Abby. Who belonged to another. Who'd married a few short months after he'd left for Germany. He wondered what she'd done with the travel money he'd sent so she could join him. Probably used it to set up a home with a man Josh despised. Sorrow for all he'd lost burned in his chest.

How would he face her?

How would he live in the same town with her and Liam Sullivan?

* * *

Abby observed her family that night as she stitched a patch on the knee of Daniel's pants. Her oldest brother, Brendan, his expression grim, sat across the room playing dominoes with Daniel. Thomas, her younger brother, sat carving a delicate bird. Her father, Michael, watched them all like the benevolent patriarch he was.

Her eyes drifted back to Daniel. When he'd come in late for dinner, she'd known he'd been crying. He knew his father was in town. She was sure he did. He'd been so solicitous of her since coming home, despite his own pain, it made her heart ache even more.

"Daniel, it's past your bedtime," she said. "Come give us a kiss and run on up. I'll be up soon to tuck you in."

Daniel's face went rigid. "You work too hard. You should rest. Uncle Thomas can come up, can't you, Uncle Tom?"

"Daniel Sullivan! As if Thomas has a life of leisure!"

Thomas stood without hesitation. "No bother at all. Can't think of anyone I'd rather spend my time with." Thomas swung Daniel onto his shoulders, his jade-colored eyes soft with an innate kindness that was so much part of his gentle nature. Abby smiled, then let her head fall back against the rocker. She closed her eyes against a rush of tears. She couldn't ask for better fathers for her son than her brothers.

Except for Joshua, taunted a traitorous voice inside her. Then a vision of his face drifted before her mind's eye. At fifteen her mother had called him a golden boy. But then manhood had beckoned and his jaw squared and his shoulders broadened. His hair went from the color of corn silk to a rich tawny gold. That same golden color had spread across his chest and his playful teasing gave way to seductive glances. Friendly shoves turned into stolen kisses. Yet two things had never changed—his sky-blue eyes or her love for him.

Her father's voice rescued Abby from her foolish trip into the past. "What did you tell Danny, Abaigeal?"

"Tell him?" Abby opened her eyes and glanced toward her father, knowing he wouldn't let the night go by without settling his household properly.

He sat in his chair by the fire, the flames reflecting in the white that liberally threaded his once ink-black hair, a blanket draped across his left leg and what was left of his right. He had arthritis in his shoulders and his hands. It made getting around on crutches painful now, so he rarely went out anymore. But make no mistake, one look into his intelligent, deep-green eyes and it was plain nothing, but nothing, got past Michael Kane. "About Joshua's return," he said at last.

"Nothing. I'm glad now I never lied to him. You were right, Da. If I'd told him anything but that Joshua just hadn't come back for us, he'd know I lied."

Brendan spoke up, then, worry stamped on his handsome face. "I think you should leave and fast. He's returned with a woman. Suppose they marry? Suppose they decide to take Danny? You'd not have a leg to stand on."

She couldn't deny the pain just the thought of Joshua married caused, but her stomach flipped sickly at the idea of losing her son.

"Is there a weddin' in the offing?" Michael asked, rescuing Abby from the need to comment.

"I don't want to talk about weddings," Brendan snapped. "It's the boy I'm thinkin' of."

She forced herself to think logically. "Joshua has never even acknowledged Daniel's existence. Why would he want him now?"

"Because Danny is one hell of a boy. What man wouldn't want to claim him?" Brendan asked, his green eyes intent and sparkling like emeralds and his black hair gleaming in the fire's light.

"Shake your head—rocks or marbles?" Michael scoffed. "You're not thinkin' straight, boyo. Wheaton didn't want his son ten years ago and he's not going to be wantin' the boy now. If he marries this woman he's brought home with him, he'll be wantin' her and her babes."

"Da's right, but perhaps I shouldn't be taking chances," Abby said. "If we can make do till the end of the month, we're free and clear of Harlan Wheaton and his son. I say we take our wagon, all we can pack, and head west. We could make it to Independence even in winter and work odd jobs till spring. Da could stay with Daniel during the day while we're at work. What say? Let's be shut of this place once and for all. We won't be gettin' the start we wanted, but at least we'll be free."

Brendan shook his head. "Lord knows I'd love to, but we need more supplies and money to get even that far. You've done a good job saving and putting up staples, but we aren't ready. We can't do it yet, Abby. But you two could. Thomas has socked away enough money for you and Daniel to go by train. It just isn't enough for all of us."

Abby felt tears burn at the back of her eyes and throat. She pressed her lips and nodded. "You're right. Foolish talk from a desperate woman. But I can't go alone. It would be going from frying pan to fire. Without the respectability of traveling with my family, I'd be but a poor widow at the mercy of men who would think I'm no better than I have to be. I'll have to wait even though the talk here will be worse now." She sighed, then tried to smile. "Isn't this just like my luck. I'd nearly earned the right to hold my head up 'round here again."

"You've always had that right, Abby girl." Her father's eyes narrowed. "It's that son of Satan who hasn't. He's the one who abandoned you. You did nothing many a young girl hasn't done since Eve. You loved the wrong man too soon. 'Twas a sin to be sure, but it wasn't the crime small-minded folks make of it. Now, that said, I'll be takin' meself off to bed."

Nearly overcome, Abby jumped up and hugged her father. "Thank you, Da."

"Don't be thankin' me. It should have been said long ago, and I should have protected you from it ever needing to be said. I failed you." He sighed tiredly, and patted her cheek. "Now not another word."

Once their father was out of hearing range Brendan looked up from his reading. "I wish you'd go alone, or I at least wish we could protect you, but we can't."

"We should all go. We don't owe much to Harlan now," Abby pleaded. "We could do it! We could all just leave."

"Da needs a chair. We all know he does. Thomas could build one but even the parts would be costly and set us back further from leavin'."

Abby stuffed her mending in the bag hanging from the arm of her rocker. "Da was hurt in Wheaton's mine and it's him that'll provide a chair if I have to camp on his doorstep to get it."

"What about Joshua?"

Swamped suddenly by roiling doubt, Abby stiffened her spine. She would not be cowled by the likes of Joshua Wheaton. "He can step over me same as anyone else, including his guests. Let him explain who I am."

"Oh, sister, that won't be botherin' the likes of Helena Conwell. She's sniffin' after a man her guardian will approve. No matter what she'd be sayin', that's all that could matter to the likes of her. Comfort is all she's ever known. How could it be any different?"

"So you think they're to wed?" Abby asked, hating herself for caring what Joshua did with his life, and wondering why Brendan was suddenly more melancholy than angry.

"Luther Dancy says so but it's not official."

Abby cursed the surge of joy her brother's words set to blooming in her heart. *It isn't too late.*

"'Tis ten years too late!" Abby hissed, then felt her face and neck flame when she realized she'd spoken the words aloud.

Fortunately, Brendan put his own thoughts to her words. "True. Had another girl been in the picture back then, none of us would have let him within a mile of you. We should have protected you then. He fooled all of us. Ma, as well. To think I called him friend. I hope he's bright enough to stay out of my way, or we may be run out of town rather than be leavin' on our own." Brendan sighed. "I best turn in. Don't you be stayin' up too late at your mendin'."

Abby stared after Brendan. He'd championed Joshua the longest, keeping her hope alive until after Daniel's birth. He'd been the one to encourage that last shameless letter she'd written. Brendan had just grown quiet about the subject when no answer came from Germany. In fact, he'd never spoken a word against his former friend until tonight, and now he was filled with anger and threats. She wondered why the change but shrugged off the thought. Perhaps as with her, Joshua's return had opened the wounds of betrayal.

Chapter Two

Joshua stopped outside his father's study. When they'd arrived Harlan had been sleeping, so Josh had decided to unpack. When he'd seen his room redone in an adult—if not an ostentatious—decorating style, he'd let himself hope his father saw him as a man now. But when Henry brought word that Harlan wanted to see him, old feelings brought doubt. He wondered if he'd ever truly be his own man in Wheatonburg. Here he felt like a rich man's puppet. His father's puppet.

He forced himself to remember who he was—who he'd become. He was one of the world's most sought-after mining engineers. He'd answered to no one for years, and had a reputation for being an independent thinker. Straightening to his full six foot one inches of height, Josh opened the study door.

"Son. Come in. Come in," Harlan called.

Joshua braced himself for the sight of his once robust father confined to a wheelchair. But he wasn't prepared for how old the man looked after ten years. His blunt Germanic features were now rounded with excess weight. His once muscular chest seemed to have caved in, the rubble falling in an enormous bulge on his lap.

Forcing himself forward, Josh wanted to allow his father as much of his dignity as possible regardless of the bad blood between them. He advanced steadily and shook Harlan's hand.

"It's good to have you home, son," Harlan said. His voice wobbled a bit. It gave Josh hope that the old man really was glad to have him back and willing to accept him as he was.

"It's good to be home," Josh answered, though he qualified it in his mind as feeling only a bit better than he'd expected.

"Sit down, Joshua. I asked Franklin to sit in on this meeting for several reasons. First, I thought there should be a witness." Harlan reached beside him, and picked up a set of keys and a piece of paper. He handed each to Joshua in turn. "Here is the combination to the safe, and these are the keys to this office and all the buildings owned by Wheaton Coal. As I agreed, you're free to run the mines as you see fit. It's what I've always wanted. A family business. There are only two of us, but I'm sure there'll be more soon."

"There is no woman in my life. I thought I'd made that clear," Joshua countered. "I'm not averse to marriage, as I told you. But I haven't met anyone in recent years I'd want to spend the rest of my life with."

"You have to forget what's past," Harlan groused, shifting restlessly in his chair. "You can't go back. There's too much water gone over that dam. Which brings me to the second reason I asked Franklin to be here. We'd…Franklin and I… uh…"

Gowery chuckled. "What your father is trying so carefully to say is he and I would like you and Helena to make a match of it. As soon as possible."

Joshua blinked. "Pardon me?"

"I want you to marry my ward."

"Franklin, don't take this as an insult, but, no. I scarcely know her."

"You must admit she's a lovely young woman."

From the implacable expression on his father's face, Joshua knew there would be no diplomatic way to extricate himself from this situation. "Be that as it may, I don't want to marry her."

Gowery nodded. His patronizing expression irritated Joshua even before he spoke. "I am given to understand that there was once a girl in your life. Are you still in love with her?"

Joshua sucked a breath through gritted teeth. This came too closely on the heels of that heart-wrenching glimpse of Abby in town. "She's out of my reach, Franklin, not that it's any of your affair. My father had no right to speak of my private business."

"Helena also loved unwisely. Her husband will need to overlook her error, however, if you take my meaning. She isn't in the family way, fortunately. You needn't worry about that. The man is completely unsuitable and as Helena is all alone in the world, I am obligated to see to her future. We've never been close but her father was a friend. You should know Helena is heiress to a considerable fortune, which will be turned over to you when you two marry."

"My father should have warned you, Franklin. I can't be bought." Joshua's comment snapped like a whip through the room. He glanced sharply at Harlan then added, "Or threatened. He tried both ten years ago and hasn't seen me since."

Gowery laughed. "I would hardly call being made a millionaire for marrying a lovely young woman a threat. Nor is it a bribe. I like you, Joshua. You're from a good, solid family and I know my friend's daughter would be well taken care of as your wife. She has to marry. Why not take advantage of a windfall?"

"I should think you'd want more for the daughter of a friend than to be considered a windfall. Love for instance?"

"Love is a much lauded but stupid emotion. It leads people to foolishness, desperation and heartache. You've learned that. Helena will accept it, as well. What Harry Conwell wanted for his daughter is the kind of alliance I have with my wife and your father had with your mother. Under the terms of Harry's will, I must approve of the man or she doesn't inherit."

Joshua suppressed a shudder, remembering his parents' cold union, and the poor German widow forced into an illicit alliance to fill the private needs his father's wife refused to deal with. Josh would die alone before he'd live the way they had. "I suggest you look elsewhere."

"At least consider it?" Gowery asked. "Squire Helena about for a day or two. Get to know her. There is another man I'm considering who is from just as good a family. I'll settle on him if you refuse even though Helena seems to despise him."

Poor Helena. Maybe it wouldn't hurt to agree to spend time with her. He could give her a reprieve for a little while. She was a pleasant person and certainly not hard on the eyes. Harlan's chair creaked, drawing Joshua's attention. He sat back in his own chair and looked toward his father again. "You've been surprisingly quiet, Father."

"I think you would be wise to think about Franklin's offer. He's only trying to do his duty by the girl and it isn't as if arranged marriages among people of our class are unusual. Don't turn it down out of hand just because I've endorsed the girl."

Joshua smiled. "That would be rather childish. If I remember from our recent communications, we've decided I'm a man now. I'll run the company and escort who I wish and, as it so happens, it suits my purposes to be Helena's escort while she's here. If we decide to pursue a relationship, it will be because *we* choose to for personal reasons—not financial gain or because you two have meddled in our lives. Is that clear?"

Both men nodded, but considering their personalities, Josh was sure it was only a temporary capitulation. "Pressure either of us and even this much of a concession is at an end," he added.

By the time dinner was over, however, Josh knew he couldn't marry Helena. She clearly hated him for some unknown reason. After thinking it through, he went downstairs to tell Harlan of his decision but got a nasty earful instead. What he overheard chilled him and placed him in the most difficult position he'd ever been in.

It seemed his father had left out something rather important when he turned the company over to Josh—like having hired Pinkerton agents to act as spies within the mining community. Josh understood both Gowery's and his father's desire to eliminate the threat from the thugs who'd taken over the failed American Miners United union. His father had been shot by one of them, after all. Josh's anger initially came from being left in the dark but then he heard something that made his blood boil.

"I want evidence gathered on one man specifically, Brendan Kane," Josh heard Gowery say.

"Is this because he seduced Helena then discarded her?" a voice unknown to Josh asked.

"He's miles below her in station. He had no right to even talk to her let alone have his way with her. I want him to swing—if not for that then for Harry Conwell's murder," Gowery demanded.

"We have no proof that Helena's father was even killed by

a miner let alone her lover," the undercover Pinkerton agent said. The man's British accent seemed to be tinged with a touch of Irish. "I was there," he went on. "I held Conwell as he died."

Newspaper accounts of Harry Conwell's murder had placed both Gowery and Jamie Reynolds, the Earl of Adair, at the scene. Did that mean that for some reason an earl was working undercover for the Pinkertons? Joshua had to agree with the man's assessment of Helena's father's death. Josh was sure Brendan Kane was innocent of everything except seducing Helena.

Josh wished he could simply warn Brendan but that might not be wise. He was trapped, Josh thought as he made his way to his room upstairs. If he didn't agree to the marriage, Gowery would just take Helena and leave town.

He had to talk to her.

Since Josh rarely put off unpleasant tasks, he went immediately to her room and tapped on the door.

"Joshua?" she whispered after cracking the door open.

"I need to talk to you. I know it's late, and that this is irregular, but may I come in?"

Helena's shadowed figure grew rigid. "I don't know what Uncle Franklin told you, but I assure you, I will not allow you to sample the merchandise!"

She started to close the door, but Josh pressed his shoulder against it. "I said *talk*. That's what I meant. Look, I don't want to sound melodramatic but this is a matter of life or death."

Helena considered him, then stepped back and silently motioned him inside. She had a lamp burning low on a table between two chairs at the far end of the room. She walked to one of the chairs and sat, gesturing to the other.

He sat. "I'm sorry to disturb you, but—"

"I was awake." Her tone was flat and preoccupied. "I don't sleep well anymore."

"You're very resentful of me. Why?"

"You're a man," she snapped. "I doubt you have the capacity to understand. What exactly is the plan for tonight? Compromise the little heiress and gain control of her fortune?"

Josh raked a hand through his hair. What if she resented Brendan? "I came here to ask your help," he explained. "You don't want to marry me and I don't want to marry you. My father married my mother for her money. I was merely the second clause in the negotiations. She had little choice, and it seems you don't, either. Am I right?" She nodded. "If I don't marry you, Franklin will go looking for another man for you."

"He has another man all picked out to step in line." Helena laughed quietly but it was a sad sound. "I can't marry the man I love, because he's poor and Uncle Franklin is sure he's after my money. It's perfectly acceptable, though, to hand me over to you or some earl who is probably bankrupt and obsessed with me. There'd be no pretense of love in the marriage on my end, but one of you will have my money as a reward. With him I'd be the Countess Adair. What do you have to offer?"

She'd answered the question of why a man of consequence like an earl would be foolhardy enough to become involved with spying on the AMU. He was trying to find the man who killed the father of the woman he loved. So where did all that leave Helena and Brendan? Poor Helena was closer to a slave than the miners. "Do you still love him and does Brendan Kane return your feelings?"

She looked up in surprise at the mention of Brendan's name and a tear glistened at the corner of her eye. "He loves me so much he won't see me or talk to me. He thinks he's not good enough for me but that isn't true. He's wonderful. And noble. All he worries about is that he can't give me what I've always had. He's bitter about losing me but he's as stubborn as Uncle Franklin. I wanted to run away with him, but he says he won't rob me of my inheritance. How did you find out his name?"

Joshua leaned forward and took her fisted hands in his. "I just got an earful outside my father's room. Franklin wants retribution, Helena, and he's using your earl to get it. Have you ever heard of the American Miners United or the term *Workmen?*"

"Of course, Uncle Franklin says it was members of the AMU who shot your father and killed mine. And they've threatened Uncle Franklin. Workmen are what their members are called."

"Do you think Brendan Kane could be a Workman?"

Fire shot to her eyes. "He'd no more shoot a man in cold blood than he would his own father! And he wouldn't belong to an organization that would!"

He'd needed to know what she thought. She thought Workmen had killed her father. She wouldn't harbor one. "I hadn't thought so but I haven't seen or heard from Brendan since I left here."

Helena's eyes widened. "You know Brendan."

"He was my best friend. Your guardian is trying to frame Brendan as a Workman. They have Pinkerton spies all over Schuylkill County. A man named McParlan is close to getting a membership list in his sector. If they bring the men involved with the AMU to trial, many will hang. Your guardian means to see Brendan's name added to the list."

"I'll warn him," Helena burst out.

Josh shook his head. "No, you can't. Neither can I. He may know men who're in the AMU. They could be his good friends. There's no sense in tempting him to warn a friend. If he did and something happens to one of the Pinkerton agents, and especially the earl, Brendan could be implicated."

Joshua thought of Brendan as he watched emotions and

thoughts race across Helena's face. He didn't like the idea of his friend being in the kind of pain he himself had been in for years. He didn't want him to feel the emptiness that goes with losing love. For long minutes, the only sound in the room came from a clock ticking in the corner.

"According to the terms of your father's will, will you ever be able to marry as you wish?"

"When I'm twenty-one. In three months time, I inherit, married or not. I'd hoped to put him off but Uncle Franklin is determined to choose for me before then. I can't let another man touch—" She stopped and shook her head, a blush staining her pale cheeks. "I won't marry anyone but Brendan."

Joshua stared at the young woman across from him. Helena seemed strong enough to bear up under the strain of a plan forming in his mind. In a way, it would be less pressure than she was currently under.

"What you need is a diversion. What I need is to keep Franklin here in Wheatonburg where I can watch how his trap for the AMU unfolds and so I can make sure Brendan isn't caught in it when it's sprung."

"How do we accomplish that?" she asked, her eyes wide with excitement and dread at the same time.

"By letting everyone think we're considering marriage."

Helena simply stared. "So," she said slowly, "we pretend you're courting me and Uncle Franklin takes me off the auction block."

"Yes, but we have to find a way to keep Franklin here so I can watch him."

Helena shook her head. "He won't leave me here. The last time I was here I met and fell in love with Brendan. He'll want to make sure we stay away from each other. I'm just afraid Brendan will think I've given up. He keeps telling me to, but

I swore not to." Her lips turned up in a sudden mischievous grin. "I suppose it would serve him right for his lack of faith."

Josh found himself grinning, too. "Are we agreed then?"

Helena nodded. "How will I ever be able to thank you?"

"By making plenty of pretty babies with Brendan and naming one after me."

Helena tilted her head and stared at him for several seconds. "You sound as if you'll never have a son of your own. Someday you'll meet the right person."

Josh shook his head. "I don't think so. I met her years ago. She was the daughter of a miner."

"And you lost her?"

"I had better go," Joshua told her, standing abruptly and hastening from the room. He knew it wasn't fair but he couldn't talk about Abby so soon after his first painful glimpse of her.

Chapter Three

Helena grew visibly nervous when the town came into sight the next morning. "How *did* you meet Brendan?" Josh finally asked, hoping to get her to relax.

Helena smiled. "Uncle Franklin brought me here when he had to go away on business. He thought I'd be well chaperoned, but I was only here a couple days when your father was shot. While the house was in turmoil, I had a groom saddle a mount, and I rode into the mountains. I was quite lost, and enjoying every minute of it, when I came upon Brendan fishing."

"And that would have been it for Brendan. You're everything he used to say he wanted in a wife."

Helena looked confused. "But he sneers at my money. He wants a ranch and I could buy one for him but he won't hear of it."

Brendan was clearly the more practical of the two. Which meant he'd changed. Had he changed enough to warn a friend if he learned of the Irish-sounding earl who was undercover for the Pinkertons and hunting his hide?

As they rode through the outskirts of town, Helena said, "It's so dreary. I've wondered why they stay here."

"They were lured here with a promise of a better life. They stay," Josh answered, "because men like Gowery and my father promised to be their saviors but keep them enslaved to debt."

"That angers you, doesn't it? Imagine how terrible it is to be told where to go, who to see, who to love." Helena blinked away a mist of tears.

Joshua felt her hopelessness. The life she described was clearly her own. "Helena, this *will* work. You'll be safe and we'll keep Brendan safe. We just need to resist the temptation to warn him about your earl. The man sounded honest if angry over your relationship with Brendan so I doubt he'll manufacture evidence against him."

She nodded and glanced away toward the company store. "Look. There goes that boy from the station yesterday."

Joshua pulled the carriage to a stop. "Ever been in a company store?" Helena shook her head. "Then you need to see how the miners get enslaved to debt. You'll notice the prices are ten to fifteen percent higher than what you're used to seeing in the stores near Philadelphia. Mining companies pay in script. That forces employees to buy their equipment, explosives and all their staples from their company store. They run up a bill, and then can't leave till it's paid," he explained as he helped her down from the carriage.

Helena looked around town. "You should have just whisked your girl away from all this. Was she very pretty?" she asked as Joshua opened the door to the store.

He followed Helena inside and found himself looking at that long-remembered face. "Beautiful, in fact," Joshua whispered, staring at Abby as she spoke with Mr. Prescott.

She looked just as he remembered...a little thinner perhaps but the years had been more than kind. Her long auburn hair was pulled into a tight bun, but just as in her youth it refused to be tamed. Tiny ringlets had pulled loose to softly frame the delicate high cheekbones of her lovely face. Josh felt his heart seize in his chest. *How can it still hurt so damned much?*

"Are you all right?" Helena whispered.

Josh couldn't tear his gaze away from Abby.

"Oh, that's her, isn't it?" Helena asked. "Your father says she broke your heart by marrying another man."

"My father talks too much," Josh growled. He didn't need reminding that the tormentor of his youth had stolen Abby.

"She *is* beautiful," Helena went on, throwing salt in the still open wound. "Her hair is like fire in the sunlight."

He wasn't ready for this. He took a step backward, but Helena turned into a proverbial pillar of salt holding him in place. Then in a flash she turned into an iron horse, all but dragging him across the room.

"Come along and introduce me," she ordered. "Get this out of the way. You've come back here to live. You can't hide in the manor house."

Joshua cleared his throat when they reached the counter. "It's been a long time, Abby," he managed to say in what he hoped was the neutral tone of a man greeting an old acquaintance.

Abby sucked in a deep, shocked breath. Seeing Joshua the day before hadn't prepared her for the sound of his voice. If she had prior warning, she'd have fled but now she had no choice. She turned to face the man she'd once loved and the woman she'd heard he intended to marry. The meeting was inevitable, but she wasn't ready, and that wasn't fair.

Because he obviously was.

He sounded as if they'd been no more than childhood play-mates. But they'd been more—*much* more. They'd created a child together. A child he'd abandoned to grow up in poverty while he traveled the world and found another woman. Righteous anger rescued her pride. "Joshua. I'd heard you'd returned. Planning to suck the miners and laborers even dryer? A little warning—they can't squeeze their budgets tighter without starving. And if they died, who'd go down into those death traps your father calls tunnels?"

"Things are going to get better now, Abby. I'm back and with enough power to make some real changes. All the changes we'd planned."

"Well, I beg your pardon but I'll not be believin' a Wheaton'll honor his word. I learned that long ago."

"Why so hostile, Abby? You should know what I've always dreamed of for this town and its people. I *do* intend to carry on with all those plans and promises I made."

"You're ten years too late to keep a good many of them! Nobody trusts the word of a Wheaton, least of all me."

"My, you two *are* intense," Helena drawled before Joshua could respond to Abby's indictment. "Darling, introduce me to this lovely, dusty creature."

A perplexed look come across Joshua's features before they hardened. "Abaigeal Sullivan. Helena Conwell. Helena is my intended."

Helena Conwell seemed flustered but then the neighbor girl Abby cared for in the mornings skipped up. "Mrs. Sullivan, Daniel said to ask if we could have a candy stick?"

"I'll try my hand at a bit of candy-making when we get home."

Two candy sticks suddenly appeared in a large masculine hand. "Hope you like cherry, sweetheart. It's the only flavor Ethan Prescott ever stocks from what I can remember." Joshua held the candy out to the children and smiled at little Susan. "If Abby hasn't improved on her candy-making skills, she'll likely burn the house down. She nearly did to Mrs. Henry's kitchen when she was younger."

"I'd rather take brimstone from the devil," Daniel snarled, having come upon them. With that said, he kicked over a bucket of dirty water, soaking the skirt of Miss Conwell's lovely gown, then ran out the door.

Helena gasped in shock and stepped back, holding the sodden material off her limbs. "That boy is a little animal!"

Joshua stared down at Abby, fury burning in his eyes. "He and I had words yesterday at the train station. I forgave his behavior because it was directed at me, but this is too much."

"I apologize for my son, but you should understand his resentment."

Josh felt dizzy. The air left his lungs, and he sucked in a strangled breath. *Her son.* He'd assumed the boy was her brother. The one her mother had been expecting when he left for Germany. Her mother's condition had been the chief reason Abby had refused to go with him. So the boy was Abby's son. He should have been theirs but instead he was proof she'd betrayed him within months in the bed of a man Josh despised.

"He needs a good trip to the woodshed with your husband," he said, then wished instantly he could take it back. The boy had been wrong, but Liam Sullivan was a brute.

"I've no husband, as you well know!" Abby spat at him.

Josh blinked. "Of course you do. Liam Sullivan."

"I'm widowed, you fool. How long do you think he lived the way he was?" She turned her gaze on Helena, who stood gaping. "'Tis sorry I am for what Daniel did. He really does have his reasons. I truly feel sorry for you to be marrying a blackguard like Joshua Wheaton. You'd better be askin' what has the boy so upset! Come along, Susan."

Josh would have followed Abby but Helena said, "Take me home. Please, Joshua." She pulled a face and held her sodden hem away from herself. He guided Helena to the carriage and helped her in, but his mind stayed on Abby. Something didn't add up. Why was she so angry at him?

"You need to find out who that boy is," Helena demanded as he climbed into the carriage.

"He's Abby's. And *Sullivan's.* He looks a lot like Abby's father. I thought he was her brother. Except for his eyes now that I think about it. All the Kanes have one shade of green eyes or another," Joshua added absently. Something about his statement bothered him, but another thought replaced it. "Abby isn't married. My father never told me Sullivan had died."

"You should find out why. Especially since your father is so anxious to see us marry immediately. Speaking of which, why did you call me your intended when we agreed to hold that in reserve?"

Josh's heart sank. Abby's hostility had pushed him over the edge and he'd made a mess of things. He'd wanted her to think he'd moved on they way she had. But he hadn't and had learned too late she was free. It was too late for them anyway since she clearly hated him now, though why was a puzzle. He'd been the one wronged.

"It'll be okay. This is about saving Brendan's life and you from the earl. But I need to find out why my father never told me Sullivan was dead," he muttered, his mind trying to put the puzzle together.

Josh flicked the reins and started the carriage toward home. Even after ten years, the thought of Abby with Sullivan made his stomach turn. "I'll never understand how her father allowed her to marry such a miserable excuse of a man."

"Perhaps there was a good reason."

"What reason could he have to let his daughter marry a drunken lout?" Josh demanded as he pulled the carriage to a stop at the front entrance of his father's house.

Helena stared at him, her expression hard. "I'm not going to tell you," she told him as he helped her down. "but you'd better find out. And while you're at it, find out why men are so blind and stupid!"

Mystified, Joshua watched as Helena ran up the stairs and through the front door. He winced when she slammed it behind her. What the hell had he done? This was no way to play happy couple.

He stared after her for a moment then returned to town. There he found that Abby and Helena weren't the only ones who held him in disdain. Every time he approached anyone from the mining families, and Father Rafferty as well, they snubbed him. Three different times women who had once been his and Abby's friends refused to acknowledge his greeting. Frustrated and angry, he decided to go inspect the mines.

Joshua's first impression was that little had changed there. Then he looked past the mud and coal dust. More tunnels had been added and consequently there were more ore cars and tracks converging on the spur that linked the mine to the railroad. There were more men milling around, as well. The supervisors all carried rifles and wore sidearms now, a legacy of the problems with the AMU. AMU's Workmen had given mine owners the excuse they'd been after for years to arm their management.

A man who'd once been chief engineer came out of a shed and headed toward him. "Joshua, I'd heard you decided to come back."

"I hadn't heard you had. You left town before I did."

Helmut Faltsburg had aged but he was still a formidable sight. "Ya, we've both come home."

"I'm back because Father made concessions. Actually he capitulated completely. I'm in charge now. I hope you won't mind working with a younger man."

"I have grown used to being ordered about. My boss may have problems adjusting, though."

"My father?"

Helmut shook his head. "I speak of Geoffrey Williams."

"Who in hell is Geoffrey Williams?"

"A man a friend of your father's recommended to run things." Faltsburg shrugged. "I tried to tell your father Williams is not as good as Harlan was told, but your father, he is not a good judge of men. I stay and try to keep things as safe as I can but he is not—"

The door to the shed crashed open. "I didn't say you could leave. If you don't start showing me some respect, old man, you're going to find yourself fired." The man stared at Joshua with a narrowed, mean gaze. "What are *you* doing hanging around the mines? It's against company rules."

Joshua moved toward the tall man, who stood in the doorway. "What rules are those?" he asked.

"We don't allow any unauthorized people near the mines. Leave or I'll have a guard escort you back to town."

"Maybe you should talk to Harlan first."

Williams frowned. "Wheaton didn't tell me a thing about hiring a new man."

"How odd. Helmut was just telling me he'd been looking forward to my taking over."

The man's jaw dropped then Helmut stepped forward, his shoulders a bit straighter, his tired eyes lively. "This is Joshua Wheaton."

"Mr. Wheaton," Williams stammered. "I had no idea you'd arrived."

"That's quite obvious. I've asked Helmut to take me on a tour of the yards. I'll see you later to discuss my findings."

Joshua followed the old supervisor toward River Fall tunnel. The first thing he noticed was the breaker shed, instead of being separate, was over the shaft that held the ventilation furnace. It was a clear safety violation. He stood at the edge and paced off the distance to the second shaft. Then back again.

"Is there another entrance I don't see?" Josh asked. His one-time mentor shook his head. "But the second shaft is twenty feet too close to comply with current mining law."

"Williams said one hundred and thirty feet was as good as one hundred and fifty feet."

Josh arched his brows. "He decided to just ignore a congressional dictate?"

"Most owners ignore the 1870 Mine Act."

"It isn't nearly as strict as the one enacted by Parliament in England. We complied over there and still made a handsome profit."

Helmut's only answer was a shrug.

Joshua growled and picked up a Davy safety lamp. Safety would be an uphill battle, waged inside the mine and in the engineering shed. The miners were supposed to use safety lamps on days when the barometric pressure was as low as it was that day. The Davy lamp was a safety breakthrough but it was far from efficient. It was too heavy to wear on a cap, so it had to be set down away from the actual work and didn't give off as much light as an open flame. He knew he'd find the men inside with naked flames blazing on their caps, the flame teasing the flammable gas the miners called firedamp to explode.

They reached the breaker shed housing the cage and pulley system used to transport men and coal to the surface. Helmut introduced Josh to the shed supervisor.

"I think you ought to wait before you go in there," he said. "The men are clearing a crush. Can't tell how much firedamp it'll cause."

Joshua turned back to the man. "It's no more dangerous for me than it is for them."

"But what if something happens to you, sir?"

Joshua smiled and clapped the man on the shoulder. "I take full responsibility for my actions. Shouldn't take long."

But it did. And he was appalled. The open flames on the miners' caps continually elongated as pockets of methane flowed through the tunnel, proving the old-fashioned furnace didn't ventilate nearly well enough. In England, the shaft would not only have been closed, but it also never would have been opened in the first place. Anger felt as if it had burned a hole in Joshua's gut by the time he reached the surface.

"Pull the men out," he ordered, fury rife in his tone. "I counted five violations. Each one could cause a disaster. There are too many men in each breast. They've robbed the pillars to the point of insanity and the wood's either rotted from the water or too light to start with. And the ventilation system's a joke."

"If we pull the men out they'll be furious, as will your father," Faltsburg protested.

Josh pinned him with a steely look. "Close it down, Helmut."

"Joshua, I know you're thinking of the safety of the men but what about their families? We shut it down and they go further in debt to the store. You know how it works. The men would rather take chances. That's what this business is about."

Through gritted teeth Joshua repeated his order. "Close… it…down! I won't risk their lives for money. Gather them around the engineer's hut. When I get through firing Williams, I'll talk to them. As for my father, he wouldn't relish spending the rest of his natural life behind bars. If even one of those engineering violations results in loss of life, he could. And at this point, I wouldn't lift a finger to stop it."

Forty-five minutes later Joshua emerged from the engineers' hut. Williams had been fired exactly forty-two minutes earlier. Josh had checked the specs. Engineering plans hadn't been followed. Corners had been cut. Dangerous corners.

Chapter Four

Joshua stopped on the boardwalk outside the shed to talk to the miners and laborers milling about on the snowy ground. Their faces were blackened with coal dust. Their hands buried deep in their pockets. "Some of you may recognize me," he began. "But for those who don't, I'm Joshua Wheaton. I've returned to Wheatonburg to take over my father's mining operations. The first thing I did was close down the River Fall shaft until it's brought up to government standard."

"And what are we supposed to be eating on until then?" a voice shouted.

"You'll be paid an hourly wage to equal your best week during the last quarter. I'll expect each man to work to his full ability. I see no reason why we can't have River Fall in operation by the New Year. The furnace will be replaced by a top of the shaft ventilation fan. We'll replace a good portion of the timbers, clean out the gob from the crushed-down breasts, add more brattles and construct safety doors to get the air currents moving. I'd also like to implement a better system for pumping the water out of the mine." Joshua glanced down ruefully at his soaked trouser cuffs and boots. "Easy to see why it's called River Fall."

Several of the men laughed, giving Josh hope that he might be able to come to a pleasant accord with them.

"Ve all get paid the same?" a man with a German accent called out.

"This is not specialty work. If you object, you needn't work. I'm sure Prescott would issue you credit but that would increase your debt."

"It sounds like a fair shake," another man shouted. "I say we go along. We lose nothing and even gain since no one can dig as much in winter as summer."

"It's fools you are to believe the word of a Wheaton. The same old Biddle fans sit where they've put in topside ventilation. How's he going to be getting Harlan Wheaton to go along with buying new fans?"

Joshua scanned the crowd looking for the familiar face that went with the voice. It had matured but Brendan Kane's Americanized Irish brogue was still easily recognizable. Josh fought to hide his hurt. Brendan was the best friend he'd ever had. First Abby, then the people he'd met in town and now Brendan. He didn't understand.

"I don't know what's been happening around here, Brendan. But I'm now solely in charge of the mines. I'll get the fans. In fact, Helmut, wire Bannans in Pottsville. Tell them to send the two Gribal fans I had them hold for me."

The men murmured amongst themselves for several minutes before Joshua drew their attention. "So what do you say? Will you give me a chance to turn things around?"

"What about the men in the other shafts?" one man shouted. "My son and brother are working Destiny and my cousin's at Lilybet."

"I'll personally inspect them, too. If we have to halt production there it will be done in the same way. Digging on the new tunnel will be stopped until the rest are brought up to European standards. Those who want to work on the cleanup show up here at your regular time tomorrow. You have the rest of the day off with pay."

Joshua watched the men break up and head for town. He wondered what they were saying. Once he would have been privy to their opinions but everything had changed. Deep in thought, he didn't hear the footsteps.

"So you've come back, have you?" Brendan Kane sneered. Joshua turned to his old friend and was met with a solid punch in the jaw that sent him sprawling. Joshua looked up into the blazing green eyes of his one-time friend. "Stay away from Abby and Daniel or I swear I'll kill you." Brendan didn't wait for a response. He just pivoted on his heel and stalked off.

"What the hell was that about?" Joshua asked aloud, not expecting an answer. He pushed himself to his feet, while rubbing his sore jaw. Then he heard a sound often heard around mines—a hacking cough. Dolly McAllister sat on the edge of the raised boardwalk of the engineering shed. Josh had once made two promises to the old man. He was on the road to keeping one, but he knew he might never keep the other.

The first real contact Joshua had had with mine workers occurred during the rescue attempted for Dolly's son, Daniel. He'd met Abby that day, as well. Harlan had been out of town and Josh had tried to fill shoes too big and soiled for a boy of thirteen. He'd dug with the rest of the men after Abby had shamed them into allowing him to help. Joshua had vowed to make mining safer, and to name his first son after the Daniel they had been unable to save.

"Well now, it seems no one else will be tellin' you what

the community thinks of what you did. Nor about how your return might cause more hurt to those hurt enough by you already."

"I came back to make a difference. To help, not hurt."

Dolly pinned Joshua with a measuring look. "I don't doubt you believe you can, or that you'll fail where mining is concerned. But I'm talkin' about Brendan's feelin's on the matter. 'Twas Brendan who had to pick up the pieces of Abby's life after Sullivan was gone. 'Twas Brendan who's had to support her and the boy all these years. He's had to be a father to a boy who's sneered at by most of Wheatonburg."

"I went away to school. I didn't tell her to marry Sullivan," Joshua growled.

McAllister shook his gray head. "Just goes to prove book learnin' don't mean a hoot in hell without common sense," the old man continued with exaggerated patience. "Who else was to give your bastard son a name, boyo?"

Joshua stood stock-still. His body went hot then icy cold. He felt as if his breath had been sucked from his lungs. Surely his ears were playing tricks on him.

"What did you say?" he asked in a voice so choked it sounded more like a gasp.

"I said, boyo, that Sullivan gave yer boy a name, since you didn't care to. Nice that he did something decent before he passed on. Abby kept your promise by namin' the boy for my Daniel."

"Abby's son is…*my* son?"

"I think you'd better be sittin' down, boyo. You look a bit pasty."

Joshua sat on the edge of the boardwalk, his thoughts whirling. No one but Abby knew how he'd begged her to join him. No one knew about the money he'd scraped together and sent her for travel, clothes and food. Abby had taken his offering, but she hadn't joined him. She hadn't even written. By the time he'd sent the money, she must have known she was with child, yet she hadn't joined him. She'd married another man. Given his son *Sullivan's* name!

Forgetting Dolly's presence in the face of his pain he muttered, "How could she do that to me? To our son?"

"To you?" Dolly asked in a high, excited screech.

"Did staying here with her family mean so much that she'd deprive me of my son and the boy of his birthright?"

"You've got a perverse way of viewin' the past. 'Twas your father and you who did that!"

"My father knows Daniel is my son?"

"'Tisn't Philadelphia, you know. He knew. Mike Kane even went to Wheaton, but he wouldn't send for you, so Mike struck a deal with Sullivan."

Joshua stood. His knees shook as much as his voice. "Thank you for your honesty, Dolly. At least Abby named him Daniel. He has one of the names he should have. I need to think. Find someone to take the buggy on home for me, will you?"

Brendan shouldered his way into the saloon, flexing his hand and hoping he hadn't broken it. After buying a beer, he heard Sean Murphy call his name from the center of a group of miners. *This is all I need.*

"What is it brought you into our midst? Wheaton's return drivin' you to drink already?"

One of the men with Murphy said Brendan would need to lock Abby in the house to keep her away from her former lover.

"I'll not hear talk like that said about my sister," Brendan growled and hoped the men would back down. His punching hand was damaged enough as it was.

"And I'll not be hearin' it, either," Murphy chimed in.

Dooley snickered at Sean, but muttered an apology to Brendan, then slipped away, leaving Brendan and Sean at the bar.

"I was thinkin' I'd ask Abby to the social on Saturday. With Wheaton back it'd be a good thing if she went with me."

Brendan felt sorry for Sean. He'd been the butt of jokes for years and he could be particularly annoying when he bragged on imagined alliances with the AMU to make himself important.

"Sean," Brendan said and clapped the other man on the shoulder. "She's never seen you in that light. Besides, Joshua Wheaton is engaged to be married, so there shouldn't be anything for people to talk about. Thanks for defendin' her just now, though. I promised to pick up something for Abby at the store so I best be on my way."

Sean smiled. "I'll walk with you. Maybe I'll get a glimpse of Abby as we pass your house."

Brendan sighed and silently cursed his rotten luck. He was uncomfortable with Sean's undying affection for Abby. She'd bluntly refused his courtship and yet he remained devoted.

"You get what you came for and I'll just look about," Murphy said at the store.

Brendan waited at the counter for Ethan Prescott. Several minutes later Prescott pushed aside the curtain to his back room and stepped out. "What can I do for you, Murphy?" he said, staring right at Brendan.

It had not been a good day. "How long is it going to take for you to tell us apart? I'm Brendan Kane, Prescott. My sister works for you. I know one sooted-up miner looks like another to you but…" Brendan stopped, noticing Prescott's bored expression. "Oh, forget it. Ten pounds of flour."

"You want this on your account, don't you?"

Brendan nodded and signed for the flour in the account book. When Prescott returned with the sack of flour, Brendan slung it over his shoulder. He turned to leave and found Murphy staring at him with an odd look in his eyes.

"Problem, Sean?"

Murphy shrugged. "I forgot I've something to do. Tell Abby I said halloo."

Brendan watched him rush away, grateful for the reprieve, but disturbed…as well. The only thing he could think Sean would find more important than another attempt at courting Abby was going off to try ingratiating himself further to AMU members. Murphy was not only odd, he had dangerous leanings.

Joshua walked in the hills for hours. He felt like a ship set adrift on becalmed seas. Lost. Hopeless. He thought of the years he and Abby had shared. First as friends then finally as lovers. He remembered the innocence of her sparkling eyes. He remembered her laughter when life should have held nothing to smile about. He remembered her guilty tears the night their son must have been conceived and the argument they'd had when she'd refused to leave town with him. Remembering. Hurting. He walked for hours scarcely noticing when the sun slipped behind the hills.

He arrived home long after dark. Dinner was thankfully a memory. With guests in the house, he would have been obligated to be civil to Harlan during the meal. Josh couldn't have done it.

"Is Harlan in his room, Henry?" Josh snapped when Henry met him at the door. The butler stepped back, his eyes wide. "I apologize, Henry. I'm not at my best. I just found out I've been a father for nine years but no one has ever seen fit to tell me. I'll show myself in. No need to risk him snarling at you, as well."

"Thank you, sir," Henry said, then seemed to scurry for cover.

Wise man, Joshua thought as he stalked toward Harlan's lair. Since learning about Daniel, Josh hadn't thought of Harlan as "Father" even once. And if he didn't get a damned good explanation Josh probably never would. The old bear wouldn't hide from him tonight! Without knocking, Josh slammed through the door.

"Joshua! What in heaven's name is wrong?" Harlan shouted.

"Wrong? What could be wrong?" Josh asked, his tone biting. "This morning I realized half the people were treating me like a leper and the rest snickered when I passed. Then I went to take a look at the conditions in the mines. How does *appalling* sound?"

"Well—" the old man noisily cleared his throat "—I haven't had my hand in there for some time now. Crippled the way I—"

"Don't!" Josh roared.

Harlan blinked. "Don't what?"

"Don't try weaseling out using your condition. We'll talk about the mines, and what I've decided to do with them at another time. Right now, I want to discuss why people acted the way they did toward me. Abaigeal Sullivan."

"What about her?"

"Abby's a widow. She has no husband. She *does* have a son, though. *Mine!*" The word reverberated through the room.

Harlan sat a bit straighter. "You believe that claptrap?"

"Believe it? Why wouldn't I believe it?"

"Because she married another man as soon as I tossed the two of them, their demands and lies out of my house. Michael

Kane went so far as to threaten me. He's lucky I thought he was amusing."

"Threats? What would he have to threaten you with?"

"Hmmph! Kane said my grandchild would grow up in the coal patch, hating its rightful name. I assume he's turning him into a Workman just like the rest of the rabble."

"What did you say to that?" Josh asked, already having dismissed the very idea that any Kane would be mixed up with the AMU. Daniel clearly did hate his rightful name, though. What made it hurt worse was they'd chosen to give him the surname of a man everyone knew Josh hated.

"I said my son wouldn't be held responsible for Kane's daughter being a tramp."

Fury surged anew through Josh. "Abby was *not* a tramp!"

"How do you know what she did when you weren't around?"

No matter how much she'd hurt him, she'd been innocent. He wouldn't retract his defense of her. "Because, you dirty-minded old bastard, she was a virgin! The night Daniel was conceived was the only time I took us that far. Abby was… Dear God…she was so guilt-ridden afterward it tore my heart out. I made her a promise that it wouldn't happen again until we were married. A little over a month later you and I fought over you trying to make me give her up."

Joshua had the pleasure of watching Harlan pale. He was clearly worried now. "But he doesn't look like you. I've asked. Don't you think I haven't!"

"If you'd bothered to see him yourself you'd have noticed he has my eyes."

Harlan scowled. "So he has blue eyes. That proves nothing. I kept the two of you apart for your own good. She was a miner's daughter. There's nothing you can do about it all these years later," Harlan added uncertainly.

"Oh, there's something I can do, all right!" Joshua snarled, his fist clenched. "I can find out why she took my money and didn't join me. I can find out why she didn't let me know about Daniel. I already know why *you* didn't tell me. God help you if I find out you did more."

"I did what I thought was best for you," Harlan said.

"What you thought? You think you're better than the men who die making money for you. Michael Kane is a better man than you could ever hope to be and he was more a father to me than you ever were! I had a right to be that kind of father to *my* son. I also had a right to be here, not wandering around Europe, unable to face living so close to Abby and her husband. I could have come home years ago. Just how long has Sullivan been dead?"

"I hoped you'd forget her if you thought she was married. I hoped you'd meet someone else."

"I *loved* Abby." Joshua stared at him, trying not to hate him. It was too late.

"Where are you going?" Harlan asked when Josh turned away.

"I'm not going to pack and leave if that's worrying you."

Seeing the relief on Harlan's face, Joshua added ruthlessly, "But not because of you. I'm staying because my son is here in Wheatonburg and I intend to get to know him. If I can, considering he loathes the sight of me. I'm also staying because there are two hundred miners and laborers here along with their families. They need me to clean up those death traps you call mines."

Harlan watched his son's stiff back as he stalked toward the stairs, leaving the door open. Joshua's words had cut deeply. He was old and alone but for his son. He'd had such hope when Joshua had agreed to return to run the mines. And now, once his boy learned what he'd done, he might well pack his bags. He wouldn't leave Wheatonburg but might move out of the manor.

He told himself he'd done the right thing and all that mattered was that Joshua stayed to run the mines. It was what he'd always wanted. Now it looked as if that was all he'd get.

Chapter Five

Joshua met Henry in the hall. "I've turned down your bed, and took the liberty of drawing you a hot bath." Henry glanced askance at the condition of Joshua's clothing. "I would say you could use a good hot soak about now, sir."

"I'm going to change but I'm going out again," Joshua told the butler.

Henry cleared his throat and stood even stiffer. "Begging your pardon, but it might do to wait for morning after the brothers go off to work and Daniel has left for school. And yes, sir, there is a school. Mrs. Sullivan's doing. Badgered your father until he hired a schoolmaster. There's need of a better building but now many children attend."

Abby had gotten her school. That was two promises he'd made that Abby had fulfilled in his absence. Suddenly tired to his depths, Josh sighed. "Perhaps you have a point. Abby and I *should* talk without any interference."

Old Henry started on his way but halted almost in midstep. "Perhaps you shouldn't judge any of them too harshly, sir. The past is over. The future lies ahead." That said he pivoted smartly and left Joshua standing in the hall staring after him, realizing what had just happened. Henry had interfered and given him advice for the first time ever. Unfortunately, Josh doubted he could take it.

"Daniel Sullivan!" Abby called out the door. "Where in the name of all that's holy do you think you're going dressed like that? Those pants are torn and that shirt's nothing but a rag. March yourself back in here." Abby shook her head. "These are from my rag bag."

"They're fine. I can still wear them. You work too hard," Daniel answered.

He was sincere, but Abby could see he wasn't being completely truthful. She tried her most penetrating glare, hoping to force the full truth from him, but it failed. His implacable expression reminded her heartbreakingly of Joshua. Idealistic. Stubborn. He was indeed his father's son, though Daniel would deny it.

It made her sad, but there was little she could do to change things. She had never spoken ill of Joshua in Daniel's presence. She'd simply said he'd left before she'd known she was with child and had not returned for her.

She'd explained her marriage to Liam Sullivan, so he could understand the talk about Josh being his real father. It was common knowledge, thanks to Liam, that she had married him to give Daniel a name in exchange for nursing care until Sullivan died of his injuries. But Daniel took too much abuse from his schoolmates not to be resentful of the man he saw as the cause of his problems.

Her heart aching for her tender-hearted son, Abby kissed his nose and cheek where the bright red yarn of his hat and scarf enhanced his freckles and set off his black hair beautifully.

After letting Daniel out the door, Abby sat in her rocker

by the hearth, eyes closed and hands in her lap. The little house was silent with Daniel off to school, her brothers at work and her father still sleeping in his small room behind the kitchen. She'd learned to cherish the solitude the early mornings brought. She wasn't due at Mr. Prescott's store till noon. Some days she even caught a few more winks. But that would not be today.

A sharp rap on the front door reverberated in the small house, surprising Abby. Wondering who would be calling at so early an hour she hurried to the door before a second knock woke her father. She gasped when she pulled the door open.

Joshua!

"We need to talk," he demanded.

Abby tried to push the door closed but he was too quick. His hand came up to stop her just as he managed to get a foot in the door. "Go away!"

"You seem to forget, Mrs. Sullivan, I own this house. If I want to gain entrance, I'll do it."

Abby didn't quite know how it happened but he was soon striding through the house, shrinking it just by his presence. Abby followed him toward the sitting area near the fireplace. Her thoughts were whirling. *What can he want?*

Josh walked to the hearth then turned, propping his elbow indolently on the beautiful mantel her brother had carved. "So this is where you chose to raise my son."

"I haven't made a free choice since the night you took my virginity," Abby spat back.

Josh raised his left eyebrow. "If my memory serves, you did more than your fair share of unbuttoning."

Abby flew at him. Her fists balled, she struck wildly, raining blows on his chest, his cheekbone and mouth. Then in a heartbeat she found herself imprisoned against the hard wall of his chest.

"Stop it!" he barked.

Abby stared up at him. His eyes were like blue flames, his lips sealed in a straight line. *He still smells the same,* some stupid sentimental part of her brain remembered. His eyes changed as they held hers prisoner. His gaze was still hot and blazing but desire replaced anger. His lips came closer to hers and Abby panicked. She wouldn't survive his kiss whole.

"Bastard!" she roared at him. Catching him off guard, Abby broke away. She took several steps backward, but refused to give more ground.

"Not me, my dear. However, our son is apparently considered a bastard by the townspeople, thanks to you."

Abby hadn't thought she could get any angrier. There was no way she'd strike out physically at him again and risk getting too close, but she'd not stand docilely by, either. "Well, now that's where you're wrong. I tried to protect him from gettin' that name flung at him. I found a husband, but it was too late."

"You gave my son another man's name," Josh charged.

"That is no one's fault but yours, Joshua Wheaton. It was you who deserted us."

The fire in Joshua's eyes became an inferno. "Deserted you? I *begged* you to come with me. You're the one who refused to leave here."

"I was frightened. For God's sake, I was only seventeen. You wanted me to sneak away. My parents would have been frantic. And my mother was doing poorly. She needed me."

"I heard she died in childbirth not long after I left." Abby heard true regret in his voice, and saw a flash of regret in his expression, but she looked away. Those were the most painful months of her life what with her mother's death and Joshua's desertion.

"So you took her place," Josh continued ruthlessly. "You've

cooked for her husband and sons and cleaned her house all these years. I'm sure the townspeople have nearly sainted you for your sacrifice, but tell me how they treat my son."

"Like the bastard you made of him! I tried to hide behind Sullivan but it didn't work. And I've not been sainted but condemned as the whore you made of me."

"Why didn't you come to me?"

Abby ignored the ridiculousness of his question and countered with one of her own. "Why didn't you come back for me? You could, by God, at least have acknowledged my letters. But you chose to ignore us until now Daniel's right here under your nose. Tell me, why the sudden interest? Is the great and world-famous engineer embarrassed to be living in the same town as the little boy he fathered then ignored?"

Joshua stared at Abby; her mouth moved but he'd heard nothing since she'd mentioned having written him. "What letters?" he asked, deathly afraid to hope she'd actually tried to contact him.

"What do you mean 'what letters'? The letters I wrote telling you about the baby I was carrying. The ones Brendan sent from Pottsville to try keeping my business private. He mailed the last one for me the day after Daniel was born."

Joshua gritted his teeth. How stupid did she think he was? "Don't lie. You'd already married Sullivan by then."

Abby's eyes flashed ice. "Why in the name of all that's holy would I lie? Sullivan was dead before Daniel was born."

Joshua stared at Abby's flushed, angry face for several tension-filled minutes before responding. "Am I to believe all your *supposed* letters mysteriously disappeared?"

Abby glared at him then turned her back. "Leave. Leave now and don't ever darken this door again."

"We've already established that it's my door."

Abby whirled on him, her small fists curled up tight. "That's right! Lord it over us. The Wheatons and their slaves. You want to know what proof I have that I tried and even begged for your help? Look around you. Look at me. Do you think I picked this life for me or my son? Do you think I like decent women holdin' their skirts aside so mine won't brush theirs? Do you think I like seeing my son bleeding after yet another tiff over his mother 'the whore' and his father who used her but wouldn't marry her?"

It wasn't a pretty picture she'd painted nor did it make sense. Why *would* she have chosen that life? She *had* loved him. He'd been young and stupid but he didn't doubt her feelings back then. But why hadn't she used the money he'd sent to follow him. "Why did you stay here?"

"After Sullivan died, I thought about leaving. Fool that I was, I believed you hadn't been able to send help, but would soon. And Brendan thought I should wait for you. Then days after Daniel was born, there was an accident. Da lost his leg and Brendan had to start as a laborer. We couldn't even afford the rent on this place let alone strike out for another patch with a newborn babe and a badly injured man. But you never did come back or send help and then it was too late to leave. We had the debt we owed that just kept mounting. We've yet to pay it off. Little Tom started working as a breaker boy, trying to help, but Brendan couldn't let him continue. That's how my talented artistic brother wound up as a carpenter's helper and how Brendan, who hates closed-in places, wound up in the mines. By helpin' support your son and his mother."

So he owed Brendan loyalty for more than just past friendship. It looked as if he owed the man a new life—and he'd see he got it, too. For the time being though all he could do was protect him the only way he knew how. By spying on Gowery and his father during their meetings with the Pinkerton man and keeping silent about him lest Brendan, feeling a loyalty to a friend of his own, bring on the earl's death by sounding a warning of the man's presence.

Abby walked away then, over to the kitchen area, and stood fussing with dishes. Nervous. Flitting from place to place without any purpose. Josh looked around at the neat, tidy little shack of a home. She clearly did her best and the furniture was of unexpectedly good quality. But the structure was shabby and must barely keep them warm in the winter. "Abby, I'd like to help. I'd like to be a father to Daniel," he said in a low voice he wasn't sure would even reach her.

"No!"

Abby stared at Joshua. The morning sun slanted through the parlor window and glinted in his golden hair. *He wants Daniel. He's rich and powerful and he'll take him away,* a voice inside her warned. In his rock-hard gaze there wasn't a hint of the boy who'd been all artless charm and sincere intent. But the fulminating anger of minutes earlier was gone from his eyes. That didn't calm Abby's anger or her fear of him and what he could do. She no longer trusted any man or her judgment where they were concerned.

"What do you mean 'no'?" he demanded.

"No. You can't be a father to him."

"I *am* his father."

"You can't have him. I won't let you take him away from me!" Abby shouted, speaking from her fear and her brother's warning.

The angry fire blazed in Joshua's eyes again. "Because you won't allow it?" Though spoken in a low, quiet tone, Abby heard the threat in his question. A threat she quickly realized hadn't been there before.

"*Daniel* won't allow it," she spat back. "He loathes you."

Joshua grinned, but it was a grin bereft of humor. He looked like an irritated cougar. "I've noticed you saw to your father's threat. Apparently Michael promised to alienate the boy in retribution."

"Well, we didn't. None of us want him hating part of himself. I told him his father had gone before he was born and never returned."

"Then how did he know I was his father?"

Abby thought she would fly apart if he didn't stop questioning her and the way she'd raised Daniel. Who did he think he was to come in here and interrogate her? She pulled out the ingredients for sugar cookies, slamming them on the kitchen table. Letting the clinking of glass bowls, the sugar and flour tins and metal measuring cups, fill the air, she let her mind drift.

Abby remembered that glorious summer when young love had caught flame and burned out of control. Then she remembered she'd been the one to get burned.

Her voice low, she told him, "That you're his father is common knowledge, Joshua. We were inseparable, you and I, that summer and it was easy for people to count back once my condition became apparent. My marriage fooled no one."

Joshua moved closer, probably to hear her barely audible words. "If you never spoke against me then why does he hate me?" Joshua asked. Abby almost thought she heard pain in his voice.

Blessed anger flared in her heart. She wouldn't have it! He'd not charm her into believing he was the one wronged. If he'd lost his son's goodwill, he deserved it. "Because having a Wheaton for a father is probably a greater embarrassment to Daniel than Daniel is to you. He also has a good head on his shoulders. He's formed opinions all on his own about the kind of man you must be to have abandoned me."

"And you never tried to contradict those opinions."

"I didn't want to lie to him, either."

"But as you said, I'm his father and he's a part of me."

"More's the pity, but don't worry, Daniel's a good, honest boy who's not a'tall like you."

Joshua smirked. "Honest? That isn't what I hear."

Abby forgot their earlier physical encounter and threw a measuring cup at him but he managed to deflect it. He took two quick steps and grabbed her hands before she could hurl a second cup. They struggled. Seconds later Joshua won the contest of strength and the cup skidded harmlessly across the floor as Joshua's arms tightened around her, pinning her arms to her sides.

The encounter might have ended as before but Abby felt a bit of satisfaction this time as he held her imprisoned against his unyielding chest. She'd hurt him when he'd batted the heavy cup aside. She could see the pain in his eyes as they stared at each other, nose-to-nose, gazes locked and silently warring. Their breathing was the only sound in the room and a different kind of heat flashed between them.

Then the click of a rifle being cocked broke the deadlock and the connection between them. "I'll be thanking you to remove your hands from my daughter, Joshua Wheaton," Michael Kane growled.

Joshua released Abby at once and stepped back. Truth told, he had to let her go anyway. Angry as he was, he found he couldn't be close to Abby and not kiss her. He turned to fully face Michael Kane and flinched when he saw the crutches and the empty pants leg. This was the result of the accident Abby mentioned. Damn!

Then their eyes met and Joshua felt suddenly drained. Michael looked at him as if he were the snake come to spoil the Garden of Eden. Joshua said nothing. He had no idea how to bridge the gap that lay between them. This man, who had been a father to him, hated him now. It hurt more than the enmity between him and Harlan.

"Now I'm thinking by Abaigeal's red face that you've worn out your welcome here. Not, I might add, that you've had one 'round here in a good many years. I'd be moving on were I you. Because, boyo, this may be your house but the gun says 'tis still my home. Now off with you."

Without a word Joshua turned and walked to the door. His hands shook when he unlatched it. He stopped on the threshold, unable to leave things as they were. He looked back at Michael, standing tall and proud with the aid of a crutch and a door frame, hating that he'd lost the man's respect.

"I swear to you, Mr. Kane, I had no idea Abby had conceived my child. I'm sorry I let things go that far between us. It was my fault, not Abby's. You trusted me and I broke that trust. I'll find some way to make it up to you—to all of you. And by *damn* I'll find out why Abby's letters never reached me."

Michael glared. "I know who pushed who and I don't need you to defend Abby to me at this late date. I certainly don't need you to tell me who was at fault. Now get out!" he shouted.

Abby stared out the kitchen window at the mountain beyond, as the door slammed behind Joshua. *Could he be telling the truth? Had he really not known of Daniel?*

"Don't you be believin' that slick-tongued devil, Abby girl. The path to pain is what it 'tis." She knew she should listen, but it wasn't that easy anymore.

Joshua truly had sounded angry and as if he'd never known of Daniel. She let the joy of that thought wash over her. Perhaps Joshua really *had* loved her. Perhaps he would have returned for her if he had known of Daniel. But the joy was short-lived. What had happened to his supposed love for *her?* He had not returned for her and her alone. Tears once again filled her eyes over Joshua and his faithless love.

"I know, Da. Don't you be worrying yourself over it. He never thought of me after this town saw the back of him. Never one letter asking if all was well. I needed him. I believed in his love, but it was a lie. I'll never let myself forget that. And what, at this late date, could he think to do to make up for all the pain? He's a man promised to another woman. A woman, who by the look of her, would never accept his son from the coal patch."

"'Tis sorry I am for your heartache, Abaigeal. I wish your mother was here to comfort you, but would a hug from your old da help?" Michael leaned his back against the doorjamb and held out his long arms, calling to her. Abby ran to him and held on for dear life. Why couldn't Joshua have been half as faithful as her own sweet da?

Daniel quickly changed his pants and shirt to the ripped ones he'd had to smuggle out of the house. He sure wished his ma hadn't caught him leaving in them. Peeking around the end of the breaker shed, he checking to see if his Uncle Brendan had gone into the mine shaft. He saw no one ahead but Luther Dancy, who was almost to the breaker shed.

An arm caught him from behind around the middle and lifted him off the ground. "Now what would the boss's boy be doin' round here at this time of the day?"

"Let me go. My uncle'll beat you black and blue if you hurt me," Daniel shouted, squirming to get loose.

The big man squeezed him so tight Daniel couldn't breathe. Lights exploded in his head then everything dimmed.

"Let the lad go, Dooley," he heard in the distance. "He's not lookin' real comfortable."

Daniel looked into the kindly eyes of Sean Murphy, the man who was sweet on his ma. "Help," Daniel pleaded with what felt like his last breath.

Murphy looked suddenly alarmed. "Let the boy go now! Damn you, you drunken sot!"

Daniel felt himself falling then found himself in Murphy's arms. "Now, there's a lad," he said, patting Daniel's back. "All righty? What were you were doin' with the likes of Dooley?"

"He came up from behind me. I'm not supposed to have nothing to do with men like him, my ma says."

"And your ma would be right. That doesn't explain why you're here," the tall, dark-haired man said as he made himself comfortable on the ground next to Daniel.

Daniel knew he had to tell the truth. Murphy might be sympathetic to his cause.

Murphy scratched his head after Daniel shared his plans. "I can see your dilemma. I faced the same choice myself a while back. Tell you what. I'll introduce you to Luther Dancy myself and get you started. You can clean up at my place after work and maybe put off your folks finding out for a few days."

"Geez, thanks, Mr. Murphy," Daniel told him, wondering why so many men made fun of him.

"That's what friends are for. We miners have to stick together. And we have your mother's welfare in common, too, don't we?"

The hair on Daniel's arms stood up. He didn't know what he'd heard in the man's friendly words but something hadn't sounded quite right. Murphy loved Daniel's mother. Love was a good thing. Confused, Daniel looked up into Murphy's eyes and relaxed. His blue eyes sparkled and his smile was kind and friendly. "Thanks again for saving me," Daniel said.

"No problem a'tall," Murphy replied and smiled.

It was a friendly smile, Daniel reassured himself. He'd been imagining that Murphy wasn't what he seemed. Dooley had spooked him. That was all. He took a deep breath. That had to be all. Murphy planned to help him. Wasn't that proof of his goodwill?

Chapter Six

Six hours after being ordered out of Michael Kane's home, Joshua ordered yet another crew out of a mine shaft. It was not, he told himself, the same thing. He was trying to save lives.

Because this mine was a young one, he'd held out hope it would be in better shape. His hope had fled hours earlier. Lilybet's workers had heard what Joshua had done the day before, and they'd cooperated by pointing out problems. But those same men broke as many rules themselves as the poor engineering had.

He understood why. If they didn't cut coal, they didn't get paid. It was piecework by the ton and safety took too much time. He understood but he had to find a way to show them how foolish it was to risk their lives for pennies.

Joshua looked over the notice to be posted and he picked up the pencil to add to the list of rules he planned to have posted. *Any miner caught breaking a safety rule will be suspended.* He ran his fingers through his hair. It wouldn't make him popular, but he didn't want to be liked as much as he wanted to save lives.

Tired and worried about the deplorable conditions he'd found, Joshua glanced at the sky on his way to the main breaker shed. The sun was low, casting long shadows on newly fallen snow. A group of men trudged toward home. One of them was Brendan.

Josh wished with all his heart he could walk over and talk to him. He wanted to tell Bren the engagement was a farce. But something bigger stood between them. And that was the next thing on his agenda before the day was out.

Harlan had a lot to answer for. But still, he dreaded the coming confrontation, especially with Helena Conwell and Franklin Gowery still staying with them. Tonight there'd be no civilized meal.

Joshua strode into the shed and stopped short at the sight of the breaker boys. This was worse than the condition of the mines. They were far younger than they'd been when Josh was a boy. It was common practice to have boys do the job of separating shale from the coal. But back then, only boys older than thirteen and men too old or ill to work the mines worked the breaker sheds.

The problem was the parents of the boys often sent them at too young an age to help support their families. He vowed before the day was out he'd have a plan to get them back in the school room, where they belonged.

He looked around. *Who the hell approved this?*

Joshua went looking for an answer from the breaker boss, Luther Dancy. As he passed in front of the breaker bins, he glanced down at the boys' callused hands. But then he saw a pair of bleeding hands—a new boy unaccustomed rough work. The pain the child must have felt twisted Joshua's stomach. How dare anyone do this to a child? Josh's eyes automatically flew to search the young face.

Daniel's face!

Joshua had never known such rage. This was his son. Until that moment he hadn't felt it. Not really. This was his flesh and blood, bleeding for pennies. "What the hell are you doing here?" he demanded.

Daniel looked up at him, shocked at first, but then his little, coal-smeared chin jutted out. "I'm here helping do what you never did, supporting my mother."

Josh was struck anew by all he had lost, and by the hatred in his own son's eyes. It was nearly more than he could stand. A bad day just got so much worse. He knelt in the coal dust in front of his son and took him by the wrist.

"Open it," Josh ordered. His brows rose at the curt, profane answer Daniel spat back at him. "That may well be true but I am bigger than you, too. We can do this the easy way. Do as I say—right now. Or the hard way. I pry them open, which may just hurt them more. But either way, I will see the damage done to those hands."

Daniel, eyes hot, rotated his wrist slowly and opened his hand, palm up. "Ain't so bad. Few days and Mr. Dancy says they'll callus up real good."

"Your sorting days are over."

His chin, so much like Abby's, notched up. "You saying I'm not good enough to separate your coal?"

"I'm saying my son isn't going to hurt like that for a few measly cents a week. If your mother needs the money so badly, I'll give it to her."

Daniel's cheeks paled beneath the coating of coal dust. "She…she won't take money from you. Too little too late, she'll say."

Joshua could almost hear Abby saying exactly that but there was something about the way Daniel had grown nervous that gave him pause. "Does your mother know you're here?"

Silence.

"Daniel?"

His son's face reddened. "I hate you! You're wreckin' everything. I was going to buy her a fancy dress. Fancy as the one your lady wore. My ma is a hundred times better. She should have nice things, too. I'm gonna' give them to her. I'm gonna' give her everything you never did!"

Joshua had no reply. At least not one Daniel would believe. "Come on, son, I'll take you home so your ma can take care of those hands."

"You're not my—"

"Father," Joshua finished on a tired sigh and stood. "Tell me, Daniel, if I'm not, then why am I so damn proud to have you for a son?"

He didn't wait for a reply, but steered the boy out of the shed. His business with Luther Dancy would have to wait. It was probably just as well, Josh decided as they rode toward the Kane house. Had he seen Dancy just then he might have beaten him till his face was as bloody as Daniel's hands.

Worried over the late hour, Abby pushed aside the worn calico curtains, hoping to see Daniel. But instead, a man on horseback came into view at the end of the road. He carried a boy in front of him. It was Joshua and Daniel.

Abby saw red. She grabbed her shawl and rushed out of the house. "He was supposed to be home an hour ago. He knows better than not to come straight home from school on days I'm not in town. How dare you make him disobey me? Do you know I've been worried out of my mind?"

"He wasn't in school." Joshua dismounted, his tone betraying a tightly leashed anger. "He was in the breaker shed. He'd been there all day."

Abby turned to glare at her son. "You are in a world of

trouble, young man! Wait till your Uncle Brendan gets hold of you. You won't sit for a week!"

Daniel refused to look at Abby. Joshua laid his hand on her shoulder and Abby felt his warmth through her shawl. It sent heat curling through her. She stepped back, shrugging off his disturbing touch.

"Ab, he was trying to earn money to buy you a dress."

Having their poverty pointed out by the man whose father caused it only fueled Abby's anger. "Don't you be defendin' him to me! If you wouldn't hire them, they wouldn't be tempted to give up school."

"I'm glad you didn't send him there and believe me, I didn't know our breaker boys were this young." He turned to Daniel. "I'll pay you ten cents a day for every day you go to school."

"We'll not be accepting your charity, Joshua Wheaton," Abby shouted. "Now get out of my way, so I can take him inside where his uncle can deal with him."

Joshua stood like a rock preventing her from reaching up to pull Daniel out of the saddle. "Not until you listen. It wouldn't be charity. All the boys, nine and up, will get ten cents for every day they spend in school. I value education every bit as much as you do." He turned and lifted Daniel to the ground. He took the boy's resisting hands and held them out. "Open them," he ordered.

Abby hated him touching Daniel and it infuriated her that he had command of the situation. If only her brothers were aware of his presence. She looked down at Daniel's hands then, expecting them to be black from the coal. Her anger dissolved in a heartbeat. "Oh, my good sweet Lord! Daniel, what have you done to yourself?"

Daniel shrugged his shoulders, but still refused to look her in the eye. "It ain't so bad."

"Oh, but it 'tis," she cried and sank into the dust at his feet, taking his bleeding hands in her own. "We'll fix you up right and proper in a blink."

"So did you find the lad?" Brendan called as he walked around the corner of the house. Abby glanced up as Brendan stopped short, shock in his eyes. His jaw turned to granite. "My father told you not to come 'round here. You aren't welcome." He shifted his eyes to Daniel and raised one eyebrow, considering his appearance. "And you, boyo. From the look of you, I'd say you acted on that harebrained idea you had."

"Yes, sir," Daniel admitted quickly.

"After I told you to do no such thing?"

"But I—"

"No buts," Brendan snapped. Daniel nodded silently. "Go get cleaned up. I'll deal with you later." There was an implicit parental threat in Brendan's tone.

Joshua stiffened visibly and turned to face Brendan. Daniel moved forward, but Joshua stopped him with a restraining hand on the shoulder. "I don't want him punished further. His hands are punishment enough."

Brendan squinted against the glare of the setting sun. "Since you gave up any right to Daniel long ago, I'd say what you want is of no importance. I don't want you within fifty feet of the boy from here on out. It's obvious you aren't a good influence. He's never disobeyed me so defiantly before."

Joshua let go of Daniel and curled his hands into fists. Abby could see him trying to control his anger. "I never abdicated my right to be Daniel's father. It was stolen from me. Nothing any of you say will keep me away from my son, Brendan. Now that I know about him, I intend to see to his interests."

Brendan tossed aside the bucket and charged forward.

Josh's horse shied and Josh stepped between him and Abby and Daniel. She scurried out of the way and pulled Daniel with her as Josh gained control of his mount. As he turned away and toward Brendan, her brother threw a punch that glanced off Joshua's jaw. It rocked Joshua a bit but he ducked away and let go of the horse's reins.

Josh backed off, holding up his hand to forestall Brendan. "I don't want to fight you, but I'm getting dammed sick of you throwing punches without giving fair warning. Why is it you're so opposed to my seeing Abby and Daniel?"

"Because it was me pickin' up the pieces of what you and your father did to her."

"So you had a hand in arranging her marriage to Sullivan?"

"Da arranged it but I talked her into the marriage idea. It was all that was left to do. As far as I can see it was not so much worse than havin' her marry you. Now clear out before I hand you your head."

Abby could see Joshua try to control his temper but she could see he was nearly blind with rage. He'd hate being compared unfavorably to Sullivan.

"If you want me gone, you're about to find out what a fight with me is all about these days. And it'll be one that doesn't start with a sucker punch."

Brendan pulled off his cap and tossed it aside. "Come on, boss man. Let's see how tough your soft life has made you."

Joshua moved like lightning. Abby saw the shock on Brendan's face before he tried and failed to block the blow. Abby was sure Josh had loosened some of Brendan's beautiful teeth.

Josh threw another punch, catching Brendan in the middle, then he took a punch to the belly from her brother. When Josh's next punch sent Brendan sprawling, Daniel cried out, "Ma, he's hurting Uncle Brendan."

Abby saw the hurt in Josh's eyes at Daniel's outcry before he turned and mounted up. She couldn't let it affect her. He'd have to live with his decisions just as she'd had to for nearly ten years.

"I'm not through with you, Wheaton," Brendan shouted, climbing to his feet.

"I never wanted to fight you, Brendan. You were my best friend other than Abby."

"And we can see where that's got all of us," Brendan bellowed.

Joshua looked toward her. "Please don't have him punished," he said, his fire-blue gaze capturing hers. "Those hands are enough, and besides, you were right. If there hadn't been a job, he wouldn't have been there. The boys were at lunch when I was in there before or I'd have stopped it then." He looked at Abby, a worried frown on his face. "The ten cents? You think it will keep the parents from sending them?"

He did still care about the people. That hadn't changed. Some of her long-fought-for anger drained. "With the boys, yes. We'll still lose the girls, though."

"The girls?"

"They hire out to the hotel and the boarding houses to scrub clothes and clean the rooms."

"Ten cents for *all* the children then. I'll post it a few places in town," he promised then tugged on the reins and spurred his horse forward. He looked tired and incredibly sad as he turned away. Abby wished it didn't make her equally sad to see him so unhappy. She fought it, but sympathy still pulled at her heart. Determined to forget such nonsense, she wrapped her arm around Daniel's back. Her son deserved all her sympathy. There was no room in her heart for his father. None!

* * *

"Where is he, Henry?"

"Mr. Wheaton? In the conservatory with Miss Helena, sir."

Joshua noticed the butler's inquisitive expression. "Better lay low, Henry. We're about to have a battle."

"I'll have the missus delay dinner."

Josh pulled out his watch. "No sense making everyone wait. Serve as planned." Josh grinned. "The dining room is about as far as you can get from the conservatory. I doubt our voices will carry that far. My father can join them later."

"And you, sir?"

"I've lost my appetite," Josh growled and headed to the conservatory.

Helena's voice flowed through the open door as Joshua approached. "This is wrong! It isn't what I want. Your son is a fine man, but he isn't Brendan Kane!"

"Kane! Will that name forever haunt me? You must cease this, girl. Franklin, Joshua and I have decided this marriage is best for you. He would never mistreat you because you debased yourself with that miner. My son—"

"Is appalled that you would speak to his future wife this way!" Josh shouted as he stormed in. "You have no right to judge anyone! Helena, Mrs. Henry is serving the evening meal in five minutes. I suggest you get yourself out of ear-shot!"

Helena turned to Josh. "Did you look into the things we spoke of yesterday?" She was clearly asking if he'd learned more about Daniel.

"I know too much now, if that's possible," Josh told her. "And I understand your reluctance over our engagement. Don't worry. It'll all come out right in the end."

Helena nodded.

"Order her not to mention Kane in this house," Harlan

demanded. "The only way to handle a rebellious wife is with an iron hand."

Joshua's anger flooded back, but luckily he also remembered his role as Helena's fiancé. "Never speak to her the way you just did. In fact, if I find out you have ever interfered with my life again, I'll make you pay."

Harlan scowled. "Are you threatening me?"

"Actually, I am. Now, what happened to the letters?"

"Letters?" His gaze met Josh's and all his puffed-up bravado disappeared. "She would have dragged you down. Her father was a miner. I couldn't allow it."

"Tell me!"

Harlan pursed his lips and stuck out his chin. It was clear whatever he'd done, he wasn't sorry. "I ordered Dodd to confiscate them. His wife was ill. He needed the job so he did what I ordered."

The full import of the words hit like a sledgehammer in the middle of Joshua's chest. She'd never known. Abby thought he'd left and hadn't once looked back. Lord! He was speechless in his fury. One thought reeled through his mind.

Abby. Sweet, hurting Abby, her trust shattered, her security and good name stolen. "There aren't words strong enough or low enough to express my feelings toward you. You destroyed us. You ruined lives—Abby's, mine, Brendan's and my son's. How could you do that to your own *grandson?*"

Harlan straightened in his chair. "There was a good chance he wasn't yours."

"Like hell you didn't think he was mine. You can go on telling yourself that, but we both know the truth. You knew I planned to either stay here or take Abby with me to Germany. You threatened to cut me off and not pay for my schooling, because I wanted to marry her. I told you I already thought of her as my wife and to do your worst."

"But she wasn't your wife. You should be thanking me for ending it for you. Forget the wench and her bastard child."

"You still expect me to believe you never suspected Daniel might be my son?"

Harlan crossed his arms across his sunken chest. "I was right."

"Then why did you check to see if Daniel looked like me? Was it because you wanted to be positive you'd made the right decision or because you didn't want living proof of your perfidity nearby? What I don't understand is why you didn't pay Abby and her family to leave. You wouldn't have had to worry that I'd find out then."

"I did offer money. More money than Kane ever saw in his life. It would have been the best solution for all concerned," Harlan snarled. "I didn't want any reminder of that family here so you could come home. The damned fool refused. Said his wife was too fragile to be moved and he wouldn't settle for less than marriage for his daughter."

"Don't pretend you were thinking of my happiness. You were thinking of your plans for me. What happened to the other letters Abby sent me?"

"Other letters," Harlan said stiffly.

"Brendan mailed them from Pottsville. How did you stop those?"

Harlan remained silent but Josh knew he was guilty as sin.

"At the other end," Josh mused aloud. "You bribed Herr Schmidt. How much does a dean's conscience cost? How much did you pay to destroy four lives? Hundreds? Thousands?" Harlan shifted in his chair and the truth dawned on Josh. "The new science building. My, my. You did go to a lot of expense."

Harlan didn't bother to deny it. "What are you going to do?" he asked.

"Do?"

"About Helena?"

Even as angry as he was, Josh had to stifle a grin. Let the old bastard stew. "What I do about Helena is no one's business but mine. But after hearing she's still not certain I will tell you there won't be a wedding until I know it's her free decision. That means I'm waiting to officially announce our betrothal until she reaches her majority. You're done manipulating me."

Chapter Seven

"I thought all you Kanes could read and write," Ethan Prescott said to Abby.

"We do," Abby said proudly. "Our mother taught us."

"But your brother uses a mark in the account books."

Abby frowned and walked over to look at the account book he had open in front of him on the counter. A lump formed in her throat. *So you hate Josh, do you?*

Years earlier Joshua and Brendan had each worked out stylized initials for each other. Apparently Brendan still used his. Abby stared at the "mark" then cleared her throat. "If you look at it, you'll see that it's actually his initials. Brendan prints a *B* for Brendan then bisects the circular segments with the diagonal lines of a *K* for Kane."

"Why, that's quite clever."

Abby gritted her teeth at the utter shock in Prescott's tone. It mattered not that this design was Joshua's. Brendan's for him had been equally as clever. "Brendan has always been very clever."

The store bell announced a customer and Prescott looked relieved for the interruption. "Good day, Mrs. Freitzburg," he said, rushing out from behind the counter.

"Are my glasses ready? I've brought my son to tote them for me."

"Are they, Abby?" Prescott asked.

"I just finished counting them. They're in this barrel over here," Abby said. "There was almost no breakage."

"Good. Good. So, Mr. Prescott, I suppose you'll be getting a lot of shipments like this one once Joshua Wheaton's new house needs furnishing."

"News certainly travels fast. He only just told me this morning to expect shipments of building materials. His architect is coming to look at the site. He'll be using the piece of land his mother left him at the west end of town."

Abby sealed the barrel of glassware in a daze. Joshua was planning to build a house. A house for Helena Conwell—on *their* land.

Hilda's voice intruded into Abby's thoughts. "As far from Harlan Wheaton and the soot of the mines as he could get, you notice," Hilda said. "I'm sure his mother would be happy."

With an ache in her heart, Abby walked to the back of the store where the voices blended and faded as she gazed out the window at the dismal day. That land had been their haven from the harsh realities of life, where they had dreamed of a better future.

A future together.

But Joshua wasn't her future. He would take Helena Conwell to that fairyland setting to live where his son had been conceived. Abby gasped, shaken by the admission in her thoughts and the jealousy she couldn't afford to fully acknowledge. Daniel was *her* son. And as for the jealousy, Helena Conwell was welcome to Joshua, his big house and everything else he had to offer! Abby didn't want him. She refused ever to want him or need him again. He was an old dream and she'd replaced him with another.

The store bell rang. Abby drew herself back from her thoughts as Sean Murphy held the door for Mrs. Freitzburg and her son. He sauntered through the store, hat in hand, and smiled when he saw Abby. "And how is the loveliest flower on the mountain this beautiful afternoon?"

Abby laughed. "And how old were you when you kissed the Blarney Stone, Sean Murphy? It's a perfectly awful day. The rain's turned the streets to muck and the wind's enough to cut a body in two."

"And it's a testament to your beauty that I can smile and see the day as lovely just for having gazed on such perfection as Abaigeal Sullivan."

"You need spectacles," Abby admonished.

"No. I've been tellin' you for years. I need *you*, Abby," he said, suddenly serious. "There's a dance planned at the church Saturday night. Come with me. If not for me, then for yourself and your boy. It could put an end to some of the speculation about you and Wheaton."

"Speculation?"

Sean looked at his shoes. "They all just wonder, that's all," he muttered.

"Wonder what?"

"If you'll take up with him again."

Abby put her hands on her hips. "And why would I, I'd like to know? After all he did to me and with him being engaged to Miss Conwell to boot?"

Sean pursed his lips and stiffened his spine as if trying to screw up the courage to say something. "A lot of folks still think you've been waitin' for him all these years. Even I've wondered. You know I love you and want to marry you, but you won't even step out with me to see if we'd suit. What is it that's stopping you if not Wheaton?"

Abby thought of the feelings she'd just experienced when

she'd heard about Joshua's new house. She was as big a fool as they all thought and she was tempted for the first time to actually give in to one of Sean's intermittent overtures.

He's a nice man. Why can't I love him back? she asked herself. And she knew the answer. She didn't respect Sean. And the other thing—the one that made her tremble with fear—was she *did* still love Joshua. "I'll think about the church social. I really will," she said quickly to banish dangerous ideas.

Sean looked shocked but recovered rapidly, smiling widely. "Suppose I stop by Friday to get your answer." He turned and walked to the picks and shovels then pivoted toward the door when the shop bell rang again.

"Afternoon, Ethan," Josh called as he passed the counter and moved straight toward Abby.

Sean shot Josh a killing look. She almost called out a warning to Josh when Sean's grip on the pick tightened, but then he put it down and lifted a shovel, his expression no longer fierce.

"Now that we've both had time to calm down, I'd like to finish the conversation we started the other day," Josh told Abby.

"My brother told you to stay away from me. He meant it."

Joshua's jaw hardened. "Brendan's not going to dictate to me what I can and cannot do."

Abby started to turn away. "I've work to do. This is neither the time or place for a private discussion."

"May I come by the house tomorrow morning before you come here?" Abby shook her head and Joshua sighed. "I have things I need you to know. About—" With his jaw clenched, Joshua glanced at Sean drifting toward them. "Friday morning then?" Josh asked.

She had to protect Daniel. Abby shook her head but almost

relented when she saw sadness edge into Joshua's eyes at her answer. *I'm supposed to protect myself and my son—not him!* "No," she reiterated aloud.

"Then I'd like you and Daniel to come for dinner on Saturday evening. We could talk then. I'd like Helena to meet him at his best and I think Harlan needs to be made aware of just what he did by keeping us apart."

Abby glanced at Sean. "I've already made plans for Saturday. Sean and I are going to the church social." She felt a pang of regret for using Sean because she'd never care for him as he wanted.

"Just Daniel then?" Josh asked. "We could get to know one another."

"No. Go away. I've given my answer."

Joshua stiffened. "That's it? No? No reason, just no?"

"I don't have to give you reasons, but if you must have them." Abby held up her hand and ticked off her list on her fingers. "One—Da would have a fit. Two—Brendan would just as soon shoot you as let you take Daniel to Harlan Wheaton's home. Three—Daniel wouldn't want to go and four, I won't be forcin' him."

Instead of getting angry, Josh smiled and leaned his shoulder against the wall. Abby's heart dipped. His eyes sparkled and his mouth stayed quirked up a bit more on one side in the crooked grin she remembered so well. Oh, how she'd loved that grin.

"Your brogue still thickens when you get mad. Did you know that?" he asked, still grinning.

I will not fall under his spell again! "Go away!" she shouted, uncaring if her raised voice caused a scene. She couldn't love him again. She had to make him leave her alone.

Joshua's grin faded and his mouth tipped downward. He straightened away from the wall and raised his voice for the first time. "I'm not going to allow Michael, Brendan or you to dictate to me whether or not I can see Daniel. I'm his father and I have rights."

Daniel barreled around the corner of the aisle. "Don't you yell at my mother! I'm not going anywhere with you. I hate you. I wish you were dead!"

"Daniel! I'll have none of that kind of talk!" Abby admonished. Joshua dead was something she couldn't contemplate no matter how furious he made her.

Instead of listening to Abby, Daniel launched himself at Josh, with fists flying. Abby could see Josh trying not to hurt Daniel while fending off his fierce, pint-sized attack.

Abby had forgotten all about Sean until he stepped in and grabbed Daniel around the waist, picking him up. "Settle down now, boyo. Your mother told you to stop this."

Daniel twisted but Sean held firm. "I hate him. I hate him!" the boy shouted.

"Suppose I take him for a bit of a walk, Abaigeal. I'll try talkin' some sense to him."

Abby was too shocked to object. The two were gone from the store before she even realized Sean had spoken.

Josh raised a shaking hand to his forehead. "I'm sorry, Abby. I shouldn't have rushed you or Daniel. I really do have to talk to you, so I'll have to take my chances that Brendan will be out, and that Michael will be in a more magnanimous mood. I'll be by soon."

Abby watched him stop at the counter to talk to Mr. Prescott. Then the clock struck four and Abby gathered up her things and slipped out the back door.

Daniel squinted in the darkness as Sean Murphy rustled around in the dim light, then a lantern flared to life. Daniel was nervous, but didn't know why. Sean was his friend, after all. "That was a foolish way to act, Danny."

"Only my granda calls me Danny."

Sean smiled. "Ah, a family name. I'd like to be more to you than just a friend. I'll be straight with you. I'd like to be your father. Family. I've loved your mother for what seems my whole life, but ever since I can remember, she's only had eyes for one man. Joshua Wheaton."

"My ma hates him!" Daniel declared.

"Danny, it's more complicated than that. Do you know what they did that made you?" Daniel felt a blush heat his face, but he nodded. He couldn't act like a baby if Sean was his friend. "Well, now, that sort of thing forms a bond for a woman as good as your mother," Sean continued. "She gave him her love, and her body and she can't just forget, no matter how much he's hurt her. Now that he's back and she sees him all the time, I don't hold out a lot of hope for her and me." Murphy shook his head sadly. "If only he hadn't come back."

"I wish he was dead!" Daniel said not for the first time. Saying it made him feel good. It released a little of the anger trapped inside him.

Sean chuckled. "I'll just bet you do, Danny. I'll bet it felt good hitting him."

"Real good," Daniel said, while nodding his agreement.

"I wish I could do that and more, but I couldn't get away with it." Murphy pursed his lips. "Of course, it remains to be seen if you will, either. Hitting him is liable to get you in trouble with your ma. You best hide your feelings a bit more. Sometimes, Danny, you have to go along to get along. But a chance for revenge usually presents itself eventually."

"I just wish my Uncle Brendan could get rid of him so Ma wouldn't look worried and sad all the time."

"I don't know if you can count on that. Did you know Wheaton and your uncle used to be great friends?"

Daniel was skeptical. "Him and Uncle Brendan?"

"Oh, Danny, Wheaton's a charmer. Fooled all the Kanes once. He could do it again, I'd wager. But I've been thinking. I've some friends. They don't like Wheaton, either. Should I talk to them, do you think? See what they'll do? For a friend of mine, they just might put themselves out a bit."

"What could they do?" Daniel asked, eager to rid himself of all the trouble that had suddenly come into their lives.

Sean smiled and sat on the barrel in front of him. All of a sudden he reminded Daniel of Mr. Prescott's cat when it cornered a mouse. But he wasn't cornered.

"They could get rid of him, Danny," Sean said and Daniel forgot cats and mice. "Shall I ask, do you think?"

"He wouldn't be able to bother us anymore?"

"He'd be gone."

Daniel thought of what it had been like before he'd ever seen Joshua Wheaton. Now, at home everyone was always upset. At school, he was being teased worse than ever. And all because his real father had come back. "I think I want him gone."

"Well, Danny, I'll try to see that gone is what you get."

Daniel smiled. He'd always thought Sean was silly because people made fun of him. But he'd been wrong. Sean would be the best friend and father a boy could have!

Friday afternoon, with the best two days of the week ahead, Daniel turned to his schoolmaster, Mr. Marks, who was sweeping the drafty classroom. "Do you need anything else?" Daniel asked.

"No, thank you for staying to help, Daniel. That's a fine job you did on that chalkboard. You run along. There's someone out front who wants to speak with you."

Daniel gathered his slate, books and lunch pail. "Who?"

"Mr. Wheaton."

Daniel moved with purpose toward the rear exit.

"Daniel Sullivan, don't you dare think of sneaking out. Mr. Wheaton's a fine man. As soon as he realized our school is in the old jail, he told me he'd find us a better building. You should be proud so fine a man wants to spend time with you. I'll not have you insulting a benefactor. Now you march yourself right out there and be polite!"

Dragging his feet, Daniel walked toward the front of the building. He glanced back. No escape. His teacher continued to watch him, clearly annoyed. Sean Murphy's words suddenly echoed in Daniel's head.

Sometimes you've got to go along to get along.

Sean was his friend so his advice must be sound. He seemed to think it would be a good idea to pretend to like his father. Letting his hatred show seemed to be doing no good. His mother was still angry with him for causing a scene in the store. Even his uncles told him he shouldn't speak disrespectfully to an adult, even Wheaton. Now, Mr. Marks was angry and he hadn't even scolded Daniel after he'd played hooky to work the breaker shed.

Daniel sighed as he pushed open the door. His father stood waiting. All the girls said he was handsome, and that they wanted to marry someone just like him someday. But then they turned right around and taunted him because Joshua Wheaton had never married his mother. Sean might be right, but Daniel just couldn't pretend to like the man.

"Daniel, I'd like to talk to you," his father said when he saw him.

Daniel stared up at his tall form and an idea occurred to him. He didn't have to pretend to like Joshua Wheaton, but he *could* pretend not to hate him. "Why?" Daniel asked, curious.

"Because I want to be your father, but I don't want to make

you unhappy. I don't want to cause you to get in trouble with your mother."

"Too late," Daniel snapped without thinking.

"Well, yes, I assumed as much. I knew you'd catch it for that scene in the store. I'm sorry about that but you were wrong."

"You yelled at my mother," Daniel accused.

"And I was wrong, as well. I know you think you hate me and I understand. I know you've had problems because of what happened years ago. I'd like to make up for that."

Daniel narrowed his eyes. What was Wheaton up to? "You can't. They all make fun of me and my ma and the more you pay attention to us the worse it gets. Maybe what you should do is go away and leave us all alone."

Wheaton winced. "I can't. You're my son."

Daniel turned away. "Well, you're not my father," he said quietly. Suddenly Daniel felt sadder than he could ever remember. He whirled back, tears burning his eyes. "You didn't want me before I was born. You didn't want my mother. You didn't want either of us for years. Now we don't want you. Go away!" Daniel turned and ran, ashamed of his tears—ashamed of himself. He didn't know why he felt that way and that made it all the worse.

"Why don't you listen to the boy, Wheaton?"

Joshua looked to his left, surprised to see Brendan at that hour of the day. "Taking the day off?" he asked.

"My work habits aren't at issue here. Your hovering about Daniel and Abby is."

Joshua felt his temper flare. "Your work habits are an issue when I say they are. I run the mine now, or had you forgotten?"

Brendan's green eyes flashed for a second then his whole expression and demeanor changed. "No, I'd not forgotten.

There've been too many changes for the good to forget that. Faltsburg needed something from the store. I said I'd come because I wanted to be sure Daniel went straight home. He's been around the mines for the last few afternoons. I don't want it. He'll not wind up like me if I can help it."

"What? Wasting his life raising another man's son?"

"Daniel's not a waste, but I won't be denying I never planned this kind of life for myself."

Josh couldn't look at his former friend knowing his father's manipulations had stolen Brendan's dream. "You were going west. A ranch and horses. I remember. I'm sorry for what part I played in the loss of your dreams."

"They aren't lost," Brendan snapped. "Just put off. In fact, if you'd waited another year, we'd have been long gone."

"Gone?"

"West, boyo. The Kanes are heading west come spring. What cash Abby and Thomas earn, we save. And I've all but paid off our debt. Come late spring or early summer, we'll be shuck of this place and we'll be free."

"She said she wanted to go west but—"

"Forget about Daniel, Joshua."

Josh stiffened. "Why does that sound like a threat?"

Brendan's smile was cold. "Why because it is, boyo. It is."

Chapter Eight

Abby reached up to dust a top shelf where an industrious spider had spun its web overnight and gasped, jumping practically out of her skin when a hand rested on her shoulder. She spun around, her heart pounding, only to find no threat but an old friend.

"Amber!" she cried and they hugged. "When did you get in to town?"

Amber Dodd smiled widely. "On the noon train."

"Your uncle never said a word about you coming when I picked up Mr. Prescott's mail at the station."

"I told him not to. I wanted it to be a surprise. I have so much to tell you." Her small blond friend craned her neck toward the front of the store. "Prescott's busy with customers, so we can talk for a few minutes. I'm just bursting with the news…I did it, Abby!" she exclaimed finally in a breathless rush.

Abby blinked. "Did what?"

"After hearing you talk about going west and all the newspaper articles you showed me, I caught the fever."

"What did you do?"

"You know the way I've felt about other men since Joseph was killed."

Abby considered her friend. Her dove-gray mourning clothes did nothing to enhance her delicate blond beauty. They drained her of color and vitality. She took Amber's hand. "You have to go on, Amber. I know you loved Joseph, but he wouldn't want you going through life alone. You're a beautiful woman and some man would snatch you up for his wife. You only have to give someone half a chance."

"The way you have?" Amber asked shrewdly, arching one delicate eyebrow.

"My situation is different. But come spring, I'll be doing something about it."

"And I'm going to do something, as well."

"Are you getting married?"

Amber shook her head. "No. I can't face the idea of loving someone only to lose them. But I am getting on with my life. I've taken a position as a governess." She halted, her blue eyes sparkling. "In California."

Abby almost didn't hear her friend because something occurred to her just as Amber named her destination. With her smile so bright and her eyes fairly glowing with excitement, Amber looked enough like Helena Conwell to be her sister. But Helena was to marry a fine man and Amber's fiancé had died days shy of their wedding.

"Aren't you going to say something?" Amber demanded.

Abby blinked. "California! Are you sure about this?"

"The position is with an old land-grant family. They have three children. Two girls and a boy."

"And what will you do when they grow too old to need you anymore?" she asked, worried for Amber.

Amber shrugged. "Find a new position. Or maybe help raise their children. I will simply put off crossing that bridge till it's in my way. I'm through hiding and through waiting around for life to just happen to me."

"How are you going to get so far alone?"

"Well, at first I was going to go by boat, but Uncle Charles is paying my way on the train. I have quite a while before the position begins. The younger child won't be six years old for another six months and that's when they want to start both girls' educations, so I don't have to leave for a few months. But I didn't want to stay with Joseph's parents any longer. They had hopes I'd make a match of it with their younger son. It's become uncomfortable. I've decided to stay with Uncle Charles until I leave."

"You're staying in Wheatonburg?"

"I am." She grabbed Abby's hand and squeezed. "I understand from Uncle Charles that you need a friend right now. I wanted you to know you're not alone, and I'll do anything to help I can." A noise from the front of the store drew both women's attention. "I better be off before old man Prescott gives you trouble," Amber continued. "We'll have all the time in the world to chat these next few months."

Abby blinked back a rush of tears and went back to her dusting as Amber selected a jar of jelly from a shelf and moved toward the front of the store. Then the clock struck four and Abby put away her duster and left for home.

She hurried toward the house a while later only to be met by Daniel running down Corker Road toward her. "Ma. Hurry. Granda fell. I helped him get into bed but he's hurt. I can tell!"

Abby took off running, but there was little to do once she got there. Her father assured her his pain was no worse than usual. His dignity was only a mite dented, he added with a smile.

She left him to his bed, but could not let it go. Had he been in a chair, all would have been well while she was gone. Like it or not, he needed that chair and by damn that old skinflint Harlan Wheaton was going to provide one!

"Daniel, I've an errand," she called, tossing her shawl over her shoulders. "Stir the soup pot once in a while and watch after Granda. See that he has what he needs. I won't be long."

Ire stood her in good stead until she'd knocked on the door. But as she stood waiting, her stomach started to churn. What would she do if Joshua or his intended answered?

When Henry pulled open the door a few moments later, his eyes widened. "Mrs. Sullivan. To what do we owe this pleasure?"

Abby relaxed a bit in spite of her agitation. "Oh, come now, Mr. Henry. You know full well you'll catch almighty hell the minute I leave for not warning Mr. Wheaton who has asked to see him."

"Yes, madam. But it's so amusing to see him squirm. Come. I'll announce you. Or not," he said with a sly smile and waved her into the front parlor.

Minutes later the squeak of wheels alerted her to Harlan's approach. "You! What is it this time?" he demanded.

"My father needs a wheelchair."

"So do I. What do you want from me?"

"A chair. He was crippled in your mines. You should buy him one."

"That was years ago. What kind of ridiculousness is this? Go home and leave me in peace."

"I'll go to Joshua and ask for *his* help then," she threatened. She didn't know why she said it. It had just popped out.

Harlan shouted, "Leave my son alone! He has a chance for a good life now. Do you think I don't know you seduced him out at that land his mother gave him? He got you with child. So what? It's been happening to the lower orders since the beginning of time."

Abby stared at Wheaton, all thought of the chair forgotten. She may have misjudged the depth of Joshua's love, but she knew how he felt about his father. He'd never have shared details of that night with him. Harlan had no earthly way to know that Daniel was conceived out at Joshua's land. Unless… "You *did* do it. You got hold of my letters. He truly hadn't know of Daniel."

Abby watched panic flash through Harlan's eyes before he looked away. "I don't know what you're talking about."

Like Mr. Henry, she wanted nothing more than to see the old devil squirm. She fixed him with a steely stare. "It's time I had a heart-to-heart with Joshua. About the chair…and *other* things. Good day to you, Mr. Wheaton."

Joshua locked the engineer's shed and took a last look around. Helmut Faltsburg had left with the last body they'd recovered, the man's widow weeping in the front seat of the buckboard. Josh stared at the ground. What a terrible way to die—drowning in a sea of mud. Four lives lost.

He looked around. There was no outward sign that a tragedy had occurred hours before. But even in the failing light, the scene depressed him. Mining scarred the earth. It killed men. It made others wealthy beyond the dreams of those who dug for it beneath the earth.

Why did I have to be a miner?

He looked around one last time. He hated this place. It even smelled of death. Something near Destiny tunnel drew his eye. A man walked quickly yet furtively away from the mouth of the tunnel. He had a sack in his hand that he carried with exaggerated care. As the man stepped into the last stream of sunlight that flowed above the pines, Joshua saw it was Brendan.

There was nothing left between them now. Brendan's

threat the other day had ended all hope in Joshua that his old friend would ever come to believe the truth of what had happened all those years ago. Just like with Abby, too much bitterness and too many years hung between them.

He mounted his horse and rode toward home. Tonight was the dance at the church Abby planned to attend with Murphy. Foolish though it was, Josh was jealous. Why couldn't he do as everyone wanted?

Forget Abby.

Forget Daniel.

What was really maddening and stupid was, if Daniel were happy and secure and if Joshua thought it would be ultimately better for his son, he would be able to step aside and never see the boy again.

Not so with Abby.

Knowing she'd married a man he hated out of spite didn't change a thing. He still wanted her. He still needed her in his life. And he *still* couldn't have her.

Josh reached the end of Corker Road. To the left was home, to the right, town. He brought his horse to a stop.

What had he done to deserve this? Why couldn't he have the one thing he'd always wanted. He'd loved Abby for what seemed his whole life. Since the very moment he'd first laid eyes on her.

She'd taken him by surprise at the edge of the woods near the coal fields. He'd been staring across the clearing at the shaft and all the activity. The sound of her voice had startled him….

"You're new 'round here. There's been a cave-in. I went to see if me da's all right. Mum is home with the little one. Was your da killed?"

Josh shook his head. "Why would you think that?"

Abby pointed at his face. "And you've been cryin'. Most boys don't cry unless it's a big thing. Death's a big thing."

He didn't know why he answered truthfully. Maybe it was the kindness in her eyes or the absence of mockery in her tone. "They wouldn't let me help. I thought I should. My father's Harlan Wheaton and he's away."

"Small wonder they wouldn't welcome your help. No one likes Harlan Wheaton."

"I don't like him, either. There's nothing I can do about being his son, or how he runs his mines. But I still wanted to help. They told me to go away even though they need volunteers."

"Aren't you afraid to go down there?"

"Sure, but the miners might still be alive. I wanted to help."

She grabbed his hand. "Then you'll help or my name isn't Abaigeal Kane!"

"Is it?"

"Is it what?"

"Is Abaigeal your name?"

"Well, of course it is! What good would it do to swear on someone else's name?"

Josh blinked. "I don't know but my father does it all the time. Sometimes I wish our pastor could hear him. I'm Joshua."

Abby pulled him along as she chattered on. "You've a very biblical name, but don't tell anyone I know. I'm Catholic and we're not supposed to read the Bible."

"And I'm Baptist but I sneak into Catholic mass all the time."

"Why?"

"At first because it would make my father mad if he found out. Later because all the candles and statues and the organ music make me feel warm. That sounds stupid, doesn't it?"

"Not a'tall. Will helping today make him mad?"

Joshua shrugged. "Probably."

"Then we'll see you help. I think it would be grand to make him furious." Abby laughed and let go of his hand as they neared the huge breaker shed. She took off running, motioning him along…

And she'd done it, too. She'd shamed them all for turning down two good hands to dig just because they hated his sire. He'd wanted to hug her then and there before God and the miners.

He still did.

Why couldn't he hold Abby in his arms again? Was that so much to ask? Without further thought, he spurred his horse into a gallop. He'd get washed up then head for town. One dance. He'd claim one dance with her. Somehow.

As it turned out it was relatively easy to do. It was an especially warm night and the rectory's windows and doors were open. A small group of fiddlers and pipers played inside while Josh listened and waited in the shadows. He didn't know what he hoped to accomplish but he stayed.

Some men stepped outside. They talked about the muddy cave-in and of how surprised they were that he'd worked beside them to save the men who would have perished without quick help. Josh dropped his head back against the rectory's clapboard exterior. At least someone appreciated his efforts. But it was ironic that he'd managed to succeed at mine engineering—the part of his life that would never bring him anything but unhappiness.

The music began again and the men left. Then Abby appeared not three feet away. Josh couldn't believe his luck. She wore a light blue dress, and had a shawl tossed over her shoulders. She'd pulled her hair up so her glorious curls cascaded down the back of her head.

As she moved toward him she glanced back through the door, and Josh realized she was trying to escape detection. He watched her for precious, long minutes, wondering at the emotions chasing across her beautiful face.

"Music not to your liking, or dare I hope it's the company?" Josh asked and stepped into the light, unable to stay away from her for another moment.

Abby's hand flew to her heart. "Joshua! You frightened me!"

"I'm sorry," he said automatically, but that was a lie. He'd needed to see her. "I didn't want to intrude on the party. Have you been deserted?"

"Sean had to talk to some friends. He said he wouldn't be long. Truthfully, I'm a bit relieved. He's not a good dancer. Brendan warned me he's as clumsy on his feet as he is at setting charges. He hasn't been allowed to set his own charges for five years. I should have listened. My poor feet need a break." She sat on a wall and slipped off her shoe.

Joshua chuckled. It seemed just like old times. The two of them sharing a private moment.

"What brings you here? You didn't realize someone else is missing, did you?" Abby asked and Josh's serenity fled.

Just like old times right down to the sick feeling cave-ins always left him with. "No. I wouldn't leave the mine unless we'd gotten all the men out. "

"No. No, you wouldn't, would you? Brendan's all right then?"

"I saw him myself after the cave-in." Josh remembered how strange Brendan had looked as he'd walked out of Destiny, looking around as if he were trying to hide something.

"He didn't come home. He does that a lot after somebody

dies down there, but he usually sends word that he's not hurt. He didn't this time. It worried me. No one knew where he was."

"He's fine," Josh assured her. He was drawn to her beyond his restraint when the music that spilled into the night slowed to a waltz. "I promise not to step on your feet, Ab." He stepped backward into the shadows and reached for her. "One dance?" he asked.

Abby hesitated. "I know cave-ins are hard for you, but that changes nothing of what we've said to one another."

"Tonight I don't care about the past or the future. It's the present that haunts me. Their faces. You always helped me forget, if only for a little while."

"It isn't wise. You must see that."

"I played ball with Quinn, Ab. He was so still when I found him." His voice broke and he had to clear his throat to continue. "No one understands how I feel but you."

Abby nodded then she forced a smile. "Fine, but I'll clock you if you tread on my toes. They can't take further abuse." She was actually teasing him! His mood lightened.

"I appreciate your kindness and generosity more than I can say."

Then she was in his arms, and there was little chance he'd tread on her toes, since he barely moved. Josh drank in the feel of her against him—all soft and strong. He breathed in the scent of her, trying to memorize it for lonely times. She overwhelmed his senses. He rubbed his cheek against the silky hair on top of her head and prayed the moment would never end. What kind of a fool was he? How could a moment in the shadows in the middle of the ugliest town in Pennsylvania be the shining light of the last decade of his life? Josh didn't know the whys or wherefores but he knew it was true.

His anger toward her had vanished the moment his father

admitted to having kept them and their letters apart. How could he fault her for marrying Sullivan if he was willing to give her child a name? She must have been desperate. And how he could have thought for even an instant that she'd have chosen the life she led over one with him? She lived a life that killed most women by their forties. It had killed her own mother. He closed his eyes and willed the ugliness of past, present and future away.

"You feel so good, Ab," he whispered. "I wish we could go back but we can't. Please let me explain what happened. Let me tell you what I found out. "Harlan—"

The earth shook as a boom rolled across the valley and up the side of the mountain, drowning out the music. Then another boom thundered, and another.

"Saints preserve us," Abby gasped and stepped out of his arms. "The mines."

Joshua whirled away and ran for his horse. He rode hard and fast. One question pounded through his head and seemed to echo in the beat of the horse's hooves. Did methane or sabotage cause the explosions?

Several mine supervisors lived close to the fields and had already arrived when Josh got there. The light from their lanterns and torches revealed black dust still spewing from Destiny. An earlier scene flashed across his mind's eye, but this time it held new meaning.

Brendan walking furtively out of Destiny, handling a bag as if it contained something very fragile.

Or very explosive.

Joshua felt sick. Would Brendan commit such a dangerous, destructive act?

Michael Kane's son wouldn't consider it. The boy he'd known wouldn't, either. Helena would say the man she loved was incapable of such a crime. But Abby's brother had a huge debt to settle with the Wheatons on her behalf. Could his understandable need to avenge Abby have pushed Brendan to join the AMU Workmen? Is this what his threat had been about?

Joshua shook off the thought. He had no answers for a score of questions including the cause of the explosion. And only time and investigation would provide answers.

Abby watched Joshua ride toward the mine at a breakneck pace. She'd been foolish to let their shared past influence her. But she knew what Josh felt every time a man died in the mines. She'd been there that first time he'd gone into a cave-in. She'd been the one to shame the others into letting him help. She'd been the one he'd gone to afterward, needing to tell someone about the pain he'd felt when he'd reached Danny McAllister's still body only to realize he was too late.

That day had changed both their lives. Though years of bitterness lay between them, she knew he still cared for the men and she knew he blamed himself for each life lost. Truth be told, a bit of her bitterness had faded earlier with Harlan's revelation. Joshua hadn't loved her enough to return for her, but he hadn't knowingly deserted her in her time of need, either. He wasn't absolved of breaking her heart but at least he was of being a thoughtless coward.

Dawn brought with it the answer Josh had prayed he wouldn't hear. Dynamite or its volatile cousin—nitroglycerine—had caused the explosion. Josh held the evidence in his hand. There was no denying the truth.

By seven, the miners who'd worked Destiny that day were being rounded up for questioning. Josh watched carefully as the two Pinkerton agents his father had hired to guard the mines at night tried to get answers. He was afraid physical persuasion would have been used if he hadn't been there. He didn't like the feeling or the two Pinkertons, so even though he'd had no sleep he stayed.

Brendan hadn't been among the men called in because he hadn't been assigned to Destiny. Joshua kept silent about Brendan's presence there the night before but the mystery made his stomach churn.

By ten, all the men had been questioned so Josh left Constable Addison's office and went to inspect the mine again. The tunnel was still partially blocked one hundred feet inside the entrance where men were busy clearing away the refuse. He didn't need to close down *this* shaft. The explosion had done it for him.

Josh headed for his horse, which stood patiently waiting. He would go home and get some sleep. Then he'd think. About Brendan and the mines.

"Are you going home?" He heard Daniel ask the question from behind him as he tightened the cinch on his saddle. Josh turned around, surprised that the boy had spoken to him without being forced. Daniel glanced back over his shoulder and fidgeted nervously.

Daniel was pale and visibly shaken. "It something wrong?"

Daniel pulled on his ear then clasped his hands behind his back. "No. No. I just wondered is all." Daniel looked around again then up at the sky. "It's a nice day, huh?" he said as if searching for an acceptable topic.

It was a beautiful cloudless day, which didn't seem fair to Josh. Men had died there yesterday. He sighed. "That depends on how you look at it, son."

"I don't like it when you call me son," Daniel said quietly.

"Danny then, the man you were named for was called Danny."

"I have a friend who calls me Danny. And Granda does, too, so you can't."

Josh went on as if Daniel hadn't spoken. "Danny died in a cave-in. He died saving a lot of lives."

Daniel took a step forward. "You knew him? Don't it bother you it's your fault that he died."

Daniel's aim couldn't have been better. He'd hit a sore spot that had plagued Josh for years and only became more sensitive as the years marched on. "Shouldn't you be in church?" Josh snapped.

"They're burying them miners. I heard you knew one of them. Don't that bother you, either?" Daniel asked again.

Josh suddenly realized Daniel wasn't there to reach out to him. He was there to goad him. And something inside him broke. Josh felt it go. It was like a damn bursting its confines.

"It bothers me a hell of a lot. Sometimes I have nightmares. Sometimes I can't sleep at all. Is that what you want to hear? Does it make you feel better to know I feel as if I've killed every man ever to die in a tunnel I engineered? And do you know what, Daniel? No matter how careful I am, and no matter how many rules I make to keep the mines safe, I still send men to their deaths and it kills a little more of me each time. So you see, sooner or later, if I keep doing what I've been trained to do, you'll get your wish and I'll be dead. Now go to church or I'll tell your mother you sneaked out while she was singing in the choir."

Daniel's eyes widened, then he turned and ran as if the demons of hell were after him. Joshua mounted and headed for home. Damn. He shouldn't have gone off on Daniel. Lately all he did were things he was sorry for later.

Once he was on Corker Road, Josh closed his eyes, knowing the horse would take him home without instruction. There was no warning, just a rushing sound and a pain in his back where something struck him hard. Then he was falling. He rolled to his feet as soon as he hit the ground. Three hooded men holding clubs pressed in. Joshua turned in a circle, trying to keep all of them in sight as they came closer. They were timid, but circled with purpose.

"I don't know what you gents think I've done."

The tallest thug smashed the stout club down on Josh's shoulder. Joshua went down on one knee cradling the arm. A second blow landed on the thigh supporting his arm. He crumpled forward as another club smashed across his back just below his ribs.

Joshua tried to grab the next club that came at him. He wrapped his fingers around it, but the man punched him in the mouth as another man grabbed him from behind. He held Josh as the tallest kicked him in the stomach and groin.

Then blows fell too quickly to be counted or felt individually. Pain the likes of which Josh had never known assaulted him as they took turns with fists and clubs.

They mean to kill me. He didn't doubt the instinctive thought for a second. Abby's face burst from deep within and Josh felt like weeping. If they succeeded, she'd never know he'd sent for her.

That thought alone gave him the strength to somehow struggle free, but the short man who'd only used his club so far rammed it into Josh's belly again, driving all the air out of his lungs. Then mercifully a club came down on his head once, twice, then a third time.

Josh's world blinked out for just a few seconds, then he heard a familiar voice and forced his eyes open. Brendan stood, his father's shotgun pointed toward Joshua. He'd gladly beg for his life if only to stop Brendan from hanging for his murder. He pushed himself to his knees and looked up at his old friend. "Please," he whispered. "Don't."

Josh knew at that moment he wanted—no, needed—the time to make amends to Abby. It didn't matter that he'd been just as much a victim of Harlan's manipulations, he should never have left without her. If he'd been adult enough to make a baby with her, he should have been adult enough to think of the possibility before rushing off in a huff.

"Please, don't," Josh begged again, but even to his own ears, his shout came out a small whisper. Too weak and full of pain to remain on his knees, Josh fell forward onto the rock-hard ground. Then everything faded. He was going to die. And the best friend he'd ever had was going to be his murderer.

Chapter Nine

"Now, I'll not be tellin' you again," Brendan shouted at the hooded men crowded around Joshua. "Get off to the side and away from him. This is a right smart shotgun and everyone knows I'm a crack shot. I'll not let you do this."

"After what he did to yer sister?" one of the hooded men sneered.

"If that's what this is about, none of the Kanes brought a complaint to the likes of you. It isn't a killin' offense for an eighteen-year-old boy to knock up a girl. 'Tis cowardly to run off and leave her, but I wouldn't want to think of all those that have been guilty of it swingin' in the breeze, either."

"We were sent to do a job fer one of our own," the tall one stated. All puffed up he was. Thinking himself the leader, no doubt.

"It wasn't one of us and there's no one entitled but Abby's family."

"You stop us and you'll be next on our list!" another said.

Brendan grinned. "Then I'll have to be makin' a list of my own, won't I? Now I wonder which of your voices and builds I can put a name to. The tall one? The leader of this little party? I wonder. Could you be—?"

"All right," the tall man shouted. "We're off but we won't forget this, Kane."

"Well, that's nice, isn't it, since I won't, either. Tell your leader that Joshua Wheaton is the best chance for a decent life any of us in the coal patch has ever had," Brendan told the three men. "Killin' him is like killin' the golden goose. I may hate his guts for Abby's sake, but he's always cared about his men."

Brendan knelt next to Joshua after the three turned tail. "Come on, Josh, we've got to be gettin' you on your horse. I'll not be puttin' my head on the choppin' block only to let you freeze solid on Corker Road."

"Didn't do it," Josh said, slowly. Brendan rolled him to his back and Josh groaned. "Feel sick."

"No doubt. What didn't you do?"

"You. You didn't…shoot me."

Brendan frowned. Joshua sounded pretty simple-minded. "Now why would you be thinkin' I'd do that?"

"Pissed at me."

Brendan nodded. "Granted."

"Bag in your hand…yesterday."

"Bag in my hand?" Brendan widened his eyes in surprise. "You saw me comin' out of Destiny?" He'd been looking around to make sure Dancy wasn't watching. And he would have looked damned suspicious to someone not knowing the whole story. Joshua had no way of knowing why he'd been there.

Dancy had found a couple kittens and put them in a bag. He was going to drown them in the mine but he was in a hurry, so he'd told Brendan to do it. Brendan had hidden them instead, thinking they'd make nice pets for Daniel, as well as good mousers to make Ab's life a bit easier.

Brendan put his arm under Josh's shoulders and lifted him to a half-sitting position. "You saw me, but you didn't turn me over to the Pinkertons."

Josh tried to smile, but a groan surfaced from deep in his throat and blood poured from a deep cut on his bottom lip.

"Come on, boyo. We've got to be gettin' you on your feet."

"Pain. Can't move."

"Oh, yes, you can and you will," Brendan ordered. "And if you think you'll be givin' me trouble remember right now I'm stronger than you."

Minutes later, he had Josh in the saddle, hanging on to the pommel for dear life. Brendan watched him for a long moment to see if he'd stay put.

"Now, I'll be leadin' this fine-looking filly home," he told Josh, who nodded his agreement.

But as soon as the horse moved a couple steps Josh gasped, "Stop!"

"You're a pain in the tail, Joshua!"

"Can't hang on," he whispered.

"Dammit!" Brendan growled and pushed Josh over the horse's neck to stabilize him in the saddle as his world obviously blanked out. Knowing it was the only way to keep him there, Brendan pulled himself into the saddle behind Josh. Blessedly he stayed unconscious on the ride home.

Abby finished polishing the window and put back the washed and pressed calico curtains. They were still faded but crisp and clean. She'd come home from church, needing activity, and the curtains benefitted. Neighbors thought her a fool to hang curtains at all but to Abby they were a symbol of what she'd have once they escaped the dirt and soot of the coal patch.

The explosion had been the talk of the town. Speculation ran high all morning about whether it was the doing of the AMU or just more poor engineering. Worried about her brother and the increasing pressure he faced from the AMU, she'd left her neighbors behind.

Abby had assumed from the moment the first explosion shook the town that the AMU was to blame. Lately it was always them. They'd gotten out of hand and Abby feared when the owners finally retaliated, innocents would die with the guilty.

She glanced out at the beautiful day. A horse that looked very much like the one Joshua rode moved slowly down the lane. There were two men in the saddle. They both swayed as if drunk…or hurt. Fear had her heart pumping double time in the blink of an eye. Who was hurt? Joshua or the man behind? She ran out, recognizing Brendan. He was the only thing keeping Joshua in the saddle.

As she ran toward them, Abby realized Joshua looked half-dead. "What happened?" she demanded.

"I stumbled on Joshua and three men havin' a confrontation. He was losin'. Badly."

Abby leaned closer to the horse and peered up into Josh's battered face. His coat was splattered with the blood that poured from his scalp and mouth. "Good sweet Lord! What kind of confrontation?"

"The killing kind, I'd say."

"He'd have been safer at home. What's to stop them from coming after him here?"

Brendan's eyes were sad as he urged the horse forward. Abby walked at their side. "I know you hate him, Ab, and I'm not blamin' you, but I couldn't let him die."

"That isn't it a'tall. They're dangerous men, Brendan. And we'll be no protection if they come after him."

"I had to bring him here."

"Why?" Abby asked as Brendan stopped the horse and dismounted from behind Joshua.

Josh immediately started to tumble after him. "Whoa, there, boyo," Brendan said as one of Josh's clear blue eyes opened. The other was swollen shut.

Abby had thought often that she'd like to see him just like this—beaten within an inch of his life—but she'd been wrong.

"We best get him inside and into Da's bed. Get the door, Ab."

"This is a mistake," Abby protested, staring into Josh's face, seeing something odd in the way he looked at her. "He should be home in his nice warm house with a doctor helpin' him."

Brendan shook his head. "I'll explain in a minute and he'll have a doctor as soon as you run and get one. Come on, Josh. Time to get you down."

"To shoot me?" Josh asked, overwhelming hurt in his tone.

"Now why would I kill our golden goose?" Brendan answered as he let Josh fall over his shoulder, taking his weight and moving into the house.

"Why does he think you'd shoot him? You didn't have any part in this, did you?" Abby asked as she followed them into the back room. She could hear her father stir in the parlor as he got to his feet. He followed them, asking what had happened.

"I might throw a punch or two at him, but I'd never do anything like this," Brendan grunted as he lowered Joshua to the bed, "but he seems to think I was part of it. That's one of the reasons I brought him here. They scrambled his brains good and proper. He hasn't made much sense but enough. If anybody heard what he was sayin' I'd be in big trouble."

"Why does Joshua think you were with them?"

"I think because he passed out just after I came upon them. I guess I can't blame him. The first time I saw him, I sucker punched him and threatened to kill him if he even came near you. Then there was that fight the day Daniel decided to work the breaker and yesterday I told him to stay away again. It was an 'or else' proposition. Besides that, he has reason to think I blew Destiny all to hell last night."

"Holy mother! Why would he think that?" Michael demanded.

"Wouldn't do it," Josh said, his speech slurred.

Brendan turned and sat next to Joshua and leaned closer. "No, I wouldn't. You didn't turn me in when you had every reason to. Why?"

"You wouldn't do it." His brow wrinkled. "But the bag?" Abby saw more than confusion on Josh's battered face. She saw desperation.

"Kittens were in the bag," Brendan explained. "Kittens for Daniel and Abby. Dancy said to destroy them. I'd have heard no end of it if he knew I was such an old softy, so I hid them in an old tunnel. You must've seen me when I went in to get them to bring them home. We've got them if you want proof."

Joshua shook his head then groaned. "My head, Bren. It's coming off."

Brendan chuckled. "No, it's attached good and proper. We'll be gettin' the doc, but you button that lip and stop talkin' crazy. You'll get me hung."

Josh frowned, clearly ordering something in his head. "You didn't shoot me. You didn't blow up the mine. You aren't a Workman." Joshua's face brightened as if all was suddenly right with the world. "You stopped them. You saved me."

"You've got it, boyo."

Joshua's lips turned up in the same someone-loves-me smile he'd beamed at her the day she told him she loved him. "Still my friend," Josh said to Brendan, then his eyes rolled back and he was gone from them again.

"Go for the doc, Ab. I'm not likin' his slippin' in and out like this."

"You go. He needs tendin'. I can do that better than you."

"I don't want to leave you or Da here alone with him. Just as you said those thugs might come after him."

Abby stood staring down at Joshua. He was so still. So hurt. Oh, this was wrong! He'd wronged her, but he was tryin' to clean up the mines double-quick. "It doesn't make sense, does it? Why hurt him when he's tryin' so hard to fix everything he can?"

Brendan frowned. "No. It doesn't. Now go. He needs help. I'm not likin' his breathing or his color now, either."

"Ma," Daniel called as the front door slammed shut, "what's *his* horse doing here? Ma? Where are you?" The worry in Daniel's voice wrenched Abby's heart. It had been a mistake to let the boy go on thinking the worst of his own father.

She met Daniel at the doorway to the back room, where Michael stood with the aid of his crutches. "Your father's been hurt. Attacked actually."

"He's not my father!"

"Yes, he is," Abby said.

"Well, I'm glad he's hurt. Now he'll be afraid and leave town." Daniel squirted past her and stood at the foot of the bed behind Brendan. Abby knew he couldn't see Josh yet when he shouted, "Do you hear that? I'm glad you're hurt. I hope you die!"

Brendan stood up and pivoted, his eyes blazing. "Have you ever seen a man beaten within an inch of his life?" He stepped aside and pointed. "Die is exactly what they wanted and still might get. Is that what you wanted to happen to the man who gave you breath, who found you workin' your fingers to bloody stumps and offered to pay you and your chums to go to school instead?"

Daniel just stared, suddenly pale. "He's going to die?"

Brendan tousled Daniel's hair. "I'm hopin' not, boyo, but I'm not sure I got to him in time. Suppose you run get the doc. Make up a bit for what you did."

Daniel paled even more. "Did?" he asked, his small voice quaking.

"Wishin' him ill at the store and just now. You haven't done anything else, have you?" Brendan asked.

"I wished he'd go away, but I didn't want him to really get killed. I—I didn't," Daniel cried.

Abby put her arm around her son. The poor boy fairly shook as Brendan squatted down in front of him, staring at him through narrowed eyes. "I'm not accusing you of this, Dan. Why would you think that? You couldn't cause this with angry words."

Daniel stared over at Joshua's still form and nodded. "I'll be back real soon," Daniel promised, then turned and dashed from the house.

Abby paced back to the kitchen then turned as footsteps approached from her father's room. Doctor Burke stepped out carrying his mug of coffee and leaving Brendan with Joshua. "How is he?" she asked.

Doctor Burke took his spectacles off and smoothed his salt-and-pepper hair off his forehead. "He's not good. Not good at all. He's concussed for sure and might even have a fractured skull. It wouldn't surprise me. He has several broken or cracked ribs to go along with a body that's bruised head-to-toe. I stitched the cuts on his scalp. Most of the blood came from them. I gave the bottom lip a couple stitches while I was at it. I've never done that before but knowing Harlan Wheaton, I thought I'd better give it a try. I'm surprised Wheaton hasn't found a way to get here or at least demand his boy be moved."

"Oh, Good Lord. No one's told him. We were all so concerned for Joshua we forgot about his father."

Doctor Burke frowned and stared at Abby with a narrow-eyed look that made Abby feel as if she'd exposed her soul. "I'll say this, they'd have killed a lesser man. Your concern was well-founded. Brendan saved his life. There's little doubt of it. He's awake again but he'll bear close watching. If he makes it past the next forty-eight hours—"

"If?" Abby all but shrieked.

"I have every reason to think he will, but head injuries can be tricky. He could be bleeding inside, as well." Burke handed Abby a piece of paper. "I've written down some instructions and warning signs. My wife will know where to find me, if I'm needed."

Abby stared down at the instructions trying to focus on the words, but one small word took hold of her thoughts.

If.

The very idea of him not making it was abhorrent. Somehow the world without Joshua in it somewhere would be wrong.

"How do we go about moving him safely?" she asked. "Wheaton's going to insist his son be brought home. He won't want the Kanes seeing to him."

Shaking his head Doctor Burke set his coffee down. "The man might intimidate me because he owns the hospital, but I won't bend where the health of a patient is concerned. We shouldn't consider moving him for at least a week. I'll go up to the manor and tell him and Miss Conwell. By now they're probably frantic over his whereabouts."

Abby remembered for the first time since looking up into Joshua's battered face that there was a woman waiting for him to return. A woman with the right to worry. A woman he planned to build a house for. A woman who should have been dancing in the shadows and comforting him the night before.

She told herself she didn't want that right. She refused to want it! She had new plans and dreams for herself and her son.

But a truthful corner of her heart shouted over the practical, hurt and angry voices in her head. Want that right she did!

She saw the doctor to the door, all the while burning with anger and resentment for the perfect-looking creature she'd met in the company store. And at Joshua as much for coming home and stirring up feelings she could never trust as for leaving her behind in the first place.

She remembered Joshua as a young man. Everything he'd done since returning said he hadn't changed so much as matured.

According to the wife of the Baptist minister, Helena Conwell had visited back in the late summer and early fall about the time Harlan had been shot and was recuperating. No doubt she'd passed whatever test she'd been given—the same test Abby herself had failed. She wondered if Harlan had told one of the servants to hide a pea under Miss Conwell's mattress to see if she was worthy of the prince of the realm.

The prince of the realm now lay on a crude straw mattress and rough muslin sheets. It was hard to believe she and Josh had danced as if ten years hadn't happened. Abby remembered the feel of his hard chest and his breath in her hair. She closed her eyes, recalling how he'd held her and rubbed his cheek against her hair. Tall and strong of body, he'd needed her to heal his sore spirit. Needy and hurting, he'd come to her.

Her!

But she'd failed the test, and he wasn't hers to comfort. He'd chosen another. It shouldn't matter. She'd plans of her own. A future away from him and Wheatonburg and condemning glances and sneering comments.

Abby walked into her father's room and stared down at Joshua. Her anger fled and her heart gave a lurch. She preferred to think it was caused by the severity of his injuries and not the sight of his muscular, hair-sprinkled chest or the lock of hair that fell softly on his bruised forehead.

Even battered, he's beautiful.

And battered he was. His lower chest was wrapped in deference to the broken ribs, and the rest of him was bruised purple. His nose, by some miracle, wasn't broken but his eyes and lips were swollen. There was a small cut on his high cheekbone and even one of his ears was scraped raw. How on earth would the shallow woman he was promised to ever deal with what he'd look like in the morning?

Abby couldn't fight the thought that Helena Conwell wasn't right for Joshua, but she put it away. He was no longer right for her, either. If all the animosity and anger suddenly vanished and Joshua came to her wanting to make good on his ten-year-old promise of marriage, she would have to say no. His life was here and hers was out there somewhere in the vastness and freedom called the West.

"The doctor's gone to tell his father," she told Brendan, who sat near Josh's bed. "I don't even want to think what Wheaton's going to say about this situation."

Joshua heard Abby's voice and opened his eyes. He could hardly believe she was there. His mind still wasn't clear, but things were starting to make sense. Brendan had stopped the men intent on killing him and had brought him home with him. Home to Abby. He tried to lift his hand to her. "Abby," he whispered.

"I don't know why he brought you here," Abby said. "You've a home of your own and beds a-plenty. And a lady you plan to wed. I shouldn't be carin' for you. 'Tis her place."

Brendan got up and walked stiffly to the window. Josh could only imagine what scene Brendan was remembering.

Probably Helena in a sunny meadow in high summer. It was how he'd remembered Abby all these years. Now his memory saw her as angry and resentful instead of happy and in love. He understood, but he hated that she felt that way, and he hated watching Brendan be hurt by talk of his wedding plans.

Josh couldn't stand her hostility or Brendan's pain any longer. He felt like a prisoner or a man trapped by ten tons of rock.

"Brendan," he called and his old friend turned and came back to the bed. His eyes were hard and his posture rigid until their eyes met.

Brendan grimaced, then his expression softened and he smiled. "And what can I be doin' for you now, boyo."

"I need you to help me."

"Now isn't that what I've been doin' since about half past ten this mornin'?"

"Take me home."

Brendan's eyebrows rose a notch. "Are you refusin' our hospitality?"

"Abby doesn't want me here. I've caused her enough grief. Take me home. Now. I'm putting your father out of his bed, too."

"I don't want to sound selfish here, old friend, but I need you healthy and able to talk to Constable Addison. If I take you out against doctor's orders, I might as well put a noose around my own neck and start diggin' both our graves. Besides, Ab's just worried that your family would rather have you at home than in this drafty old room of Da's. It isn't real healthy for you. Isn't that right, Ab?"

Abby glanced at Brendan and then Joshua. "I don't want you dead, Joshua. The doctor said you were to stay here, so here it is you'll stay. I'm uncomfortable with you here and I'll not be denying it. You nearly destroyed me and I don't like having to deal with you."

"But I didn't mean to. I didn't know about Daniel. I swear it. Harlan confessed. He paid the head of the university to have my mail censored. I never got your letters or any at all from Wheatonburg if others were sent. Harlan forced Dodd to confiscate my letters home, too."

Abby seemed to wilt before Josh's eyes. "Mr. Dodd?" Her voice broke. "I see. I'd figured out about my letters to you—"

"I spoke to him. Harlan had him over a barrel. His wife was ill and in need of medicine. Harlan threatened to fire him if he didn't cooperate. The only news from home came from Harlan. I thought everyone from here had forgotten me. I *did* send for you. I even sent money for passage. I'd saved it up by doing odd jobs. Then Harlan told me you'd married Sullivan. That's when I gave up on us."

Abby looked up, tears shining in her eyes. "I'm sure he feels justified. After all, now you're marrying the kind of lady he always wanted for you."

Joshua nearly came off the bed. "Do you think I give a damn what Harlan thinks?" He gasped as pain went shooting through his body, then he closed his eyes and gave in to despair. He wasn't engaged to Helena but he couldn't tell Abby. He prayed sleep would come before the tears burning at the back of his eyes betrayed him.

He was trapped. Trapped by his own plan. Trapped by the needs of others for revenge and power. Now more than ever he had to protect Brendan. Josh could do no less for the man who'd saved his life.

"Damned, if I don't believe him," Brendan barked after they watched sleep overtake Joshua. "And damn Harlan Wheaton for what he's done to all of us."

"I can hardly take it all in. I never thought someone could be so hateful." Abby thought back over every one of her encounters with Joshua since his return and sighed. "I'd put some of it together after I went to the manor about a chair for Da. Harlan let something slip that only Josh would know but I'd put it in one of my letters. I hadn't even considered Mr. Dodd holding his letters to me."

"I'm so sorry, Ab."

"It all fits, doesn't it?" she asked Brendan. "Joshua and the way he is. It being so out of character for him to abandon me and his child. His anger when he returned and learned of Daniel. His father'd told him I'd married Sullivan, though."

"I wonder how much he told Josh about your marriage? I wonder if Josh knows about the accident? That Sullivan was crippled and dying?"

Once again Abby considered the depth of Joshua's anger. "No, Harlan Wheaton wouldn't have told him the deal struck was for care till Liam died in exchange for his name."

"Ab, maybe there's a chance for the two of you. Joshua still looks at you the same way he did."

Abby sighed. "Our time's past, Bren. His father saw to that. Joshua's taken another woman into his heart. And I've replaced my dreams of a life with him with one I have no choice but to go after with everything in me. Heading west is the only way Daniel will have a decent life, and be able to grow into the good and decent man I know he can be."

"But Josh—he can't even know her, Ab. Not like I…I would need to know a woman before pledging my life to her. You said so yourself. And he obviously still cares for you!"

"Yes, he obviously does care about Daniel and me, but that isn't love and *love* is what I'd need of a husband."

"But you could build on all you meant to each other. You have a son by him, for God's sake."

"But for Joshua's sake as well as mine and most of all Daniel's, I can't let that be enough. You know him and how responsible he is. He's come back here and found a son and a woman his father caused him to wrong. I didn't want him that way. He just feels obligated to make it right because of Daniel."

"Are you sayin' you don't still love him?"

"That's exactly what I'm sayin'!" Abby cried. She thumped her chest over her heart. "Somethin's died in me! I can't trust a man with my heart or myself to choose the right one to give it to. All that aside, you see how much Joshua cares about the miners. He couldn't give up his dreams for Wheaton Mining nor would I wish him to. Too many other people's happiness depend on his success here. And I can't stay here. I just can't."

"He'd see any talk stopped. He'd stand by you."

"But where would that leave us? I'll tell you where! In a sham of a marriage like the one that produced Joshua. Did you ever wonder why he always tilted after windmills and looked for love and acceptance anywhere he could find it? He never found purpose or affection in his own home. I'll not live that way, I'll not give my son a life like it nor will I condemn Joshua for the second half of his life."

Brendan stood, shoulders slumped as if her answers had destroyed his dreams and not hers. Apparently, he'd never really given up hope for her and Joshua. "I know you once loved him like a brother," she said. "I'm sorry, but it just can't be."

"'Tis your life. I'd best get at choppin' some wood. I've put it off too long. I'll take Daniel with me to keep him occupied and get him out of Thomas's hair for a while."

Abby watched Brendan leave and wondered about his deep disappointment. It was her happiness in tatters, not her brother's. Shaking her head, she glanced at Josh and was surprised to see him awake again.

Abby put her hands on her hips. "You're supposed to be sleeping."

"I'm sorry to be such trouble."

Abby's heart wrenched at the look in his stunning blue eyes. Actually it was only one eye. Such sadness and heartache were written there. She didn't know how she knew his feelings but accepted that she did. She should have known he'd never have abandoned her and his son. And now it was too late for all of them.

"What is it, Joshua?"

"Doc Burke said I still may not make it." His voice cracked on the last word and ripped out another chunk out of Abby's battered heart. "Please don't hate me. And don't let Daniel hate me if I don't have the time to make amends."

"Daniel doesn't hate you," she lied and looked away.

You can't die before Daniel gets to know the man you really are. We'll still leave but he'd at least take good thoughts with him.

"Don't talk nonsense," she continued. "There'll be no dying on my watch. You hear me, Joshua Wheaton?"

"I hear," he replied, shutting his eye. "Talk to me, Abby. I just want to hear your voice. Tell me about Daniel. Tell me about my son. At least that way maybe I'll know some things about him in case I—"

"Only if you promise to get a more positive attitude about the future. You'll have one. You have to believe!"

His swollen lips kicked up in a little smile. "Yes, ma'am."

"All right then. We'll talk of Daniel. He was Daniel right from the beginning. Kicked the daylights out of my ribs for months, then came into the world squallin' like a banshee. There was no doubt he'd arrived."

"Wish I could've been there."

Abby reached out and covered his hand with hers. "None of that now. Put that sort of thought out of your head. We're celebrating life here. Daniel's life. *Your* life. He was such a fine-looking babe. All gums and smiles for the longest time and such a head of hair! There was no waiting a year for his first haircut. And you'd have thought he was Samson being shorn by Delilah the way he screamed that day. Brendan laughed himself silly while poor Da snipped away."

"Did he walk early?" Josh asked, visibly more settled now.

Abby pulled a purposely silly face. "The little imp wouldn't even give it a try. Hold him by the hands and he'd let those little legs collapse. For nineteen months we all carted him around and the size of a three-year-old he was by then. Then one day Thomas carved a little duck and put it on wheels with a stick attached. He gave it to Daniel and showed him how it worked. And off he went scootin' it about all over the kitchen as if he'd been born on the run."

"He seems to have a lot of energy," Josh said, his voice weak and sad as if his heart was breaking.

Abby went on hoping to distract him. "It seems like yesterday that he brought me my first flower. A weed it was, but so precious to me. He was about two and a half years. Thomas and I had him in a meadow to play. He bent down, plucked up a violet and came running with it. It was mangled and smashed but the most beautiful violet I'd seen in a long time." She thought back and smiled.

"I used to bring you violets all the time. Remember?"

Abby forced the pain away. Josh needed peace and things to perk him up. "It's a chip off the old block he is. You should see him whack a baseball. Brendan and Thomas spent all of last summer chasin' his ball hither and yon. He ran them ragged."

"Maybe by summer he'll let me field for him."

"Now there's the spirit," Abby said, feeling guilty for the hope she'd put in his eyes. By summer the Kanes were heading west. Daniel with them. There was no choice. Their son would never grow up whole in a place that reviled him as a bastard. And she could not live day in and day out watching Joshua sire other children with Helena Conwell.

Josh's hand touching her cheek snapped Abby back to the present. "So sad. Why?"

Abby opened her mouth to tell him but couldn't. She shook her head. "I don't like seeing you like this. They shouldn't have done it. You don't deserve their anger. You've tried to make things better. Why can't people live in peace?"

"Because of greed and jealousy. Because people like Harlan squeeze the men till they can't take it any longer. Now they're so bitter they've gone out looking for blood. Today it was my blood." Josh closed his eyes. "I'm afraid Bren's going to be next. I shouldn't be here, Abby."

"Well you are and here you'll stay till Doctor Burke says you can safely be moved. Now sleep."

He never heard her. Josh had already drifted off again.

Daniel rushed out the door of the new schoolhouse. He wanted to get home and make sure his father was still all right. It had been a week and he got a sick feeling in his belly when he thought of how hurt he was. It wasn't what he'd wanted. It wasn't what he'd wanted at all.

He skidded to a halt and swallowed around the lump of fear in his throat when he got to the outskirts of town. Standing in front of him blocking the road were three large boys nearly his Uncle Tom's age. They were boys who had never gone to the new school. Before he knew it they grabbed him.

"We have a message to give your folks," the largest boy announced. "Tell 'im to send Joshua Wheaton packing or they'll come after him there."

"And tell them they won't worry who gets in the way," the one on his left whispered. "It don't matter a whit that it was you who asked for the job. It was your uncle what saved him. You got it, Danny?"

Still held by the two other boys, the larger one punched Daniel in the stomach. He doubled over and the other two loosened their grip and started hitting him, too. Daniel knew he had at least one thing in common with his father. He knew how it felt to be held down and hit. And he knew something else. He deserved this. It was punishment for what he'd done. Because now he knew for sure that the AMU had beaten his father because he, Daniel, had told Sean Murphy to ask his friends to get rid of Joshua Wheaton.

Daniel didn't cry out as the fists landed. Uncle Bren said Wheaton hadn't cried no matter how hard they'd hit him and Daniel wouldn't, either. He deserved this after all, so he had to be just as brave as his father had been.

So when the big boys pushed him in the dirt, Daniel got himself to his feet and stuck out his chin as they ran away. Halfway up Corker Road, though, he heard his Uncle Brendan call to him from behind, and the tears he'd kept at bay welled up.

He'd tried to be brave, but he was so scared and hurt and ashamed. Daniel dropped his things and ran back into the safety of his uncle's strong arms. But he didn't even feel safe *there* anymore. It was one thing to fight with boys his own age, but another thing altogether for boys almost as big as his Uncle Tom to hold him and hit him. Daniel didn't think he'd ever feel safe again.

Chapter Ten

Abby closed her tired eyes while stirring the soup she'd made the night before for tonight's dinner. Doc Burke, Joshua's poor condition and an early blizzard had conspired to keep Joshua under her care for nearly a week now and she'd slept little in all that time.

It wasn't that Josh was much of trouble. He wasn't. He asked for nothing, never called out for help and slept most of the time. Weak tea and broth were the only things he'd managed to eat as yet, so he was no financial burden. Especially since even as ill as he was, he'd noticed she'd missed work because of him. So being Joshua, he'd insisted on paying her lost wages.

No. He was no trouble, but his presence caused a kind of tension in the house that was like a living, breathing monster. It robbed Abby of sleep, Thomas of the stillness that usually allowed him to sit for hours carving and Brendan of an appetite that had rarely failed before. Da seemed unaffected except that he spent most of his time staring at Joshua as he slept. But it was Daniel's reaction that was the most disturbing and was as much a cause for everyone else's disquiet as was Joshua himself.

Daniel was afraid. He swore he wasn't, but she'd caught him several times peeking in at Josh. Once he'd run to her, swearing Josh was dead. He had terrible nightmares, too. He said he didn't remember what they were about, but Abby knew her son, and he was lying.

During his few hours awake, even Joshua had noticed Daniel was not himself. Watching him move about on cat feet, trying to be a perfect child, gave Abby a feeling of impending doom. It made no sense but there it was.

She nearly jumped out of her own skin when a thunderous pounding echoed through the small house. It sounded as if someone were trying to kick down the front door.

"Abby," Brendan shouted. "Open up."

She rushed to the front door, which was bolted from the inside for safety because Joshua was there. And that was when she heard Daniel crying.

"What's happened?" she asked as Brendan carried him inside. Her boy was quaking and sobbing in his uncle's arms.

"They beat him, Ab. There were three of them."

Abby felt her temper fire as Brendan sat at the kitchen table with Daniel in his arms. His sweet, lower lip was split, his right was eye bruised and he was holding his stomach as if it hurt terribly.

"How could little children hate this much? Oh, their parents have a lot to answer for. Who was it, Daniel? Who were they?"

But Daniel wouldn't look at her. He only shook his head and clung to Brendan. Abby looked once again into her brother's troubled green eyes. "Bren?"

"They were older boys. This was a message. About Joshua."

"Glory be to the Father. So they're pitting children against children now." Abby turned at the sound of the wheels of her father's new wheelchair.

The chair had arrived in a carriage with Helena Conwell. The young woman had not been as haughty as she'd been in the store. She'd been polite, asking to see Joshua if it wasn't too much of an inconvenience. She didn't want to intrude if Abby's hard-working brothers were at home and by the way there was a chair for her father she hoped would help repay their kindness.

Abby hadn't been able to turn her away, much as she'd wanted to. It had been too kind a gesture to be ignored and too desperately needed to be turned down. So Abby had swallowed her pride and shown the pretty young woman to the room off the kitchen. They'd spent a surprisingly short amount of time together, then she'd left never to return again.

Her father brought her thoughts back to the present. "Abby, latch the front door again and give me my shotgun."

"I'll do it," Brendan growled, then stood and set Daniel on the table. Abby stepped to Daniel's side and her son clung to her now. She gathered him against her and held him for all she was worth. She couldn't imagine such hatred in the young. What was the world coming to?

Her Daniel was a fierce little boy who got into brawls when taunted by the other children, but he'd never run home crying when he lost. Eventually his sobs slowed and she asked again, "Can you tell me if you're crying because you're frightened or in so much pain? I can't help if I don't know."

Daniel nodded and took a deep shuddering breath. "He said to tell you to throw Joshua Wheaton out or they'd come after him here. Not the big boys. AMU Workmen. The other one said one of you might get hurt if they do."

Abby's fury burned.

"Did you recognize them?" Brendan asked, returning.

Daniel hesitated, trepidation in his blue eyes, then shook his head. "They were working in the breaker shed the day I was there."

"But no names?"

Daniel just shook his head and laid it on her shoulder, snuggling deeper as if to find a safe haven.

Josh held on to the doorway for dear life and prayed he didn't wind up in a heap on the floor. When had the world gone so insane?

"Bren," he said quietly, "I think you'd better get me out of here."

"Doctor Burke said you weren't to get up! What are you doing out of that bed?" Abby cried.

Josh had never felt so powerless. His son had been beaten and was crying. That alone told him how badly hurt the boy was. Nothing made Daniel cry—at least not where anyone could see him. Josh understood and respected his son's strength and the tender heart he kept hidden. But just then that heart showed in the way the boy held on to Abby, his arms wrapped about her slim waist, his head nestled against her breast. He wasn't afraid for himself but for his mother.

"I don't care what Burke says," Josh told Brendan, his teeth gritted against pain. "I'm a danger to all of you." He grabbed onto Brendan's arm for support. "And I don't think Abby or Daniel should go anywhere alone."

"Daniel, I concede, bears watching in light of what happened. Especially since everyone knows you've taken an interest in him. But no one in their right mind would hurt me to get to you," Abby countered.

Josh wondered how she could be so blind. Her brother simply nodded in response as if it were a given that Josh still cared for Abby, then he gestured to the nearest chair. Josh nodded and let Brendan help him get there. "Abby," he said, "the AMU is obviously furious that Brendan stopped them, and that you've taken care of me. They found one way to get at you two and they might try another. Please don't wander around by yourself."

Abby's eyes blazed. "Cowards they are. That's for sure. I'll be careful. You've all got my promise." She walked Daniel out of the room.

Josh watched her leave. He was the cause of the danger and he couldn't even stand on his own, let alone protect her or their son. His pride stung. "If Dakota's still here, will you help me get on him?"

"Your father had someone fetch the horse, besides which, you can't sit a horse," Brendan told him.

"Your wagon should do just fine then."

Brendan shook his head. "If I go borrow your father's carriage, it would be a smoother ride."

"I don't want to cause you more trouble than I already have."

Brendan raised a mocking eyebrow and turned to leave but stopped and came back. He looked hesitant, worried and terribly sad. "I'd been thinkin' they might go after your fiancée before they'd ever think to move against Ab or Daniel again. You should think seriously about a guard for her."

"Don't worry. I will," Josh said quickly, once again burning to tell Brendan the truth about their engagement. But he couldn't tell him the reason for the engagement without possibly putting the Pinkerton man in jeopardy. He also couldn't risk that Gowery would leave town if Josh cried off. He'd lose track of the investigation and endanger Brendan.

It was ironic that Josh had come back to this town thinking himself free of constraints, and now he was more boxed in than ever.

Several days after Josh insisted upon returning home, word reached Wheatonburg of a tragedy in another town. Pinkerton men broke in to the home of a suspected Workman. The miner's sister was killed in the fray. Clergy called her a slain innocent. The *Miner's Journal* out of Pottsville claimed she was a victim of her family's illegal activities. The miners called her a martyr.

Women on both sides of the mining business suddenly felt vulnerable. Some women had been witness to the murders of husbands and brothers in the past but they'd always been safe from acts of violence.

Christmas came and went and Abby had an escort everywhere. She neither saw nor heard anything from Joshua. She began to think he'd decided to leave her and Daniel alone. And if that brought with it a soul-deep sadness, she refused to acknowledge it.

Instead she and her friend Amber continued to plan their exciting new futures in the west. Abby made clothes for Daniel for the trip as advised in the literature she'd gotten on travel by Conestoga wagon. Their debt was now paid to the company store and their meager savings grew slowly. Abby took heart, knowing her precious son would soon be free of the stigma of his birth, free of guards following his every move and free of the threat of the AMU Workmen.

In the manor on the hill, Joshua and Helena continued to play out their arrangement, counting the days until they were both free. They spied on meetings, Helena planned her future with Brendan and Josh dreamed of sweeping Abby off her feet when summer flowered the meadow where they had once lain in ecstasy.

June had been selected for their supposed "wedding," because Josh had insisted it be well after Helena's twenty-first birthday. He'd refused to marry her if it was against her will, and said he wanted her inheritance in her own control and removed as a coercion to their marriage.

Franklin Gowery, therefore, was unable to leave since he knew Helena wasn't happy about her impending marriage. He took her with him on a visit home at Christmas, but Josh insisted she spend most of her time with him, so they could grow to know one another. Gowery returned with her by the New Year.

The plan to keep Gowery in town worked well. Joshua was able to monitor all the late-night, secret meetings between Harlan, Gowery and the Pinkerton agents. Josh burned with resentment that Harlan had excluded him, but admitted Harlan knew him well. Joshua would never have cooperated fully and not at all in framing Brendan.

As planned during Helena's visit with Josh at the Kane home, she'd taken his place spying until he could take up the job. McParlan, one of the Pinkerton spies, had tried to quit because his information had led Alan Pinkerton to the home where the woman was killed. Like Josh and Brendan, McParlan now feared for the women of the region. Gowery promised there would be no more vigilante raids, so McParlan reluctantly stayed.

Joshua's memory of the days just after his beating were fuzzy and muddled. He did remember that Brendan had saved him, and that he'd had a plausible explanation for his presence and actions at Destiny before the explosion. But keeping Brendan safe from prosecution as a Workman was even more difficult than he'd thought and he couldn't even share the reason with Helena.

The company store accounts for December had been submitted to him by Prescott. There was a disturbing entry. Two days before the explosion, Brendan Kane had purchased his explosives just as he usually did around that time of the month. But then three days later he'd bought another month's supply. Josh was again forced to wonder if Brendan had used the first batch on Destiny. Brendan had saved Josh's life, but Josh wasn't sure that proved anything. It was also entirely possible Prescott had doctored the store records as dictated by his father or Gowery. Or the AMU could be framing him for their sabotage because Brendan had refused to cooperate with them.

Joshua didn't know what to think. He only knew he couldn't do anything until he was sure of Brendan. Because even if Brendan was innocent, and Josh prayed he was, the evidence against him was convincing enough that a jury might find him guilty.

The last day of January saw Joshua returning to the coal fields. Helmut Faltsburg had carried on in his stead but had put off any work in River Fall. He wanted Josh to make a more in-depth inspection when he wasn't furious and determined to do the impossible.

The day was cold and snow threatened again but Josh and Helmut rode the eleven hundred feet down into the mine. The timbers, which he'd noted before were too far apart in the breasts, hadn't been put in place to hold up the mountain, but to warn of imminent collapse by their creaks and groans. There was an old miner's saying, "When the timbers start talking, it's time to start walking," and that day the timbers were shouting.

Josh stopped by the store, needing at least a glimpse of Abby. She was dusting shelves when he walked in. Prescott rushed to help him but Josh waved him off. He didn't like the storekeeper's knowing look when he noticed the direction of Josh's gaze, but he just couldn't leave. He needed to talk to her.

"You're looking better," Abby said, twisting the dust rag in her hands as he approached her.

Wanting to put her at ease, Josh chuckled. "Since I looked three days dead the last time you saw me, I'm glad to hear it."

"But you do look tired," she added.

"I went down into River Fall today. I'd hoped it wasn't as bad as I remembered."

"But it was. I've heard Brendan talking about it to Da. Did you see Brendan?"

"We nodded a greeting," he told her absently, staring at the sunlight in her hair. "I'm sorry I can't really talk to him, but I have to keep my distance. I don't want to make him more a target than helping me already has."

Abby nodded.

"So about River Fall. I'd hoped to open it again soon. Today, I had to extend the shutdown order until a new shaft can be completed."

"Is it played out?"

Josh smiled. How Abby had grown up around mining while managing to avoid all but the most elementary knowledge of the business he'd never understand. "There's plenty coal. That's not the problem. Wide pillars of coal are supposed to be left to hold up the rock above. If too much coal is taken out of those pillars, you get a collapse. It's a danger for anyone to be inside any of the existing breasts. And there's a huge ventilation problem down there because of the explosion. That was supposed to be the purpose of the new shaft but today we found a fault line. Helmut and I decided to clear out Destiny and combine the two tunnels. We'll ventilate through Destiny. That should bring the mine up to government standards."

"Isn't that going to be expensive?"

Josh sighed. "Very."

"Are you… Is Wheaton Mining in trouble?"

Josh raked his a hand through his hair. "If we don't get a tunnel open and damn soon, we will be. I can't fail, Abby. I have to prove safer mining can be profitable."

"But what if you go broke?"

Josh grinned. "I won't go broke. Harlan's mining company may but I won't. I've put every spare cent I've ever earned into diversifying and so has Harlan. I'm worried because if this doesn't work, the mine shuts down. That puts the men out of work. I know I've gone about this wrong. Changes should be gradual to be at all practical, but I can't bring myself to do it that way."

"Leaving the River Fall shaft open would have been practical. Is that it?"

"Not without sending good men to their graves. There'd be men asphyxiated or an explosion because of the volume of gas down there or an eventual cave-in would kill them."

Abby granted him a sad smile. "You're a good man, Joshua Wheaton."

Joshua smiled wearily. "I thought you'd forgotten."

Because of his worry for Daniel, Joshua found himself knocking at Abby's door the following afternoon. Her eyes widened when she saw him. "Afternoon, Abby," he said, tipping his hat. "Might I have a word with you?"

Abby stared for several long seconds. He wished she wouldn't look up at him with such worried eyes. "Talk?" she asked at last. "What…is there to talk about?"

"Daniel." He put up his hand up to forestall her objections. "Before you go off half-cocked let me explain. I'm sorry for a lot of what I said to you when I found out about Daniel. I didn't understand about the letters then. Daniel has to get to know me and learn I'm *nothing* like Harlan."

Abby looked away. "I have no objection as long as you don't try to take him away from me."

Josh felt a tide of anger rip through him but he clenched his hands behind his back and controlled it. "Do you believe I didn't know about Daniel and that I *did* send for you?" She nodded. "Then what have I ever done that would make you believe I'd do something so damned rotten? I want to get to know him. Is that so impossible to understand?"

"No. It isn't. I trust you about your intentions toward Daniel."

"Just so you know how important Daniel is to me, I've changed my will. The way things have heated up with the AMU I thought I'd better do something immediately. Daniel is my sole heir."

She clearly didn't know what to say. "I'm touched you'd do that, but I don't like to think it's a necessary precaution." She glanced over his shoulder again. "You shouldn't have ridden here alone. Not after what happened in November."

Josh sighed in disgust. "There's a Pinkerton just around the bend. Harlan and Gowery insisted."

Abby laughed. "It's glad I am I'm not the only one with a shadow these days."

"No, you're not, believe me." Joshua grinned, but sobered when he saw Michael wheeling his way toward the door. How was it Michael managed to look so much more of a man than Harlan sitting in the same kind of chair?

"Good afternoon, Mr. Kane," he called over Abby's shoulder. Abby's father had said little to him during his short stay except that Josh shouldn't worry that he'd put Michael out of his bed. Still, it galled Josh that he'd let the man down by leaving Abby alone and pregnant.

"And a good afternoon to you, too, Joshua. And I'm hoping it will continue to be a good one," he finished pointedly.

Josh nodded, understanding the message. If Abby wanted it, Michael expected him to leave but he didn't know if he could. He'd lost so much time with Daniel already.

"So what do you say? Could I have a few minutes with Daniel after school today?"

Abby sighed. Joshua looked so vulnerable, standing on her stoop, his blue eyes reflecting the afternoon sunlight. He'd looked the same way the day before—as if the weight of the world sat on his broad shoulders. And she supposed it did. Their small corner of it anyway.

"Suppose you go tell your Pinkerton agent to go on home until about eight. You can come on in and stay for dinner and some talk later. I think it'll be easier for Daniel to warm up to you if he sees us do the same."

"Stay? You want me to stay for dinner?"

Abby suddenly remembered that he had a fiancée. "Unless Miss Conwell will object, that is."

"Helena? Her encouragement helped me get up the nerve to come to today."

Was the woman daft? Abby longed to ask, but instead— kill her though it did—she said, "That's very generous of her."

"That's Helena, generous to a fault," Josh replied. Abby noticed a wry tone in his voice and could have sworn he colored slightly. What was going on with him?

"I hope my staying won't be a problem?" he asked.

"My father and brothers defer to me where Daniel is concerned. But he'll be a problem. Don't be thinking otherwise. There's a wealth of bitterness in him. I give you my word, it wasn't put there by me or my family. It's this town that caused it. Not for a minute has that boy ever been allowed to forget that he's Harlan's kin and that you thought so little of him and me that you left town rather than claim us. I understand what happened but Daniel has suffered."

Looking pained Joshua nodded and he stepped inside.

"We're having company for dinner, Da," Abby told Michael.

"It's a start," Michael told them, looking entirely too pleased. "I just heard your brothers 'round back."

Abby glanced at the elegant clock on the mantel that Thomas had just finished. "Their baths are ready. I finished heating the water a bit ago. Call Daniel, will you, Da. Joshua, why don't you go sit near the fire and warm up?"

Josh went into the sitting room as Abby suggested. He looked around at the room, ashamed. He'd only claimed ownership of the house on his first visit to get Abby's goat. In truth, he was anything but proud of being part owner of these hovels his father called dwellings.

He sat uneasily in a comfortable chair near the fireplace. Josh found the room cheery and warm. Then the mantel snared his attention so he stood to study the workmanship. It was out of place with the possession house as was the wooden furniture scattered about. It all matched the mantel perfectly.

He examined the clock Abby had glanced at. It was a work of art. "Abby," he called, "where did you get the furniture?"

Abby returned from the kitchen, beaming and obviously proud. "Thomas. He builds it in his spare time. He wants to be a cabinetmaker."

Josh looked up from the glowing coal in the grate when Abby's brothers entered.

"Joshua," Brendan said, worry in his tone. "Is there some problem?"

"Abby invited me to stay for dinner so I can get to know Daniel."

Brendan's eyes went hard for a second, then he smiled, albeit an obviously forced one. Josh understood. Brendan had probably played the role of father for nine years and now along came Josh to take away the honor at the same time he stood engaged to the woman Brendan loved.

"'Tis as it should be," Brendan told him, "and it's sorry I am I won't be able to stay. Sean asked me to have dinner with him at the boarding house."

"This is the first I've heard about it, Brendan Kane," Abby scolded from off in the kitchen.

Brendan's green eyes seemed to catch fire as he turned her way. "Since I just got home and since you weren't me mother last I looked, I can't see a reason that you should've known before now. If I'm wantin' to accept an invitation that's what I'll be doin'. Don't go waitin' up for me, either," Brendan ordered. He slammed his cap onto his head and turned to leave. "Good luck to you, Joshua. 'Tis a fine thing you're doing, trying to get to know the boy, but don't expect too much."

With that said, and before Josh could respond, Brendan backed out the door. He hadn't the time to think about Brendan's parting statement before Daniel shot into the room from above stairs. A sneer replaced his smile in a heartbeat. "What is he doing here?"

"*He* is your father and I'll thank you to keep a civil tongue in your head. Joshua is here to share a meal with us and catch up on old times."

"That's real simple. We're dirt poor and he's still a Wheaton."

Josh thought Wheaton sounded more like a disease than a surname in Daniel's mouth.

"And so are you and don't you be forgettin' it," Abby snapped. "Since when were you ever taught to judge one person by the actions of another? Would you like to be thrown in with that lot of thugs callin' themselves the AMU because you're of a mining family?"

Josh thought he saw tears in Daniel's eyes before the boy took to studying his shoes. "No, ma'am."

Abby stooped down and lifted Daniel's chin. She understood children and her child specifically. They often acted opposite of the way they wanted to. This man mattered to Daniel and he was afraid to admit it. He'd been deeply hurt by the taunts he'd lived with for so long, plus for some reason he continued to carry a wagonload of guilt over what had happened to Josh on Corker Road. It all made for one confused little boy who didn't know what to do with his feelings.

She softened her tone. "I've been wrong not to correct you before. And I'll admit I was angry at Joshua. It served my anger to let you go on feeling as you did. But I've learned he didn't know I was with child. He never knew about you until he came back to Wheatonburg. Joshua's a good man, and I want you to try getting to know him."

Chapter Eleven

Josh looked around the table. It wasn't going well. The silence in the kitchen was damn near deafening. It hurt. One of the memories that had sustained him, and conversely tormented him, during his years away was meals at this table. The noisy chatter. The good-natured teasing. The unconditional love.

Because of his presence the only thing heard tonight was the clicking and scraping of eating utensils. He couldn't stand it! "So…ah…Daniel," he said into the torturous silence. "What did you learn in school today?"

Daniel looked up from his plate. He hadn't really been eating, just pushing the food from one place to another. The boy stared at him as if he'd grown a second head. Then his eyes, eyes so like his own, narrowed. "We learned about the Emancipation Proclamation. We talked about how it only abolished slavery in the states in rebellion. The rest of the slaves were supposed to be freed by the states that hadn't seceded and that happened in 1865 when the Thirteenth Amendment was passed."

"We were at war and some said Mr. Lincoln took advantage of his increased powers to foster his own goals. What did you think of what he did?"

Daniel looked away toward the far wall, his eyes narrowed. Then he turned his head and his lip curled. "I think Mr. Lincoln should have said what slavery really is. That way you and your father couldn't keep people here when they'd rather move on."

Now even the sound of utensils clinking against dishes halted. Josh stood, uncomfortable, ashamed of his own name and by his own son. "Well, if you know anyone in that position, Daniel, you tell them to come see me and I'll forgive their debt and tell them they're free to go."

He looked toward Abby. "Thanks for the meal. I'd better be on my way. I don't want to wear out my welcome. Thomas. Mr. Kane," he finished, nodding to both men with a forced smile. He moved quickly to the door then, and grabbed up his coat and hat as he passed the coat tree near the door. He felt angry and hurt and hopeless.

"Joshua," Abby called as he opened the front door. "I'm sorry about his mouth. I'll be giving him a good talking-to."

Josh closed his eyes at the feel of Abby's hand on his shoulder. Even now, when he felt flayed to the bone, Abby's nearness made him vibrate with need. He turned to face her.

"Not on my account, please. It'll only make him resent me more. I knew this wouldn't be easy, but…"

"But you didn't think his constant rejection would hurt so much." Abby stood near, her voice pitched low to keep their words private, then she reached out and gripped his forearm. Even through the coat he'd draped over his arm, Josh swore he could feel her warmth flow into him.

His pain, her understanding, his need, her nearness…all conspired against Josh's better judgment. He stared into her emerald eyes then traced her beloved features with his gaze.

This wasn't what the evening was supposed to be about. It was as if he stood outside himself, watching in a mirror as he bent and pressed his lips to hers.

They were soft. Softer than misty memories.

Sweet. Sweeter than old times not forgotten.

His heart took off at the speed of the newest locomotive on the tracks. Then Abby's hand came up to caress his cheek, and he reached out to pull her against him. But the second his hands settled on her waist, she was gone from him—the mirror broken, the reflection shattering in a million pieces.

Abby pushed out of his arms and stepped back, her fingers pressed to her lips. "Don't, Josh. Don't confuse my concern for you with something that's long gone."

"I'm not the one confused."

"Yes. Yes, you are. Of course, you are."

"You don't know what I'm feeling," Josh retorted and knew he was right. She hadn't the slightest idea of his feelings.

"I feel your pain but that's all. Oh, Joshua, you've always been rich in money and poor in all the important ways. I guess that's another thing I didn't teach Daniel well enough. Money can't buy the important things, can it? But you have a shot at it now. You have Helena, a woman your father approves of and who you obviously care for. You can finally have the life you've always wanted—a rich wife, and control of the mines where you can do the most good."

Josh felt profound sorrow take over his soul. How could she know so little about him when she was the one person who should know what really mattered to him? How could she see so much yet be so blind to the truth?

"Good night, Abby," he said quietly, then turned into the night.

"Joshua," she called out. He stopped to listen but didn't look back and when she spoke he thanked God he hadn't.

"We're one of those families Daniel spoke of. We need only the wherewithal to make it west and these next months will give us that. Me and mine are going west. It's the only way Daniel will ever have a life away from anger and resentment."

Abby watched Joshua mount and ride away, then with her heart in her mouth she saw a shadow melt out of the woods along Corker Road to wait for Joshua. She waited, praying for his safety, until Joshua acknowledged the man and she knew it was probably the Pinkerton agent.

"So, how was the meal?" she asked once back in the kitchen. No one said. "Daniel, have you lost your appetite or is it not peppery enough for your liking?"

"No, Ma. It's just fine."

"You're sure you wouldn't like a bit more pepper for that spicy tongue of yours?" she asked.

"No, Ma. It really is good. See!" Daniel shoveled in a large fork full of stew as proof. "It's real good," he added around the mouthful of food.

Thomas snickered and Abby shot him a quelling glance. She picked up Josh's plate—a plate that still held a good portion of what she'd dished him. Shaking her head, she took it over to the sink then came back to her place and sat down.

"'Tis odd," Michael said to no one in particular. "Joshua leaving so sudden. Always loved that stew when your mother served it up and you do just as good a job as herself."

"And he was hungry when we sat down," Thomas added, thoughtfully.

"Remember how much he always loved eating with us?"

"How could I forget?" Abby said. "Meals in that edifice on the hill were so awful." She shook her head. "So, so awful."

"Was his cook that bad at it?" Thomas asked as if they'd rehearsed.

Abby shook her head. "The food wasn't lacking but the love was. Joshua always craved love. His parents didn't love each other and used Joshua as a pawn in their battles."

"And didn't he always want someone to love who was all his own," Michael said, shooting Daniel a quelling glance.

"Can you imagine how lonely he was wandering Europe all those years," Thomas said, seemingly musing aloud. "And then to come back and find that because his letters went misdirected, he'd lost touch with his childhood sweetheart and had a son he hadn't know of."

"So sad." Abby sighed and stood. "I'll clear, Daniel. I think you should brush up on your history, especially on slavery, and exactly what it was and how the slaves got here in America in the first place. I'm rather sure it wasn't their idea to come here."

Daniel stood. "Yes, Ma," he said then raced from the room.

"Think he listened?" Abby asked her father.

"If he didn't, I'll be havin' another talk with him. One that's a bit more direct," Michael said and backed his wheelchair away from the table. "We—all of us—owe Joshua a second chance. Daniel isn't the only one who needs to think on what you said tonight, daughter. So do you."

"I can't afford to think about it, Da. I have to get Daniel away from here. West is where his and my futures lie. It's my son's only chance at happiness."

Amber Dodd ambled up the road to Abby's. Happiness bloomed in her chest for the first time in years. She loved being the bearer of good news. And she had some for her childhood friend. Abby answered on the second knock and Amber smiled widely.

"What are you up to?" Abby said and put her hand on her

hip as she leaned the other on the edge of the open door. "I haven't seen that cat-that-swallowed-the-canary look on your face since you talked me into spying on Wheaton and Hilda Mauze."

"It's nothing so provocative and not at all heartbreaking," Amber replied. "Goodness, I'd forgotten all about that poor woman's plight at his hands. It's nothing improper. I promise. I have a wonderful idea for us. I've been making myself useful at my uncle's house. I found some trunks full of my aunt's things and even some material she never used. Uncle Charles said he's ready to get rid of it all.

"Now for my idea. I thought we might use the dresses for material if nothing else. I could sell what we make in town and we could split the money to go west. She had some beautiful things. With two of us working it would take less time. Mr. Prescott said I could use a corner of the company store. I could be there in the mornings and you could take care of our things in the afternoon when you're there. And then I'll take over for you till he closes at six. What do you say?"

Abby smiled. "That we have nothing to lose but our time. And as that's free there's little risk." The smile slipped a little as she added, "How much of a cut does Prescott want?"

"Not a thing. A favor to my uncle. Prescott feels obligated to me through him."

Abby laughed. "Wait till he finds out I'm involved."

"Oh, I told him right after he agreed." Amber chuckled.

She'd come to Wheatonburg after her parents and brothers died of the fever. A good and decent man, Uncle Charles had adopted her, but wouldn't let her call him Da—a name he said owed her true father. She had however honored him by insisting on taking his last name.

She would miss him. But she had time to talk him into following her and seeking employment with the Southern

Pacific. She thought he might like to leave Wheatonburg behind. His part in the ending of Joshua Wheaton's contact with Abby haunted him.

After the evening meal a week and a half after Abby asked Joshua to dinner, someone knocked on the Kanes' door. The family had gathered around the hearth as usual since it was the warmest place in the house after the kitchen stove cooled. Brendan answered the door and returned with Josh in tow.

"Well, now. If it isn't Joshua come for another visit," Michael said as he grasped Josh's proffered hand while glaring at Daniel. A silent message that he'd better behave.

"I'll be goin' for a walk, if you'll all be excusin' me," Brendan said.

"I'll come, too," Daniel called out as he jumped up from the corner where wood shavings told the story of his attempt at whittling.

Joshua turned back to Brendan. "Actually, I'd appreciate your staying. I have something I'd like to put to Thomas and he might like your opinion. I know *I'd* like it."

Brendan nodded. "If you need me here, then here I'll stay." But he didn't look happy about it.

Abby couldn't look away. Joshua's presence never failed to spark something deep inside her. And tonight it was more evident.

Excitement.

It was in the air and had come into the room with Joshua. He looked as if he hadn't slept in days but, though he looked tired, he seemed full of energy. She smiled. That about him hadn't changed. She finally shook herself loose from her spellbound state and stood. "Can I get you some coffee or a bit of pound cake?"

Josh shook his head. "I don't think I could eat. In fact, I didn't. I had to tell someone. I've been looking for something else, you see, and I think this would work. If Thomas was willing, anyway. Otherwise everyone might resist the whole idea."

Brendan chuckled and clapped his hand on Joshua's shoulder. "Now why don't you sit down and fill in the blanks you've left in your idea, boyo. That is what you just said, isn't it? You've had an idea that involves our Thomas?"

"Isn't that what I said?" Joshua asked as he sat in the chair Thomas had pulled into the circle about the fire for him.

They all laughed. No, this about Joshua hadn't changed. His thoughts always rushed out in a jumble, when he was at his most brilliant. She was glad he'd come here with his idea and his excitement and not to Harlan. If he'd seen Joshua like this, with all his boyish enthusiasm showing, his father would have cut him apart just as he'd done in years past. Joshua would have hidden the hurt as always, but he'd have felt it just the same.

At that precise moment, she pinpointed the biggest change she'd seen in Joshua. He was usually more guarded now. Tonight that trait had gone missing.

"I had an idea for the town," Josh said finally.

"Could you get to it?" Thomas all but begged.

They were all as impatient as her impatient brother and again they all laughed. All but Daniel. He sat expressionless in the same position he'd sunk into when Brendan had quashed his escape.

Josh took a deep breath. "It's about your furniture. It's beautiful, but I'm sure you know that. I didn't want to say anything until I'd checked out my whole idea. I sent a letter to a friend in Philadelphia and a telegram to a man in Germany. I got answers from both men today. The telegram from Germany arrived about five o'clock. That's why I couldn't eat."

"Fascinatin'," Brendan retorted. "Get on with it!"

"They all said yes. So if Thomas is interested we're going to start a furniture factory here in Wheatonburg."

"We? What would I do?" Thomas asked.

"Design the furniture. Teach the men to build it. One of the letters I sent was to a man named John Wanamaker. He's starting a large store in Philadelphia. He's going to be selling all sorts of items under one roof. He calls each section a department. He's agreed to sell our furniture in one of the departments."

"How does he know about the quality?"

"Because you sold a cabinet like the one over there to Charles Dodd. I noticed it when I went to see him one day. I borrowed it from him and sent it with the letter. And we'll also sell out of another store in New York that we'd own."

Thomas flushed. "Joshua, it sounds like a dream come true, but a dream nonetheless. Good tools are expensive and not everyone is cut out to build furniture. In fact, I'm not at all sure I am. I've had a few disasters of my own. I built Abby a bed and she wound up on the floor three or four times before I got it right."

"That's where the telegram to Germany comes in. I know a man who has a furniture-building business in Hamburg. Wilhelm is willing to teach you everything you need to know. You'll need to learn fast, but you're talented and you've learned a lot already. He's also agreed to help you lay out a factory on paper. His manager wants to come to America, so he would help run it. We can probably have the factory built by the time Wilhelm's done with you."

"Where will the other workers come from?" Brendan asked.

"The mines. Men who can't work there anymore, but who can still do some manual labor. Or men who are sick of working in the dark, or who never wanted mining in the first place. I know you didn't, Bren. The men will have a choice this way. Mining won't be the only way in the area to earn a living. Who knows, if the idea does well enough, maybe we won't need the mines at all by the time our grandchildren are born."

"I'll do it!" Thomas stated, determination stamped on his features. "When would I leave?"

"Just like that, you're going off without a thought to your poor old Da?" Michael teased, not too successfully hiding a smile. "And who was it who taught you to whittle, I'm askin'?"

Thomas's face fell.

"I'm teasin', boyo. I'm hopin' you can keep my hands busy once this factory gets goin'. I can't walk, but I can still carve. That's what you're meanin' about men not able to work the mines anymore, isn't it, Joshua? You don't care if I'd have to get there on crutches or in a chair."

Abby gazed at them. Thomas and Da both seemed to have forgotten the west. Was she forcing them to leave here? She didn't know but Brendan hadn't said a word. He hadn't given up his dream of a ranch and she wasn't giving up hers of a little dress shop or maybe a little homey restaurant with long tables and cheery gingham cloths covering them. Josh's voice called her back from her dream to his.

"If a man can add something to the business, I don't care how he gets to work. And from what I remember of Wilhelm's factory, he installed elevators to move the wood up and the finished furniture down. We could do it, too, so you could use them. Or we'll go with a one-floor operation. I've plenty of land."

Michael nodded. "Fine idea but will Harlan go for it?"

"I have money of my own. It's going to be Thomas's and mine. Kane Wheaton—Fine Furnishings."

Thomas frowned. "Joshua, I don't have money to buy into something like what you're proposing."

"You have the ideas, the talent, the designs. We'll work out an arrangement. Half the profit will be yours. You can pay me back out of that."

"That's truly generous, Joshua. I don't know what to say."

Josh smiled and shrugged. "Nothing *to* say. You already agreed, remember?"

Thomas smiled now, too. "I did, didn't I?"

"Where will you build it?" Abby asked.

"One of the parcels of land my mother left me is west of town away from the coal fields but runs along the train tracks." He stood. "I just wanted to ask Thomas's help on all this. I'm glad you're interested. I think it has a shot at success. I'll be in touch after Wilhelm's letter arrives with more details.

"Good night, Abby." For the first time since entering, Josh's eyes wandered to Daniel. "Good night, son. Maybe some day you can work with your Uncle Thomas. That's a mighty fine frog you've carved there."

Daniel looked at the piece in his hand then back at Josh. "I don't want to work in any factory you have a hand in. I want to work for the railroad. The Southern Pacific. Out west where my Ma's going to take me." He looked at Abby. "We're still going. Aren't we?"

"Even if we have to walk all the way," she promised him and her words seemed to echo in the room. She was sorry to have put sadness in Joshua's eyes but she couldn't change her plans. Not for Joshua. Not for herself were he suddenly free. Daniel deserved to hold his head up and he'd never get that chance in Wheatonburg or in any other town in the coal patch.

* * *

Abby tipped her face to the sun, soaking up its warmth. There was no doubt there were still cold days ahead but this one was a promise of the coming spring. Off to her left was the thaw-swollen creek where she and Josh had often sat dreaming a future far different from reality.

Without a thought to her plans for the morning, Abby veered toward the flat rock that hung out over the gurgling water. Holding her skirt out of harm's way, she carefully tiptoed across the stepping-stone bridge Josh had set in the creek bed almost exactly thirteen years earlier to the day. Abby's thoughts drifted with the current when she sank down on the big warm rock to watch the water swirl and eddy.

So much had changed since that long-ago day when Josh had asked her to follow him and she'd shaken her head....

A teasing light had entered his eyes. "Now, don't tell me the invincible Abby Kane is afraid to get her toes frozen!"

Hands on her hips Abby had replied, "I am not afraid. But these are new shoes and I can't get another pair as easily as you can." Abby had hated the look of not only embarrassment but shame that had rolled across Joshua's features.

But then as she had seen so often since that day of the cave-in, he stiffened his jaw and a look of determination replaced the guilt. "Then I'll build you a bridge."

With utter disregard for his own shoes or feet, Josh stepped into the stream and began rolling larger rocks into a straight line. Abby could only watch in utter amazement as a stone bridge took shape.

Josh bowed low over his creation when it was finished. *"Mademoiselle,"* he said with a wide sweep of his hand.

Abby giggled. "You sound like Mr. Henry."

"'Not mister, Miss Kane. Just Henry'," Josh replied in a perfect imitation of his father's unflappable butler. "And speaking of Henry, I have some news. He's back from his holiday in England. And guess what he brought back."

"What?"

"A W-I-F-E. Mother is all excited about her arrival. To hear her talk Henry got married solely to secure the house a new cook. Speaking of which," Josh said as he dug into his breast pocket, "she bakes."

He handed over two cookies. Abby wondered if they were still warm from the oven or from the warmth of his body. That thought gave her a strange dizzy kind of feeling in the pit of her stomach. Hunger, she decided. What else could it be…?

The smell of oatmeal cookies and the sound of Joshua's voice jerked Abby back to the present spring day. "Saints preserve us, Joshua Wheaton, you scared the life out of me."

Joshua chuckled. "It'd take more than the sound of my voice to do you in. Hungry?" Abby focused on the fist full of oatmeal raisin cookies he held in front of her nose.

"Are those Mrs. Henry's cookies?"

"Would I go to all the trouble to smuggle them out of the kitchen if they weren't? They're still warm," he confided and waved them at her again.

Abby grabbed one and took a hearty bite. "Still the best baker in the state, she is." Then she chuckled, remembering their youthful speculations about the name Henry.

"Let me in on the joke."

"Mrs. *Henry*. Have you solved the mystery?"

Joshua laughed, nodding. "But it took until last week to get up enough nerve to ask. Henry's parents had the poor taste to…yes, you guessed it. Mr. and Mrs. Henry. We had much better names picked out for our children."

Abby sucked a quick painful breath as the blood drained from her head.

Josh reached out and gripped her hand. "Ab, I'm sorry. It was so nice to just talk to you and now I've spoiled it."

She could see his regret and felt some of her own, too. She had to get used to the real past and Josh's part in it. "And I'm sorry I let it upset me. It happened, Joshua. We spent time together. We made plans for a future and loved each other enough to create a wonderful little boy. We can't avoid any mention of all that. It won't go away, because we wish it would. And I can't wish that, because I'd be wishing away our Daniel."

"That isn't what I wish, either, Abby," Josh whispered and was suddenly closer. He cupped her chin in callused palm, and Abby felt again that curious mix of hunger and anticipation his touch, his nearness, even his genuine smile had always stirred in her. His thumb stroked her cheek and when their eyes locked the feelings escalated. "It's the rest I'd change. I wish you were mine. I wish you'd come with me or I hadn't gone. I wish Harlan hadn't been so dead set against us. Then maybe he wouldn't have done all he did to keep us apart."

Abby thought again that Joshua seemed determined to blame his father when he could have stayed with her in the first place. But she didn't have the strength to give voice to her thoughts. Her strength—strength she should use to stand and leave—had left the instant he'd touched her. And now as his lips sealed over hers, she was glad she'd been unable to move.

It was foolish to revel in the feel of him, the taste of him. It was just plain stupid to savor the unique scent of him—a scent she'd never forgotten. And it was dangerous to twine her fingers in his thick golden hair as he deepened the kiss because if he could ignite her senses with just a look, he could incinerate her sanity with a kiss. But when Abby felt the hard warmth of the rock under her back, she finally came to her senses. This was emotional suicide.

She pushed him away.

"Abby." Somehow he turned her name into a plea.

But she could only shake her head, cursed tears springing to her eyes. She hid them by sitting up and putting the sun at her back. "It's too late for this. For us. It was a lovely past we had together but it's over. I can't be forgetting that. Fact is fact. Past is past. Go home and kiss your intended. She's your future. And somewhere out there," she said pointing westward, "is mine and Daniel's."

He was off the rock before she could blink. Agile as always, Josh touched only three stones before landing on the bank. He never even looked back. Abby held her tears until he was out of sight.

Chapter Twelve

Abby watched the unfolding scene through the open door of the company store, and it made her chest ache for both Joshua and Daniel. She heard Daniel's suspicion of his father and watched the mistrust in her son's tone register on Joshua's face. She loved him as much as she ever had. Maybe more since now it was a woman's love and not a foolish girl's. She had to admit it to herself, but even a threat from the hounds of hell couldn't make her to admit it to him or anyone else.

It was seeing how much Daniel was hurting Josh that forced her to admit what she'd known deep in her heart for weeks. It was love that had his pain costing her more anguish than simple empathy would. And what made the anguish worse was that she couldn't let love matter. Even if he were free, Wheatonburg was Josh's destiny.

And Daniel's and hers couldn't be there.

"You won't owe me anything for it," she heard Josh tell Daniel. "I just wanted you to have it. It's a gift."

"Why?" her boy asked with narrowed eyes.

"You were using a jackknife when I was at your house.

This one is safer. I asked your Uncle Thomas what kind to get you before he left for Germany."

Daniel's eyes held a keen desire that belied his words. "Uncle Thomas gave me my knife and it's just fine. I don't want or need nothing from you," Daniel said, then turned without seeing Abby in the doorway and ran off toward home.

She waited until Daniel was out of earshot. She'd have words for him later. "Joshua, you just stood there begging that boy to take a gift from you," she said, hands planted on her hips.

"He didn't want it. I was trying to get him to take it."

"Didn't want it. Think again. He's asked for that knife once a week for six months. You can't buy his love."

Anger surged into Josh's eyes. "I wasn't trying to buy his love. I worried that the jack wasn't safe. Before Harlan moved Mother and me here, I had a friend who nearly cut his finger off with a jackknife when it closed by accident. Getting a new knife into Daniel's hands is all I was thinking about. Maybe he'd take it from you."

Abby took a deep breath and tried to ignore the familiar scent that besieged her senses as Josh neared. She stepped back, gaining herself a bit of breathing space. "It goes against everything I believe about raising children to reward poor behavior but to let you know he's safer I'll take it and see that he uses it."

Josh gave a quick nod. "I appreciate it."

"But that's not to say that I don't intend to have a stern talk with him about the way he's treating you. As for you, take a little advice—stop *letting* him treat you the way he just did. Its effect isn't attractive on either of you."

Josh nodded. "I'll try." He pursed his lips. "I guess I have a lot to learn. But I will learn, Abby. I'll be a good father to him."

As he walked off toward the railroad station, Amber came

out of the store and stepped next to Abby. It was clear from her expression she'd heard what Josh had said.

"How he can be so blind?" Abby asked. "He'll never be a father to Daniel. Brendan and I talked long into the night. With what cash we've put together he thinks we can leave in the end of June and have a good start when we arrive in California. Because it'll just be me, Daniel and Brendan now that Da and Thomas are staying behind, we're going to travel by train and get what we need when we get where were going."

"Where exactly in California will that be?"

Abby laughed at her friend's hope-filled question. "We aren't sure. We both decided we'll know when we get there."

"Oh, I hope you settle near San Francisco. It would be wonderful to have you close."

"Do you think you and…?"

"I'll not love another and that's that. So did you decide what to do with that awful hat of my aunt's?"

Abby grinned at the change of subject. "Why not come by this afternoon and see? I doubt there'll be a run on our corner of the store from then till closing."

Amber nodded. "I'll walk home with you when you leave at four."

They chatted and traded fashion ideas as they walked along Corker Road that afternoon. They'd just turned off the road, having reached the Kane house, when a flash of light and a piercing explosion stopped them in their tacks. Before either woman could take another breath, a blast of dry heated air sent them sprawling backward.

"Daniel! Da!" Abby shouted as she scrambled to her feet. She looked over to check on Amber and stumbled on her skirts. Amber too was pushing herself up. She seemed fine so Abby tugged her skirts knee-high and ran toward the house only to be forced back by the heat of the flames as she neared the front.

"Daniel! Da!" Abby screamed again, then ran toward the back of the house. Daniel flung the door open just as she reached it. He struggled with the wheelchair, trying to get Michael outside. Abby and Amber joined in and had him safe moments later.

"Oh, thank the saints you're safe," Abby cried, giving them both a hug when they were away from the house.

"Aye, we're safe," Michael told her, "but the whole place'll go up and all Thomas's lovely furniture with it. Damn them! Damn them all to hell!"

"There's a bucket brigade forming," Amber said. "I'm going to join them."

"Can I help?" Daniel asked as Amber ran back the way they'd come.

Not wanting Daniel to feel helpless, Abby nodded. "But not close to the fire," she told him and followed, pushing Michael around to the front and over to their nearest neighbor's front porch. He settled there, looking frustrated. And who could blame him. It wasn't much but it was the home where he'd raised his children and watched his wife and their last little one die.

With tears in her eyes, Abby raced back, picked up one of the discarded buckets and pushed her way into the fray. She saw no way the efforts of twenty or thirty women and their children were going to overpower the flames licking at wooden structure.

At her insistence the women formed two lines, fighting the fire on both sides of the doorway. If they were to save the house, they'd have to stop it from spreading too high up the wall. If that happened, only water from a hose and a high-pressure pump would do the job.

Abby glanced toward the road and the sound of hoofbeats.

Josh nearly flew from the saddle and hit the ground at a full run. He stopped halfway to the house and looked around frantically.

Like most of the children, when not taking turns on the pump, Daniel ran a bucket full of water toward the house and tossed it low on the wall at the outer edge of the fire. Josh saw Daniel then he and ran toward him. Just as he got to the pump, Josh grasped Daniel by the shoulder and bent low. Daniel pointed in Abby's direction and then at Michael, then Amber Dodd ran up to them. Josh checked his watch, dropping it in the mud in his hurry. Daniel scooped it up, handed it back, nodding at whatever Josh said.

After shoving the watch into his jacket pocket, Joshua spared an instant to watch Daniel run off toward the horse. Amber followed, boosting Daniel into the saddle. The boy rode off at a gallop on Corker Road toward the mines.

A bucket being shoved into Abby's grasp snapped her attention back to the task at hand. She had no warning when Josh pulled her out of line and into his quaking arms.

"God, I was so afraid for you and Daniel," he murmured, tightening his hold even more.

Abby felt safe and protected from the ugliness of what had been done but only for a few seconds. Then she noticed several of the women staring their way. "Let go," she yelled as she pushed her way out of Josh's fierce embrace. "We haven't time to wallow in fear. The house is burning and the water's due to go off at four. Even if the fire wagon comes, there'll be nothing for them to fight with."

"That's where I sent Daniel. The water won't go off. And the hoses should arrive any minute. They sounded the alarm as I left town but let's see what we can do till the wagon gets here."

Joshua shed his coat and tossed it to the ground. He worked

side by side with her and the other women who battled the fire with only buckets of water. As Josh had promised, a pumper wagon arrived not long after he'd joined the bucket brigade. They had the fire out in minutes.

After the fire was out, Josh watched two men go inside to inspect the damage and open windows. He noticed Abby take off after them at a stumbling run. He shouted for her, afraid she'd be hurt. But Abby forged ahead. He found her standing motionless in the sitting room staring at the ravages of the smoke and water.

He'd made a promise to himself to keep her at arm's length, because her constant rejections hurt so damn much. But Josh forgot the promise when he saw her looking so forlorn standing in the smoky room. Her sorrow-filled expression stripped him of his resolve in a heartbeat. He moved behind her, and wrapped his arms around her slim waist, pulling her against him. "It'll be all right. I'll see the house gets repaired as quickly as possible. The furniture can be saved and maybe even your curtains."

Abby sank back against him, surprising the hell out of him. But then she spoke, her voice hoarse from the smoke and suppressed tears, and he understood her small surrender. For the first time, she showed him a hidden part of herself. He thought it might be the first time she'd even admitted to herself that she was a tiny bit bitter about the burden of her family and her life.

"After I wash and iron and scrub. I just did all that. That's all I do. Wash! Iron! Clean! I want to do something that won't have to be done again next week. I envy Thomas. If he makes a chair, even if he makes another just like it, it still stays made. I scrub a floor or wash a window and by the next week its so full of filth it doesn't look as if I've ever touched it.

That's part of the reason I hound Harlan for improvements for the town. Once he gives in, I don't have to do it again."

She laughed, sounding a little hysterical. "And what do they destroy? Supplies I've been squirreling away for the trip west. All the things I made for our new life—none of them embedded with coal dust. It was supposed to stay done!"

"Oh, Ab," Josh whispered, his heart aching. She was killing him with her pain *and* her plans. He was going to lose her—either to the AMU and their revenge for the aid the Kanes had given him, or to the west—unless he did something to protect her and to keep her there. Josh tried to quell his rising fear.

"Let's get you out of here," he whispered and steered her out the back way, his heart aching to do something to ease her pain—something to keep her with him where she'd be safe.

He settled her on a bench Thomas had built just outside the back door near her newly tilled garden patch. Brendan was with her when he returned with a glass of water.

"I'm so sorry," her brother was saying, his back turned toward Josh. "This is all my fault."

"The stand you've taken is the right one. All you did was back away from the rest and tell them to leave all of us alone."

"So what do I do now that the time for threats is over?"

Josh felt weighed down by it all. It was clear Brendan had had more contact with the AMU workmen than that day on Corker Road. He didn't know if what he'd just heard was an admission of Brendan's past membership in the AMU or proof he'd resisted at all costs. Whichever it was, it was clear they were unhappy with him.

"You could talk to Constable Addison and tell him what you know of the AMU," Josh suggested, giving away his presence. Brendan's head shot up and he frowned. "Addison's an idiot and you know it. I did tell him. Unfortunately, all I knew was how many shadowy figures I saw one night setting fire to the Mulgrew house. I put it out as soon as they'd left. But Mulgrew is a miner, after all, so our esteemed constable made nothing of it."

"Damn him! Anything else?" Josh demanded.

"Just that I have a good idea of the height of the men who beat you. And they can write because they've written threats in childish block letters and tacked them to the door. I could guess at who I *think* is involved, but I could be wrong. If I am, I'd ruin the life and eternity of innocent men. They'd jail them with no investigation followed by a mock trial. Then the church would turn 'round and excommunicate them."

"What do they want from you?" Josh asked.

"Cooperation."

"They want you to join or rejoin?" he asked as causally as he could.

Abby came alive instantly, her green eyes catching fire. "How dare you? Does that look like the way they treat a friend?" she demanded, pointing toward the smouldering house. "You said you believed Brendan."

"Abby, you have to understand—"

"I don't have to understand a thing other than what you just accused my brother of being part of!"

Brendan put a hand on her shoulder. "Ab, Josh has a right to be suspicious. This is what they do to convince men to stay who try to leave. Everyone knows it's them because the charge is clearly set by an expert. And with only the porch goin' it's likely no one would be hurt. In its way, this makes me look guilty as sin. It's like they're trying to force me to join by tarring me with the brush of a Workman. And now the gloves are off. I won't join their ranks, so they'll go after me either here or in the mines. They could easily harm you, Daniel or Da if they come after me here."

"Abby…" Josh reached out to touch her.

Abby pushed his hand away. "Go away. Just get away from me, my son *and* my brother who you think is a criminal."

"But—"

"Joshua, you'll not be gettin' through to her now." Brendan pulled him several yards away where Abby couldn't hear his low-pitched voice. "Try again, in about a week. She'll not keep the boy from you no matter what she says. She wants you to have the time together while the boy's still here."

There it was again. Not a threat. A promise. They were leaving and taking his son with them. Josh put that thought away focusing on the present. Right then, neither Abby nor Daniel was safe. And he wanted them safe.

"Not this time," Josh said with a definitive shake of his head. "I can't back off again. What if they *do* come after you here? What if Abby or Daniel gets in the way? They're coming home with me until we at least have the windows and doors replaced. I'll see the carpenters get started in the morning."

Brendan chuckled. "Good luck, boyo. Without a whale of a fight you'll get neither Daniel or Abby to spend time at the manor."

Josh had to concede he did indeed have a rough task ahead. "Have I your permission to do what's necessary to ensure their safety?"

Brendan studied him. "One question. How will Helena feel about Abby staying there?"

Josh smiled at the bent of Brendan's mind. He was mighty anxious to watch out for Helena's feelings, especially for a man supposedly unconcerned with her future. "She'll be glad for the female companionship. She knows exactly where Abby fits in my life."

"And where's that?"

Josh turned and walked away, saying enigmatically, "You

know me better than anyone—even Abby. She's the mother of my son. You figure it out."

He found Daniel washing up near the pump. "Son, you and your mother are staying at the manor until this place is cleaned and repaired. Go inside and bundle up some clothes for yourself."

"In a pig's eye!" Daniel spat and turned to walk away.

Josh took him carefully by the arm. "Listen to me. Do you want to put your mother in danger? She can't stay here so neither can you. She needs you with her to protect her reputation from all these gossiping old biddies. Now go get your things. Have your uncle bring you along!"

Daniel seemed to weigh his options. "For Ma's sake, I'll come. It's my job to protect her from the likes of you."

Josh scratched his chin as Daniel stomped off. That had been easier than he'd expected.

"If Abby Kane heard that boy speak like that to an adult, even you, she'd take him down a peg or two, I can tell you," Amber declared.

Josh laughed. "Women! You can commiserate with a man and insult him in the same breath."

She gasped. "Oh. I'm so sorry. I didn't mean—"

"Of course you did, but I'm not really as bad as I seem."

"I know that, Joshua, but you must see that it can't matter to Abby. Her son has to come first."

Josh frowned. He didn't want to hear more reasons why he had to lose the woman he loved and his son. "How would you like to earn some extra money? And before you think I've made an indecent proposition, I'd like you to hire a crew of women to clean the Kanes' home before Abby returns. The carpenters shouldn't take long and the clothing and things could be worked on before that. If the curtains aren't repairable, have new ones made and charge the material to me at the store. Hire as many women as you think it will take. I'll pay five dollars a day."

"Five dollars!"

Josh gritted his teeth. "I won't let the AMU win. This happened because Brendan Kane saved my life. Five dollars a day if it's all done and cleaned in time for Abby to come home."

Amber gave him a cheeky smile and reminded him startlingly of Helena. "I'll do it," she said, "but I don't want Abby to know. She'd kill me!"

"She's going to try to kill me anyway in a few minutes, so I may as well take the whole brunt of her anger. Deal?"

"Deal," she agreed with a sharp nod.

Josh mounted his horse and walked him to where he'd left Abby. She was still talking to Brendan but was standing now. He spurred the animal to a trot, scooped her up and pulled her into the saddle in front of him, pinning her arms at her sides.

She looked at him, her eyes wide with shock. "What in the name of all that's holy are you doin'?"

"I'm taking you home where you'll be safe and warm and dry. The roof has holes from embers that settled and burned through, the windows are blown out and it's going to rain any minute."

Abby twisted. "You'll be doin' no such thing. Let go of my arms and put me down."

Josh gritted his teeth as she wiggled her bottom against him. He felt himself growing hard. *Dammit!* "Hold still. I'm not going to give in this time and if I let go, you'd hit me. I don't like pain, thank you very much."

"Let go! Brendan, *do* something. Make him let me go!"

"Not on your life, Ab." With a huge smile her brother added, "That's my boss and you know how I value my job."

"You hate your job, Brendan Joseph Kane!"

Josh chuckled. "No help from that quarter. Give it up,

sweetheart, and don't think you'll get away from the manor, either. Try it and I'll drag you back and lock you in your room."

Abby hung her head forward and sagged against him. "Please don't do this to me."

Josh almost relented at the defeated, near-tearful tone in her voice, but he stiffened his resolve, when he remembered how close Amber said they were when the explosives went off. "I'm sorry, Abby, but I can't let you and Daniel stay here."

All placidity left her. She stiffened, then arched her back, almost sliding out of his grasp. Josh had just enough time to tighten his hold and haul her back into his lap.

"Stop it!" he shouted.

"The hell I will! You can't *let* us stay here? And who is it you think you are? God Almighty Himself?" she demanded, twisting wildly again.

"Settle down, dammit! It's who you are at issue here. You're the mother of my child. I refuse to stand by and watch Daniel lose the only parent he's ever known, just because you're too stubborn to see how dangerous it will be there for the next day or so. Don't try that again. You could have been hurt if I hadn't caught you."

"But I'd have been out of your…your—"

"Embrace," Josh whispered helpfully against her ear.

"Clutches is more like it," she muttered acidly.

Josh laughed. "That sounds like a line from a bad play."

"And you're a character from my worst nightmares."

Josh sobered. "So I still star as the man who walked off and left you alone and pregnant. *I didn't know!* I've tried to tell you, but you don't seem to care about explanations. I didn't *know.* Harlan kept me from finding out. I'd told him I loved and wanted to marry you so he made sure we never had the chance."

"He let slip where Daniel was conceived and it was *knowledge* he spoke, not just a guess. I know he took the letters. But you never came to get me, did you?"

Josh thought of all the years he'd stayed away unable to face watching her with another man. *And you're a character from my worst nightmares,* she'd just said. He'd never stopped loving her and all she cared about was traipsing off into the wilderness and leaving him behind. He refused to expose the anguish he'd experienced thinking of her as another man's wife—in another man's bed. Nor would he tell her how much worse that pain was now, knowing she'd been free all along.

"I never wanted to come back," he said truthfully, "and I only did because Harlan begged. There's no other way to handle the next few days so give in gracefully. You aren't the only one this stay will be difficult for."

Abby winced. Of course it would be difficult for Josh to have her and Daniel under the same roof with his fiancée. He couldn't want this any more than she did.

But what neither Josh or Brendan could have understood was her objection to the arrangement was about the danger to her heart. If she had to live in close a proximity to Josh, she knew she'd begin to want more from him than he could— or would—ever give her. Abby faced the truth of that and she sank back against him—all her fight gone. She wanted his love and to share his life though not in Wheatonburg. But he wanted a younger, far prettier, and well-bred society woman.

Helena Conwell was all the things she could never be. And Joshua Wheaton represented all the things she could never have.

Chapter Thirteen

Abby stared at Joshua's hands on the pommel. They were barely visible in the darkness, but she knew they were there. So close. Every time the horse's rhythm changed even slightly, she found herself tossed forward and those torturously still hands brushed her stomach, igniting further the fire that burned deep within her. It was a fire whose flames only Joshua had ever sparked. A fire that had burned once and left only devastation in its wake.

Abby clenched her jaw. Why had she tried to get away? She'd only made matters worse. After she'd tried to slide free of him, he'd ordered her to sit astride in the saddle in front of him. She was more than a little sorry for her bid for freedom because, though Josh wanted nothing from her, his body certainly had other ideas. He was fully aroused and pressed against her. The horse stumbled slightly and Josh's hand came up to steady her, splaying across her middle. She gasped at the heat that blazed through her.

"It's all right, Abby. The horse can see better than we can. We'll get there safely and soon."

"I'm not afraid of the dark," she whispered.

Joshua chuckled and the low-pitched sound sent sinful fingers dancing up her spine. Abby shuddered

"Then you're chilled?" he asked.

"Just the opposite," she muttered under her breath, then bit her tongue.

"What was that?"

"Not a thing."

"I heard you say something. You shivered. Why, if not from cold or fear?"

Cornered, Abby came out spitting. He'd never know how she felt about him if she could help it. She had precious little in life, but still had her pride. "Fine. You want to hear what I said? I hate having you touch me. I've tried to overlook my distaste for Daniel's sake, and in honor of past feelings between us, but it's rather difficult when sharing the same saddle!"

Abby found herself alone on that same saddle so quickly she nearly lost her balance. She grabbed the horse's mane and the animal stopped in his tracks. Joshua snatched up the horse's reins and pulled. His horse heeled then like a well-trained dog.

She knew she'd hurt him and regretted it. But what else could she have said? *How about the truth or nothing a'tall?* a voice she knew as her conscience asked.

"Joshua, I—"

"Shut up, Abby."

They rounded the last bend, still climbing toward the manor, high on the hill. The lights gleamed, but it wasn't the cheerful sight her own home would have emitted.

"But—"

"Not another word!"

"Joshua, I'm trying to apologize."

Now at the foot of the walk, Josh stopped and turned, his

eyes glittering in the light of the lantern. "Are you saying what you said was untrue or are you only sorry you insulted me?"

Abby wasn't sure exactly how to answer, so she sat in silence.

"Not sure?" he asked as he pulled her from the saddle. "Suppose we find out." Josh let her slide slowly down his body. The contact scorched ever fiber of Abby's being. She closed her eyes and reveled in every hard-muscled inch of his torso she felt through her thin dress and threadbare petticoats. The cool night air suddenly shimmered with heat. She trembled violently when his arousal pressed against her. Then Joshua pulled her even closer and bent his head to capture her lips. His demanding kiss reflected his anger and hurt. It was punishment, pure and simple.

At first, Abby was sure the anger, though it burned brightly for a short time, would soon fizzle, but it didn't. And she felt fear in his arms for the first time. Rather than burn itself out his anger built. She struggled but soon remembered just how strong he was when the hand on her chin forced her jaws apart. His tongue stabbed inside her mouth, plundering what she would once have willingly given.

A whimper escaped Abby's throat. Her worry for her pride had destroyed something precious—his innate gentleness—and she wanted it back. Hot tears flowed down her cheeks and onto his, as well.

And Joshua froze—the storm ended. His fingers gentled and he broke the kiss, staring in horror at her before closing his eyes and meeting her swollen lips with his again. This time they apologized for his aggression. And in that instant, Abby was lost.

She could have fought her feeling thanks to his anger, but never his remorse. He lovingly—carefully—tunneled his fingers in her hair. Dislodging what pins were left he cupped her head and she shuddered, this time from the need he unleashed in her. His tongue begged entrance and Abby granted what she'd been forced to accept only moments before. And with that small surrender, heat bloomed and spread to her core.

Josh explored—implored. And Abby followed—gave. His kisses traveled to her chin and jaw, soothing any earlier hurt, and her knees nearly gave way. His soft, questing lips opened on her neck and changed from yearning to passion.

His fingers combed gently through her hair then his hands traveled her back to her waist, spreading fire where he touched. Then one hand moved to her bottom, kneading the curved flesh, pressing her to him. Abby found herself straining to get closer to his heat. He rocked against her then, and all her senses exploded in an eruption that consumed her soul. She quaked in his arms as tiny aftershocks spiraled through her.

Josh sighed. "I apparently found my answer."

Abby opened her mouth wanting to deny the truth, but his lips claimed the lie from her lips and his tongue laved it away. "Please," Abby groaned, whether for mercy or further fulfillment she no longer knew.

"'Please' what, Ab? Please let you go or satisfy you again? Please take you upstairs and make you mine again or set you free? What is it you want of me? Whatever it is, it's yours."

Abby stared up into his eyes. They smoldered with need and desire in the light of the porch lanterns. It was the look that had given birth to Daniel. The look she'd been unable to resist. Then his words sank in. What was she to be in his life? What if she asked him to take her and Daniel away from there?

"What about Helena?" she asked aloud instead.

Joshua kissed her again and in minutes they were both

panting and breathless. "This isn't about Helena," he whispered. "It's about us and what we feel."

"But what about her?"

Joshua stared at Abby's soot-streaked face, unable to think of an explanation of his relationship with Helena. They were in this charade together. They could enlist Abby's aid, which could be risky for the same reasons he was reluctant to involve Brendan at this point. And he had no right to break Helena's confidence without prior permission.

But right then, Abby looked up at him with such love in her eyes that he knew she cared for him. And he could see the heat building in those eyes. Not a sensual heat. This was a hurt and angry heat, no doubt caused by his silence where Helena was concerned.

"Abby, I—I can't just abandon Helena. You don't understand about her and me."

"You lowdown— What am I to you? A potential mistress? You can't have two wives, now can you? You'll marry your society darling and get a rightful heir on her while you think you can bed me for your pleasure!"

"Abby, that isn't how it is at all. I'll explain it to you in the morning after I talk to Helena." To be fair he had to talk to Helena first. Her future, as well as Brendan's, was at stake here.

Abby lashed out again but not verbally this time. He was so preoccupied with the tangle his life was in Josh never saw the roundhouse punch that knocked him backward. He tripped over an ornamental rock and into the flower bed. He looked up at her in the lamplight. She looked like a Valkyrie, red hair shining and fire in her eyes. Dear God, he loved her.

"I'd pitch a tent before I'd stay under your roof. You'll talk to her in the morning? After you've had me one last time in your bed? Just when I'd begun to think of you as a man of principle, you show yourself as no different morally than your father. He had Hilda so you think you can shame me the way he did her. Well, boyo, you can forget it. Go to your proper lady because you'll get no…no *comfort* from me."

There was nothing in this world that infuriated Josh more than to be compared to Harlan. Especially if it had anything to do with Hilda!

A widow with four small daughters, Harlan had all but forced her to bed him. His mother had even arranged it to get Harlan out of her bed. She'd spread rumors of the liaison before Hilda's husband was even cold in his grave. Trapped and considered untouchable by the rest of the community, Mrs. Mauze had given in to save her children.

Joshua surged to his feet and Abby took a step back. It was more than his tentative hold on his control could stand. Up to down. Hope to despair. Torrid to glacial. His temper flared out of control for the second time in minutes.

"That's what you think of me? That I'd force you into something like that? That I'd shame you and my son?"

Abby's chin went up a notch and even in the darkness he saw that her temper matched his. "You forget you already did shame me and my son—every day for the last ten years. And again tonight by bringing me here."

"Well, I guess I may as well be hung for a sheep as a lamb," he growled, then reached out, picked her up and flipped her over his shoulder.

"Put me down or I swear I'll kill you when I get free, you great overgrown oaf!" she shouted. Never one to give in gracefully Abby kicked and pounded on his back.

Josh stalked into the house, surprising Henry, who strode into the foyer as Josh kicked the door shut behind him. There was a collective gasp from the formal dining room off to the left of the huge foyer.

He smiled, ignoring the muffled protests coming from Abby. "Oh, good evening everyone, go on with your meal. I just brought along a guest. Abby and our son will be staying for a few days until her house is livable again. Henry, is mother's room still kept ready?"

"Yes, sir."

"Good, I'll just go tuck her into that part of the master suite. Miss Abby will be busy bathing for a while then she'll be eating in her room. Please send up a tray up for her and could you have your wife find something clean for Abby to wear, as well. Her clothing will need to be laundered."

Abby punched him again, but her protests were getting weak and breathless. "What's that, my dear? You're starved? Henry, make it a large tray. She's worked up quite an appetite fighting the fire."

His temper cooling rapidly, Josh ran up the steps as smoothly as he could. He didn't want to jostle her, but he was in a hurry to get her upright. He hadn't meant for her to remain in this position for so long. He hadn't meant to take his anger out on her at all. She had a right to mistrust him and his motives. To her it would appear he was engaged to a woman inside the house while he'd stood outside begging Abby to spend the night in his bed.

Damn, what a tangle!

Josh set Abby down on the edge of his mother's bed. He was ready for another blow, one he knew he deserved. It never came.

And that worried him.

She just sat there, her hair mussed, snarled and covered her face. She kept her head bowed. His guilt nearly crushed him. Why had he let her goad him to such uncontrolled anger? Why, since returning to town, had he allowed himself so often to lose control of the temper he'd mastered long ago?

He shook his head ruefully. Because of Abby. Because she hadn't fallen into his arms when he'd returned the conquering hero. He hadn't dared to hope it would happen, but he'd dreamt the scene often.

"I'm sorry I hurt you," he whispered, wanting to reach out and gather her in his arms. "I'm sorry I carried you in like a sack of potatoes. I'm sorry you're embarrassed." Abby didn't move a muscle. "I don't intend to take advantage. I was angry."

Abby nodded, still silent, head still bowed. Josh dropped to his knees. He needed to see her face. She looked at him then with an expression he'd never seen in her eyes. It hurt him all the way to his heart and further. He didn't know what he saw there. Shame? Fear? Had that look not remained in her eyes when he continued trying to reassure her, he would have been elated. Because the one element he did not see was hatred.

"My room is all the way down the hall. Helena is in the other half of the master suite. Daniel will sleep in the nursery through that door. You can have the key to all the locks. No one, especially me, will come in here uninvited."

Silence. Nothing.

He tried again. "Mrs. Henry will more than likely nail my hide to the stable door for treating you the way I did."

Again only silence from Abby.

"Say something, Ab. You're scaring me. It isn't like you to be so docile."

"When will Daniel get here?" she asked quietly.

"Brendan'll bring him. I told him he was your chaperon. He seemed to think it would be an important job."

"Daniel's overprotective. A lot like his father."

"Abby, I don't think bringing you here is overreacting. Neither does your brother. The only people overreacting are you and Daniel. You don't need him to protect your virtue. You know that about me if you'll look past all the anger we've both been flinging at each other."

Abby nodded.

"Then why the wild protests."

"I didn't want to come here," she said baldly.

Josh grinned. "I could tell."

Abby grinned, too. A small one. A tentative one. It faded when she spoke again. "I know you've never been wholly trusted or well-treated by the miners because of who you are. I know you know what it feels like to be shunned. But can you imagine if they did it because they were convinced you were beneath them? Can you imagine how it would feel to be considered so low that, if your child were starving, they'd give their table scraps to a stray dog rather than you? Do you have any idea how your father has treated me the times I've come here to ask after improvements for the townspeople? I actually think he was afraid my filth would sift off onto his carpets."

"Ab, I'm sorry. But I've never treated you like that."

"Until now," she said, her voice as hopeless as her expression. He'd done so much damage in just a few minutes.

"I was afraid for you. I knew you wouldn't listen to reason. So I acted. Then you made me mad and I lost my temper. I had no intention of manhandling you, insulting you, compromising you and especially not embarrassing you by carting you in over my shoulder. I wanted to take care of you and keep you safe."

Abby raised a perfectly arched eyebrow. "Had it occurred to either you or my brother that if you'd come to me and explained your reasons, I might have agreed?"

Josh was stunned. "But you ordered me off the property. You were furious that I questioned Brendan."

"And by the time you came back and carted me off, I'd calmed down. I understood Brendan's explanation of how the explosion would look to others."

Still stunned Josh asked, "You'd have come?"

Abby's eyes flashed fire. "Would I *ever* put my comfort or even my reputation ahead of Daniel's safety? Do you think I don't know wild horses couldn't drag my son here without me? And can you imagine me sending him here without my protection from your father?"

"Abby, we aren't ogres. He doesn't need protection from—"

"Don't you believe it. He's behaved badly a few times and your father knows all about his pranks. Miss Conwell must hate him. He ruined her gown and much as I hate the expression, he *is* your bastard son."

Hating the title as well, Josh stiffened. "Helena would never hold a grudge against a child." He hesitated then, not sure how to proceed. He wanted peace while she was there, and hoped she'd realize life with him could be good. He reached out and covered her hand where it lay on her thigh.

"When you meet Helena again, try to remember money doesn't always cure ills. Sometimes it creates them. Being wealthy doesn't guarantee happiness."

She covered his hand with her other one. "Now how could I have known you as a boy and not learned that. A sadder lad I've never seen."

Abby thought he meant to kiss her, when he leaned toward her. "You and your family," he whispered, "soon changed that sad, lonely—"

"I hope I'm not interrupting," Josh's fiancée said from the adjoining doorway.

Josh stood quickly, but he didn't look a bit guilty or uncomfortable at being caught in an indiscretion. Instead he smiled. "Actually I was about to ask you for a favor. Daniel will be arriving soon. He'll probably be in as bad a need of a bath as Abby and I are. I wonder, would you ask Mrs. Henry to set a tub up in the pantry for him?"

Helena Conwell nodded. "Of course. I'd be glad to." She didn't sound unwilling, but she was definitely bewildered.

"His uncle is bringing him. Perhaps you could greet them and ask *Brendan* to stay while the boy bathes. I don't want Daniel uncomfortable but I also don't want the staff to be on the receiving end of his resentment. He'll cooperate as long as he knows his uncle is in earshot. I thought perhaps you could have Mrs. Henry fix Brendan a plate and then you could entertain him while he eats in the breakfast room. It's near enough to the pantry that he'd hear any ruckus Daniel might cause."

Helena's tentative smile widened to dazzling. "Of course. I'd be delighted." She patted her perfect hair and looked down at her dress. "Do I look all right?"

Josh chuckled. "Perfect." She continued to stand as if for his inspection. "Go," he said with an affectionate laugh.

"Thank you, Joshua. Oh, thank you," she said and turned, nearly flying from the room.

"She's certainly eager to please," Abby said, confused. He treated Miss Conwell like an indulged child.

"Don't let her fool you, Ab. She has a will of iron. I just asked her to do something she wants to do."

"Why would she want to entertain my brother while he eats and keeps an ear out for Daniel? Especially after what Daniel did to her in the company store."

A knock prevented his answer, though Abby wondered if he had one. She'd seen relief in his eyes before he rushed to open the door, admitting Mrs. Henry.

"Joshua, how could you carry Abaigeal in here over your

shoulder and bring her up here against her will!" she demanded.

"I've already apologized for embarrassing her, but she wouldn't listen to reason. At least, I didn't think she would, and she isn't safe at home."

"Well, she'll be safe here. Entirely! You will not come near this room again. Understood?"

Josh put up a forestalling hand. "That was my plan all along."

"It had better be! Now off with you!"

Joshua disappeared with a wink to Abby behind Mrs. Henry's back. Abby smiled. Mrs. Henry had been more a mother to Joshua than his own ever had.

"I'm too late," the housekeeper stated.

Abby blinked. "Too late?"

"Too late to save your heart. You love him. I've known you since the day he brought you home to gobble up my cookies so don't even try denying it. I've seen that look in your eyes before. Your love is written all over your face."

"No. I—"

"You love him. Lie to him. Lie to me. But don't lie to yourself, Abaigeal. That's the most dangerous kind of lie."

Abby closed her eyes. She did love him. She'd admitted it to herself weeks ago. She thought of Helena. And the way Josh had looked at her. It shouldn't matter. It couldn't matter, but a tear still leaked past the barrier of her lashes. Abby looked up at Mrs. Henry. "He can't know."

"Of course, he can't. There's Helena to think of. He was a fool to agree to marry her, but Gowery was all but auctioning the girl off to the highest bidder. Henry thinks that's why Joshua agreed. To save her. It was a rich man Gowery wanted for the girl and that's what Josh gave him." Mrs. Henry sighed. "Gowery gets what he wants and Helena gets what she needs. A caring man after more than her money."

Abby frowned. "Josh seems to care about her."

Now Mrs. Henry frowned. "Joshua cares about anyone in trouble. She treats him like a well-loved brother. Never like a future husband. Nor he her in that respect." She shook her head, clearly as confused as Abby now was. "They've reached some sort of agreement, but I confess it boggles my mind what it could be. But there *is* something between them. Make no mistake, he'll honor his agreement," Mrs. Henry warned with a shake of her finger.

"I know," Abby agreed.

"I hate seeing you hurt again, but you will be. She'll turn twenty-one in less than a week and be free to choose her husband. That's how Josh wanted it. She's to set the date at the party that's planned to celebrate her birthday. The party is bigger than they realize. It's a surprise."

Maybe Helena will refuse, Abby thought, but then she remembered how eager the girl had been to please Joshua. Abby tried to quash the hope that had flared in her heart. Helena Conwell wouldn't refuse. And Josh would marry her because he cared for her and she needed him. And as Abby had said ever since learning he'd never known of Daniel's birth, it didn't matter if he was free. She'd still be headed west where a fresh start away from ruin and name-calling awaited her and Daniel.

Abby stared down at her hands and balled them into fists. Then, painful stone by painful stone, she rebuilt the wall around her heart. She stood then, chin high and back straight. "Thank you for the warning, but it wasn't necessary. Too much has happened. Too much hurt. The most Josh can ever be is a distant friend. We're still leaving in early summer. That's how it has to be no matter how I feel about him."

Chapter Fourteen

"You aren't eating, Brendan," Helena said, breaking silence in the breakfast room. "I thought the roast was very good."

Brendan shifted in his chair, wondering how long this agony would go on. "'Tisn't the food," he replied through gritted teeth.

"The company then?"

Brendan heard the hurt in her voice. It pierced his heart. "I can't help that you attached some sentiment to a tumble in the mud."

Helena's eyes went cold with anger, then she blinked and spoke calmly. "I remember it as much more. It was a warm summer's day. It hadn't rained in a week. The meadow was tall with grass and the smell of flowers was all about us. I won't let you make it or remember it as something ugly. And I won't let you hurt me because I know you're just being nasty to discourage me."

He shrugged as casually as his stiff shoulders would allow. "It doesn't matter anyway. You're engaged to another man. A man I still consider a friend."

"Even after what he did to your sister."

"Joshua didn't know about Daniel, so he didn't do anything I haven't done to you. Holdin' a grudge would be a mite hypocritical, don't you think?"

"And after we're married, he'll be doing it to me. How does that make you feel?"

Like chewin' lead! "Haven't really thought about it," he lied aloud, staring at his plate.

"The thought of marriage to Joshua makes me feel like a prostitute sold to the highest bidder. We could have your dream, Brendan. Together we could go west and start that ranch you want so badly."

"You could marry someone else," he countered. *Please say you will. Please don't let the man who takes you away from me be Joshua!*

Helena stood and looked down at him, and Brendan wondered at the steel he saw in her now. He didn't think he liked it, and prayed he hadn't put it there.

"I don't intend to make it easy on you," she said, her eyes shooting daggers. "You think you're being so noble. Well, you're not! You're being selfish! You're being a fool! And if I didn't love you so much, I swear I'd hate you!"

In the blink of an eye she was gone. He stood, to go after her. Maybe she was right. But the door opened and Franklin Gowery stalked in. He stared at Brendan with open hostility and loathing.

"I want you to stay away from her," Gowery snarled.

Pompous ass. Brendan grinned. "I was invited here by Joshua Wheaton himself, but just for the record, I'm not interested in Helena. I got all I want out of your little ward last

summer, Gowery. And a nice little piece of tail she was."
With a jaunty salute, Brendan walked through the pantry
entrance and slammed the door behind him.

Daniel's bath had evolved into play with toy ships and a
miniature bark canoe that had probably been Joshua's as a
boy. Brendan called a halt to tub-warfare and helped dry the
boy off. "Don't you be losin' sleep over Granda and me," he
ordered. "We'll be fine sleepin' in his room till the work's
done."

Josh pulled to a halt outside the pantry when he heard his
son's voice. "But what if they come after you? They killed
my kittens when they blew up the porch. They might kill you
or Granda next."

"They're cowards, boyo. They'd be afraid to face your
granda and me on equal terms. And they know me well
enough to know I'll be prepared if they come. With you and
your ma here, Da and I can concentrate on keepin' the house
and ourselves safe. I'll be heading on home now, boyo."

Josh heard the door to the outside at the back of the
pantry open. He rushed in to stop Brendan from leaving. He
came upon Daniel clinging to his uncle's leg. Neither heard
the door or noticed him standing there.

"It'll be all right, Dan," Brendan promised.

"But I don't belong here."

Brendan ruffled Daniel's wet hair. "Oh, but you *do,* boyo.
And if some people had stayed out of it, you'd have been born
right up the stairs. This *is* where you belong. It's your birthright. Don't turn your back on something most of us would
give our eyeteeth to have behind us. Now you behave and
mind your parents. I'll be around to hear if you don't."

"Leaving so soon?" Josh asked.

Brendan looked up. "I think it'd best if I got goin'. I might just have insulted one of your guests already."

Josh sighed. "Gowery just stomped by me swearing to see you in your grave."

Brendan chuckled. "Don't be lookin' so worried. There's nothing I've ever done that would put me in a grave except become a miner."

"He's not a man to make idle threats. What the hell did you say to him, Brendan?"

Brendan swiped a hand across his eyes, looking suddenly exhausted. "I only confirmed something he wanted to believe. Of course, I had to tell the great man a whopper the size of all Ireland to do it. He believed it, though. And that, old friend, is his problem."

"He just might make it yours," Josh warned.

"I'll tell you how I look at it. Why waste breath on denials when someone doesn't want to hear the truth? It's a tiring thing. Believe me."

Josh frowned. Brendan was talking about more than his encounter with Gowery. It obviously hadn't gone well with Helena. "I thought Helena was keeping you company?" Josh prodded.

"Ah, but your Helena's a lovely lady. Treat her right, will you?"

"It's never been my intention to hurt anyone."

Eyes sad, Brendan nodded. "All's as it should be then. I'll take my leave."

As the door closed behind Brendan, Daniel turned wide uncertain eyes on Josh. "Let's go see what Mrs. Henry whipped up for our dinner, son." Josh held up a hand as Daniel opened his mouth to forestall the boy's protest. "I know. You're not my son. Well, maybe you'd like not to be, but I'll always want to be your father. Let's go," he ordered.

Abby looked down the dark tunnel. Nothing. There was nothing there. Then she smelled it. Smoke. It came up from the floor, swirling around her, reaching out with misty fingers. Then she remembered why she'd come. Daniel. She come to save Daniel. And Da. Daniel and Da were here in the nothingness and they needed her. Josh had gone ahead first, so he must be lost now, as well. She called frantically for each of them but her voice only echoed back at her.

Light flashed and she knew where she was. She was in a mine. The coal glistened in the walls, an eerie black glow that faded into nothingness again as the light faded. A rumble shook the floor and the smoke grew thicker. She screamed for her loved ones. She was their only hope. But her shouts only added to the rumble and terrible shaking of her world.

Abby grabbed some timbers and shored up the roof. "Are you in here?" Abby screamed, disregarding the possible danger to herself. She had to save them!

The smoke disappeared then and Abby breathed a sigh of relief. They were just ahead. Each held up a lantern but the flames flickered and one by one went out. Then the roof crushed in on her. The weight of the world above was just too much for the fragile supports she'd been able to erect….

Abby screamed in anguish and found herself engulfed in the warmth. "It's all right, Ab," Josh said as he held her against his bare chest. "Nothing's going to hurt you or Daniel. You're both safe."

She felt dazed and couldn't stop crying. Josh stroked her hair and rocked her murmuring soothing words. "Why don't you try to talk about it."

She nodded and he sat back but his arms stayed protectively about her. "Daniel and Da were in a tunnel. And you. You were in there, too. There seemed no way to get to any of you. There was smoke and noise and then the smoke was gone and the roof caved in. I'd tried to shore it up but I failed. It was all my fault. You were all killed because of me."

"Ab, it was just a dream. Nothing is going to happen to anyone. Please. Calm down."

She was crying again, she realized. The dream had been so real. "I'm sorry, I…I can't."

Josh engulfed her in his arms and warmth again.

"What's wrong with Ma?" Daniel asked as he climbed onto the bed.

Josh released her and let her sink back to the tear-stained pillow. "She had a bad dream," he told Daniel while wiping her eyes with the corner of the sheet. "I'll sit with your mother a while longer. You run along back to bed. You worked hard putting out the fire and you need a good night's sleep."

"Ma?" Daniel asked.

Abby could hear the suspicion and uncertainty in her son's voice. She forced herself to stifle another sob. "It's all right. It was just a dream. Run along now."

Daniel looked over at him as Josh lit the bedside lamp. "You shouldn't go around without a shirt when there are ladies present," he admonished.

Josh grinned. "Your granda teach you that?" Daniel nodded. "He's right, but I was asleep down the hall when I heard your mother screaming. I dressed in a hurry and forgot my manners, I guess."

"You forgot your shoes, too," Daniel pointed out, then scrambled off the bed and into the nursery.

Josh's eyes, gleaming with mirth, came back to Abby. Then all jocularity seemed to desert him. "Are you all right?"

"Fine. I'll be fine now," Abby promised, but as she looked at his lean, muscled chest, she had to restrain herself from reaching out to touch him again. She'd be a long time forgetting the warm feel of his skin against her cheek and under her hands again. *There goes the rest of my good night's sleep.*

Josh reached out and tugged on one of her braids. "You look like a little girl with your hair like this. It brings back memories. You wore it like this the first time I saw you, but I never saw it like this again."

"Because it was a little girl's hairstyle. After I met you, I wanted to be all grown up." Josh frowned, obviously not understanding the inner workings of a young girl's mind. "I wanted you to think of me as older," she explained but he still looked blank. "I wanted you to think I was *old* enough for you."

"Not necessary. I fell in love with you the minute you opened your mouth to defend me to the miners. Then your da and brother stepped in to support my right to help, and I was lost to the whole clan. Abby—" Josh leaned forward, his lips touching hers in a sweet salute to what had been "—you were my girl from that day on."

Abby put her hand up to push him away while she still could. It was a mistake. There would have been a second kiss and a third but Helena chose that moment to enter the room and clear her throat. "I believe Miss Kane has regained her composure, Joshua. You should be leaving."

Josh bounded to his feet and rounded on Helena. "Dammit, will you stop interfering like this! That's the second time you've interrupted us tonight."

Helena crossed her arms and arched one delicate eyebrow. "Uncle Franklin more than likely heard her cry out. Better me than him. I'll sit with her and *you* get out of here."

Josh looked angry enough to chew nails. *Odd. He's not embarrassed or self-conscious of being caught by his fiancée about to kiss another woman. And for a second time in one* night. *What kind of marriage would these two have? One pop-ulated by mistresses the way his parents had been?*

She decided she didn't want to think about their marriage and she certainly didn't intend to be his mistress. "I don't need anyone to sit with me. I'm fine and I'd like to be getting some sleep tonight." She nestled down and closed her eyes. *Not a chance in Hades I'll be getting any rest,* Abby thought as the door closed behind Josh and Helena.

Abby looked around as Josh all but dragged her toward the library the next day. Her sense of outrage over his telling her what to do again abated as one garish item after another reached out and snagged her attention.

The Wheatons might be wealthy and all of Wheatonburg might envy them this house but the inside was appalling. Not appalling in the way of the possession houses, but in its sheer ostentatiousness. Any grace that had once been present when Joshua's mother was alive had long since been buried under gilt and red velvet.

Abby had long suspected the sole purpose of the entire house was as a demonstration of the size of Harlan's fortune. It certainly couldn't have been to show good taste. The library was no different.

"You can sit in here with your feet up and rest. The quiet will do you good," Josh cajoled.

"I'd rather be helping Mrs. Henry," Abby protested, snatch-ing her arm from his gentle grasp. "I don't need to rest. My house burned. I didn't." Abby turned away, pretending to peruse the shelves.

"Here it is," Joshua said behind her. "*The Adventures of Tom Sawyer.*"

Abby whirled around, hands outstretched. "Oh, I've wanted to read this!" She snatched the volume. "I suppose Mrs. Henry can do without my help after all."

Josh laughed. "You never could resist a good book."

A squeak from the doorway drew their attention. "Is nothing

sacred?" Harlan Wheaton grumbled as he rolled into the room. "That boy's tearing around in the garden, climbing trees, spying on me in my bed and now I come in here and find the mother rifling through my wife's books."

Abby slid the book behind her and backed out of Harlan's line of vision. She moved slowly toward the other doorway, hoping to slip from the room. If she talked to the man at all it wouldn't be in a kindly manner.

Josh glanced at Abby, halting her progress toward the door with a hard glare. "It happens to be my book. You're going to have to accept reality. Abby is the mother of my son. Daniel *is* my son. We have to go forward from here and put aside our differences or we'll be at each others' throats for the rest of our lives."

Abby felt her anger rising. "Well, now that's a lovely sentiment, Joshua, but then you've been gone a long while. Perhaps you need a bit of a history lesson—a bit of catching up, you might say. When I came to this house, brokenhearted and scared out of my mind to be pregnant and unwed, your sainted father called me a lying whore. I'm to forgive that without an apology? Am I to forgive what came after as well? What you may not know is that several months later, with my mother and her tiny babe dead and me still recovering from childbirth, my father woke from the surgery that took off his crushed leg to find your father's fire boss there inquiring when my brothers could take his place in the mines, so we wouldn't lose our home."

She turned fully to Harlan Wheaton. "It's sorry I am that you've been injured, Mr. Wheaton, and it isn't a fate I'd wish on my worst enemy. But it's short on sympathy I am when my own father is in a wheelchair now. One you refused to provide but one your intended daughter-in-law sent as a thank-you gift for our care of Joshua. You remember my father and brothers, don't you? The men who've fed and clothed your grandson for years with no help from you."

Josh sighed. "Abby, I didn't mean you haven't a right to your ill feelings but—"

"But nothing! You want me to forgive and forget. That's a bit tough when your father has yet to acknowledge Daniel as your son instead of *that boy*. That boy has a name and a title he's been denied from the day he was conceived. He's a son. He's a grandson. He's a Wheaton!" Abby turned and left the library clutching Mark Twain's latest work in a white-knuckled grip.

Joshua watched intently as Abby stalked out of the door, across the foyer and up the stairs. Harlan took careful note of the look in his son's eyes.

"Are you sure you're doing the right thing?" Harlan asked.

"I refuse to have Abby or my son living in that house until it's weather tight. It's bad enough he lives there at all."

"What do you intend to do about Helena? Have you settled this matter with her? She seemed upset earlier."

Josh knew Brendan was Helena's problem. "I keep my promises. I'd better leave for that meeting with Helmut about the new shaft or I may say something I'll regret. Abby and Daniel will be with us at dinner. Try to be more welcoming and remember Daniel is my son. A request for forgiveness from both Abby and him wouldn't be out of order."

"It will be a cold day in hell before I ask your whore and your bastard son for forgiveness," Harlan shouted. "I want them out of here. Do you hear me?"

Joshua leaned down, his face inches from Harlan's. "When I walk out that door, you'd better start thanking God for this wheelchair you live in. Because it's the only thing keeping me from rearranging your face. Remember that or I just might forget how feeble you are and that you're supposed to be my father."

Chapter Fifteen

Daniel pushed his food around his plate as the silence around the table deepened. He just couldn't bring himself to lift another thing to his mouth. He remembered what his mother had said about dinners at Wheaton Manor and Daniel glanced at his father. Had it really been like this his whole life? How had he stood it? Daniel's stomach was starting to ache and feel sick. Maybe his father hadn't always been as lucky as everyone said.

"You look lovely in that shade of peach, Abby," Helena Conwell said, finally breaking the strained silence.

Daniel stared up at Miss Conwell, who was sitting next to him. Was she being nice? Or was she trying to make his mother feel ashamed of the hand-me-down dress that she'd altered that day?

"It was one of Mrs. Wheaton's," his mother said, smiling at the woman.

"Then she had wonderful taste. You seem to be of a size with her. I'd have given you something but I doubt any of my things could be altered to fit you."

Abby remembered well Mrs. Wheaton's rotund figure. "I

had to take it in considerably, Miss Conwell," she snapped then took a deep breath, trying to dispel the tension that was as thick in the room as Mrs. Henry's mashed potatoes. Perhaps the younger woman didn't know Joshua's mother had spent her days eating.

The silence returned, heavier than ever only to be shattered by Helena Conwell's sudden shriek. Abby, deep in thought, knew exactly what had happened as soon as Helena jumped up, knocking her chair over. A stain spread across her lap. A milk stain.

Abby looked over at Daniel and saw a look on his face that always spelled disaster. "Oh, Daniel."

Mrs. Henry rushed in with a towel and tried to minimize the damage to Helena's dress, apologizing profusely for the mishap.

"Joshua, that boy is an ignorant little heathen," Franklin Gowery shouted. "Do you have any idea of how much I paid for that gown?"

Harlan brought his fist down on the table! "People can't even have a civilized meal with him around."

Joshua just stared at Helena's gown, clearly shocked. Daniel in a snit had that effect on people. Then Josh turned to Daniel but Helena spoke up first.

"It's all right," Helena Conwell shouted over the din of Mrs. Henry's fussing and Gowery and Harlan's outrage. She gained everyone's attention as if they were waiting for an explosion. "It's all right," she repeated, her voice controlled. "It's just fine. I'm sure it was an accident."

Daniel, however, was too angry to accept the reprieve so graciously handed him. He jumped up. "It wasn't no accident. I hit what I aim at. You tried to hurt my ma. I protect what's mine!" Daniel whirled away, clearly ready to flee.

Unfortunately, Joshua caught him around the middle and

hauled him to a stop, then turned Daniel by his shoulders to face him. "Just a damn minute. You will apologize at once!"

"When pigs fly!"

Abby stood, too. "Joshua, I'll have a talk with him. This is my fault. Daniel is very protective of me."

"That doesn't excuse this."

"I didn't say it did. I said it was partly my fault."

"And *I* think," Helena added loudly, once again coaxing all eyes to her, "that I might have said something that was insulting to Daniel's mother. I'm sorry, Abby. Daniel. I was only trying to make conversation. I never met Joshua's mother. I gather from your reaction that being of a size with her is not a compliment. I truly *am* sorry. I'd like us to be friends."

"Helena, you've nothing to apologize for," Gowery snapped, "and you most certainly will not become friends with a woman so far beneath your station. Do you want to embarrass your future husband?"

Helena's chin lifted a notch and she looked at Gowery with icy blue eyes. "That, Uncle Franklin, is *his* problem, but you must concede that if he were embarrassed by either Abby or her son, they wouldn't be at his table. I'm going to change. Again, I'm sorry for the uproar my remark caused. And Joshua, let *me* handle Daniel." She held her hand out to Daniel. "Come with me. We need to have a chat."

"I don't think that's wise," Joshua said, clearly hesitant to let Daniel be alone with Helena. He probably thought the woman might need protection. But then seeing the look in Daniel's eyes, Abby wasn't too sure Josh wasn't justified.

Helena laughed. "Joshua, I thought you understood. I'm never wise."

Abby was intrigued by the younger woman in spite of being jealous of her relationship with Joshua. "Go," Abby told Daniel.

Surprised, Daniel shrugged and moved along with Helena.

"I want to talk to you later," Joshua said as the duo filed out.

"People in hell want ice water," Daniel retorted over his shoulder, sending Josh a mutinous glare.

"And I want to talk with you before you talk to him," Abby told Joshua, trying not to wince at Daniel's retort. Without another word she turned and left through the entrance to the kitchen, hungering for fresh air to banish the oppressive atmosphere of the manor house. At the back door, she grabbed Mrs. Henry's wrap from the hook and stormed outside. The work on their home couldn't be done fast enough to suit her!

"Abby, wait. Please."

Abby stopped and turned, trying to ignore the plea in Joshua's voice. "Leave me be. I'm here. Just as you wanted. But I'm not liking it and obviously neither is Daniel. You can't force us to be who we aren't."

"That isn't what I want, and I think you know it. I want you in my life. You and Daniel. I tried to tell you the other night. Wait! Before you go off into a rant, let me explain."

"I remember well what you wanted. You wanted me in your bed. Well, Joshua Wheaton, it's time you learned the whole world doesn't revolve around you and your wants. I have dreams and wishes, as well, and by God I'm going after them, and none of them include becoming your mistress. Soon me and mine will be shut of this town and its condemnation and sneers."

Josh stepped back, a stunned look on his face. "You and Brendan really *are* serious."

"Don't you be gettin' ideas about trying to keep us here. I won't let you stop me from givin' Daniel a life where he'll finally be able to be someone more than your bastard son. He's never been allowed to be more and never will be as long as we stay in this town. I won't have it any longer."

"But—"

"No!" Abby fairly shouted, cutting him off, unable to handle the anguish of his gaze or his nearness any longer. "In time Helena will give you children. You'll be able to forget Daniel. And we'll forget you."

Abby yanked her gaze free of his and fled to her room. It wasn't the house that stole her peace. It was Joshua.

Josh exhaled deeply, closed his eyes and leaned back against the house. He stood, absorbing the frigid air and the cold from the stone at his back. After a few minutes he opened his eyes and looked up at the moon. It would be full by Saturday. Only three more days and Helena would be twenty-one. He'd talked to his lawyer about gaining control of her finances. She'd be free to order her own destiny.

But he'd never be free.

He hadn't thought out his dream of marriage to Abby in light of what she'd been through because of Daniel's birth. Nor had he considered the life Daniel had in Wheatonburg or even the one he would have after Josh changed his name to Wheaton. His son would trade one burden for another. One source of ridicule for another. No, it wouldn't even be a trade because everyone would still look down on Daniel over the circumstances of his birth and he'd have the added burden of the name Wheaton.

Josh thought of his other dream, the one he and Abby had once shared for the town. He was well on his way to making Wheatonburg a better place for its citizens. The furniture factory would bring progress and jobs aplenty and the improvements he planned for the mines would make mining a safer occupation for those men who chose that as their way of life. He'd even thought of trying to attract some farmers to the area. In the papers Harlan had turned over to him he'd found they owned thousands of fertile acres nearby that would make excellent farmland.

Josh sighed and pushed away from the wall. He had to face his father and Gowery. He only had three more days to perpetuate the lie that kept him from telling Abby she was the only woman he wanted in his bed and that he'd never considered having her there as less than his wife. Maybe then they would find some way to work out the rest of their problems.

Saturday night Josh watched Helena descend the stairs, her composure restored. He was thankful Abby had refused to attend the party because his father and Gowery had turned the small dinner party he'd planned into a surprise gala at which they had taken the opportunity to officially announce the impending marriage—the marriage that would never take place. It had been a shock to him and had nearly undone Helena.

Almost immediately Helena had gone upstairs to regain her shaken poise and Gowery had introduced him to a distinguished man he'd invited to attend. His name was Lord Jamie Reynolds and Josh had instantly recognized the lilt of Irish in his voice. He was the man who'd infiltrated the local Workman gang. Reynolds's appearance as himself worried Josh.

He'd furtively followed the men to the study and his suspicion had been confirmed. They had quite a few plans for the night. At midnight the Pinkertons along with Constable Addison would go to the homes of the suspected AMU members and arrest them. Reynolds had produced a list that didn't include Brendan's name and Josh had been elated. But then Harlan ordered the name added and had produced the evidence of the double explosives purchase. Josh had thought he'd suppressed it but apparently Prescott had gone to Harlan himself.

Then Reynolds had happily added the last nail in Brendan's future coffin. He said he'd been told by a Workman that Destiny's saboteur had made the explosives purchase for the job himself.

Josh knew in his heart that Brendan was innocent and being framed by both sides of the conflict. The initials were Brendan's but Daniel's beating had been a message from the AMU. Even if Brendan had saved Josh to throw suspicion off himself, he would never have let anyone hurt Daniel. And Bren would hang if Josh didn't put his long-thought-out plan into effect immediately.

He met Helena at the bottom of the stairs and held out his hand. A smile pasted on her face, Helena took his proffered hand. "Must you look so grim, darling," she said keeping the smile in place.

"I've reason to look grim. Dance with me." He led her to the dance floor. Once she was in his arms for the waltz, he'd signaled the band to play, he spoke in a low conspiratorial whisper. "Your uncle introduced me to a man name Lord Jamie Reynolds. I recognized his voice as well as his name. It confirms what we thought, he *is* the man who infiltrated the AMU in this area."

Helena was visibly angry. "So it *is* him. As I told you, he's the man Uncle Franklin wanted me to marry back in Philadelphia. He'll be after Brendan's blood and he'll be determined. I threw my liaison with Brendan in his face when he told me he'd asked Uncle Franklin for my hand. That's how Uncle Franklin learned about Brendan and me. Lord Reynolds wasn't at the meetings I eavesdropped on for you or I'd have recognized his voice."

"He's here tonight because they're about to spring the trap. At midnight. He and Harlan have succeeded in doing Gowery's dirty work. And make no mistake, Brendan will hang if we don't get him out of the area now. The way I've planned this, if we don't delay, we can have him out of the county by midnight and you right along with him. Franklin and Harlan have actually played into our hands with this damned party."

"Then it's all in place?"

Josh nodded. "I'm going to give Abby a note to take to Bren. He can meet you at the church. I'll take the horses to the station. Dodd has the case with the things I packed for Bren. Is your case ready?"

"For a week."

"Dodd's niece has been ready since just after you sent her the trunk of clothes for alteration."

She grinned and looked suddenly very young. "Thank heaven you had your lawyer draw up that power of attorney for me to sign earlier today. I'll let you know where we settle and you can handle the transfer of my assets."

Josh thought a moment and the band played the ending of the waltz. "It's your life now, Helena. Yours to do with as you want, but Brendan may not be as easy to convince as you think. He'll be a wanted man until I can find a way to clear him and he may want to protect you from that. I'd better get Abby the note. Try to keep watch on Reynolds and Gowery while I'm gone. If either man makes a move, find me."

Helena cast her eyes just over Josh's shoulder. "Thank you for the dance, darling," she purred rather loudly. "You dance as well as you do everything else."

Josh recognized the mutinous look in Helena's eyes and turned to find Reynolds approaching.

"May I have this next dance with your intended?" he asked Josh.

"That would be up to Helena, Reynolds. She's her own woman. I'll see you later, my dear. I've monopolized you enough for now. But I would like a long walk in garden later. I have a gift for you and I'd like privacy when I give it to you."

Helena smiled and nodded.

Josh glanced back when he reached the edge of the dance floor a moment later, wondering if he needed to worry about being followed. Helena smiled up at Lord Reynolds as if he were friend rather than foe. She wouldn't let the man out of her sight.

Josh took the steps two at a time and burst into Abby's room. She was sitting in a window seat reading the Twain novel he'd given her. Relations between them had been chilly since the night Daniel caused the scene at dinner. Josh hadn't tried to explain his motives for kissing her again, knowing soon the need for lies and secret engagements would end. He hadn't thought the end would be quite as dramatic as it was turning out to be.

Abby stood. "Shouldn't you be at your party?"

"I need your help. Actually Brendan needs your help. At midnight he'll be arrested as a Workman."

"That's ludicrous!"

"I agree but they have evidence."

Abby stared at him. "And you believe this?"

"Of course not," Josh retorted, then sighed. "Just trust me, Ab. Brendan's life depends on it. Take this to him," he said and handed her a sealed envelope. "Tell him Helena will meet him at Saint Stephen's inside the church. She'll have money for travel and clothes that'll disguise his identity."

"Helena?"

Josh nodded. "I'm going to the station to meet the ten o'clock train and to put a couple horses on it. Dodd agreed weeks ago to help. The story is I've sold the horses and I'm shipping them to a man in Boston. Dodd has had the car ready on a spur for several weeks. His local records will show that the horses were sent to Philadelphia then on to Boston. But the box car will go the other way to Independence,

Missouri. Brendan'll take the train disguised as a business-man. How long he and the horses stay on it is his business but the confusion should give him a good head start on the Pinkertons."

"How do you know he'll be arrested?"

"I'll explain later. Oh, and don't tell Bren Helena will be at the church. Just get him there."

"Can she be trusted?"

"She'd die rather than let a hair on Bren's head get so much as rumpled."

Abby frowned. "I don't understand?"

"She's in love with him and he with her. He thinks he's given her up for her own good, but I couldn't let him lose the woman he loves. I know how much it hurts."

Josh looked away, not wanting to see her reaction to his admission, so he checked his watch then tucked it back in his pocket. "We're on a tight schedule. You'd better go. Make sure you aren't followed and no one sees you go in or out of either house. And, Abby, say a prayer the ten o'clock train's on time. I want them well away from town before the law goes looking."

"Them? What about Daniel and me? How long do I have to pack do you think?"

"Pack? Abby, Brendan's going to be a wanted man until I can clear his name. You can't go with him. It's bad enough Helena's going. You and Daniel would slow him down. We have the decoy set up for Helena, but if you disappear at the same time, they'll be able to track him too easily with your description. You can't go along and that's all there is to it. You'd put him in too much danger."

Abby watched Josh leave and just stood there trying to weigh all he'd just told her. It didn't take long to realize he was right about her and Daniel. They'd have to follow later. She shook her head. She'd have plenty of time to look at her remaining options later. Time was marching on.

Abby and Brendan approached the church with caution but it was soon apparent there was no one hiding in any of the dark shadows around the building. As they entered the little church, there were candles burning on the altar, and Brendan hissed a word that shouldn't be spoken in a church.

In the dim glow ahead, Abby saw why. Helena Conwell stood near the altar talking to Father Rafferty. Wearing a beautiful white gown, she turned and put her hand on the old priest's arm, then walked up the aisle toward them.

"What are you doing here?" Brendan growled.

"I'm sorry you aren't glad to see me. I suppose that makes this all the more necessary," she said, and leveled a pistol at Brendan, which she'd concealed in the folds of her dress.

Abby's heart sank. Why had she trusted Joshua or his fiancée. "Is this all an elaborate trick to snare Brendan in your guardian's trap?"

"Oh, no. It's my snare—to catch myself a husband." She smiled up at Brendan. "Father Rafferty has agreed to marry us, darling, and time is wasting. I'm sorry it has to be this way. I know it's my fault they went after you, but I won't forfeit a chance with you because Franklin Gowery is a poor loser."

Brendan grinned. It was a grin he'd used on Abby often enough and she'd always wanted to slap it right off his face. It had the same effect on Helena Conwell.

"You won't shoot me, love," he told the bride behind the gun.

Helena, however, didn't rise to his bait. The gun swung left. "No, but I might just might shoot your sister," she said in an oddly calm tone.

"Have ya' lost your mind?" Brendan demanded.

Abby looked at Brendan, and saw more than worry for his sister. It was mostly worry for Helena. He loved her. And that Helena indeed loved him. She also saw something gleaming in Helena's gaze and knew her irrationality was an act.

"I believe she means it, Brendan," Abby said, playing along.

"Father Rafferty will never marry us this way," Brendan suggested.

"Actually, after I told him how you'd trifled with me, then refused to marry me, he was glad to agree. This is his gun."

When she looked at Helena and realized she had spoken the truth about Brendan having been her lover, Abby's anger knew no bounds.

"After you saw what Josh's betrayal did to me, you did the same thing to Miss Conwell?"

"I lost my head," Brendan conceded.

Abby glared. "I'd say Helena lost a bit more than that. We'd best get on with this ceremony. You'll be losing one form of freedom tonight, brother mine, or my name isn't Abaigeal Kane Sullivan. And I'll be holding that pistol, Miss Conwell. Helena. You need someone lookin' after your interests. A lady shouldn't have to hold the gun on her groom at their wedding. And don't worry, if he refuses, I'll shoot him where he sits since I suspect that's near where his brains have been lately. I wouldn't kill my own brother, but just now I wouldn't mind knowing his ride west will be mighty uncomfortable."

Chapter Sixteen

Abby followed Joshua up onto the manor's rear porch several hours later. After losing Helena, Josh had to be hurting, but the rock-hard line of his jaw told her he'd die rather than admit it. Months ago she would have gloried in such a moment. Tonight, she wanted only to offer him comfort. But again, she knew he'd never admit to the need. That had changed about Joshua. Time was when he'd have turned to her—only her. But he'd become a man. A man to admire, who was still noble and tilting at windmills, but who was also stronger than ever.

"I'm worried. With Helena on the same train as Brendan, won't that lead the authorities right to him?" Abby asked. She wanted to know but she also hoped to distract both of them—he from his loss and she from remembering her own in another time.

Josh turned, but didn't look at her. He just stared out over the valley below, and shook his head. "Hear that whistle? It's the eleven o'clock train headed toward New York. I bought Helena a ticket on it, which of course she didn't use. But Amber Dodd did. I paid her fare on a clipper out of New York instead of her taking the overland route. The clipper ticket is in Helena's name. When I went to confront Dodd about holding our letters to each other, Amber overheard. I noticed how much she resembles Helena and she must have noted it, as well.

"Dodd asked if there was anything he could do to make up for what he did to us. He is truly sorry for his part in all of it. That's when I decided to enlist his aid in getting Brendan and Helena safely out of town when the time came. Later Amber walked into a meeting I had with Dodd and offered her help, as well. She agreed to lay a false trail for Helena."

He handed her a note from Amber. Abby tucked it in her pocket to read later and turned her attention to Josh. He stood with one hand on the wooden pillar, his hip cocked and one foot dangling over the top step as if he were poised to flee back into the night to outrace his thoughts.

"You were very clever," she said, thinking a compliment would lighten his mood a bit.

Josh shrugged, still staring straight ahead. "Actually Amber thought of using her as a decoy. She's a bit older than Helena but no plan is perfect."

"Won't her clothes give her away? She couldn't afford a wardrobe like Helena's."

"That's why Helena sent over a trunk of her clothes supposedly for alteration. But Amber altered them for herself. Helena took very little with her."

Abby nodded. "That surprised me. She isn't at all what she first seemed. I'm glad for Brendan's sake."

"It was *all* for Brendan's sake, Abby. Right from the beginning. And by the time anyone misses her it will be too late to track Brendan through her. Helena got Father Rafferty to promise to hold their marriage license for a while before filing it, so the ceremony won't tip our hand, either. It'll be difficult to catch up to Amber in New York. She'll be hiding there under her own name until she sails. She'll be on the high seas for months after that."

"Josh, why didn't you warn Brendan sooner?"

In a quiet undertone and still staring at the surrounding landscape, Josh unraveled the tale from the significance of Helena's twenty-first birthday in respect to her father's will, to why Brendan had broken off his relationship with her. "Bren didn't want Helena's money but he didn't want her to lose it, either.

"I didn't tell Brendan because I was afraid he'd accidentally do something to tip our hand. I knew he'd be closely watched because an agent was after Bren's blood as much as Gowery and Harlan were." Then Josh told Abby about the double explosives he'd tried to cover up for Brendan but that it had come to light anyway.

Abby put a hand on Joshua's forearm. "I haven't thanked you for all you did tonight."

Josh turned from his study of the valley, a muscle in his jaw flexing. "I did it for a friend, Abby. Brendan is the best friend I've ever had. Even when he thought he had reason to hate me, he still saved my life. At the risk of his future, he's supported my son for years. I could do no less than what I did."

Abby stared up at him. The truth unspoken lay between them. To pay a debt, he'd taken a chance on compromising his position as head of the mines. He'd set himself up to be the subject of ridicule in his community when it was learned his fiancée had deserted him, and he'd even given the woman he loved over to the care of the man she had chosen instead of him.

"I'm sorry, Josh. I know this must hurt."

"I've known all along about her and Bren."

Abby frowned, confused. She let his remark pass to be examined at a later time. "You should have seen Bren's face when Helena threatened to shoot me if he didn't marry her."

Josh laughed. "Helena is one of a kind, I'll say that." The affection in his voice stabbed at Abby's heart. He obviously loved the woman he'd given up without a whimper. He loved Helena and Abby loved him.

It would be too easy to rely on him. To come to need him in her life. She had to take Daniel west. She had to free her son of the stigma of his birth. She couldn't stay in the same house with Josh any longer now that he was free. Luckily she didn't have to. The house was finished.

"I'll be going back home in the morning while Daniel's in school. Da can't be left alone."

Josh felt the hairs on his arms stand up. A moment ago he'd seen trust and something more shining in her gaze, but now she wanted to put distance between them again. He didn't think he could handle that. Besides, Abby would be in too much danger if she went back now. What if they missed even one Workman? What if that man was the one who'd hated Brendan enough to frame him and use explosives on his house? It still chilled Josh when he thought of how close Abby had come to being on that porch when it blew up. And wouldn't Abby and Daniel still be a means to hurt him for all the arrests that night? No, Abby wasn't going back.

"Your father can come here. You won't be safe. As much as I respect Michael, he's in no shape to defend you and Daniel."

"Da would never live under Harlan Wheaton's roof and you know it. It's time for us to go back to our life now, Josh."

She didn't look all that happy to be going back to her life. But she did look beautiful in the light of the full moon. Her deep auburn hair shimmered and her eyes sparkled in the moonlight. Her skin shone as white as a bride's satin dress. Unable to resist, Josh touched her cheek with his fingertip and found it even smoother and softer than satin.

"Abby," he whispered. Sliding his fingers into her hair, he cupped the back of her head and tipped it back, taking her lips with his in a salute to her beauty and his deep love for her. Her lips were so soft under his he nearly lost his mind.

He tried to keep the kiss light, but she stepped closer. The feel of her breasts touching his chest fired a blaze of heat that went straight through him. He wrapped his free arm around her small waist and pulled her closer.

A small moan at the back of her throat broke the rest of his restraint. Knowing already the sweet taste of her mouth, he sought it with his tongue and took the kiss deeper, pressing her against the pillar. Heat flared into a blaze.

Abby quaked in his arms and moaned again, her hands in his hair now. She was clearly as on fire for him as he was for her. Josh felt as if he'd explode if he didn't have her. In his bed. In his life. He didn't know how he'd go on without her. He couldn't lose her. Lose this!

He gripped her head with both hands, trying to get still closer. The pins had long since fallen out of her hair, leaving it flowing freely over his hands like a silken waterfall. She smelled of springtime and tasted like the headiest of wines. Before he lost his control completely, Josh broke the shattering kiss and stepped back.

He sat back against the porch rail and pulled her close between the *V* of his legs, nestling her head on his shoulder. He prayed for the strength to resist carrying her off to his bed. But he wouldn't do that.

He wouldn't. He didn't think he'd ever get over hearing her tell him about the way she'd been treated these last years, knowing he'd been the cause of all her pain. After the only time they'd made love, when he'd had no idea of the consequences to come, he'd promised her it would never happen again without the benefit of marriage. How could he now after all her suffering go back on that promise?

"Marry me, Ab. Tonight. Right now. We'll go to Father Rafferty. He'll do it. You said he married Helena and Brendan without so much as a blink of his eye. Helena had no proof of what she said but no one can deny I trifled with you. Daniel's proof."

Abby pushed slowly away from him and stared into his eyes. He didn't know what it was she was thinking but he knew she wasn't thrilled with his proposal. "I won't pay for the rest of my life for a mistake in my youth, and I can't let you and Daniel do it, either."

"Is that all our love was to you? A mistake?"

"Past is past. I told you my dreams have changed. I'm leaving here, Josh."

Josh knew she meant Wheatonburg and felt a moment of total panic. "No," he ordered.

"Yes! As soon as Brendan lets us know where he is, we'll follow. It won't be as easy as it would have been with Brendan's help, but it'll be worth it when I can hold my head up, and when my son is just another little boy whose father is dead."

He wouldn't lose her again. Or Daniel. There had to be a way to stop her from going back to that damn possession house and then leaving town with his son.

*Possession…*house.

Josh wondered how much he'd learned from Helena. He wondered if he could watch hatred come back into Abby's gaze and mask his feelings. He had no choice. He'd earned back her trust once. He'd have to do it again.

Josh gripped her by her upper arms. "No, Abby. You aren't going back. You aren't going anywhere. You and my son are staying here with me where you belong. There's a caretaker's house where Michael can stay if he won't live in the manor house but you aren't going back there."

Her eyes flared, twin flames in the light of the back porch lantern. "And I'd like to know who's going to stop me!"

"I am. No one from your family is working in the mines. You have no right to that house. And further, I won't watch you and my son being treated with such utter disrespect for one more day. Nor will I let you take him away to some unsettled dangerous frontier so he can have a life free of ridicule. I'll do that for him by marrying his mother and daring one person, man, woman or child, to say another nasty thing to either of you when they need my goodwill to keep food on their tables."

Abby stared. "What are you up to, Joshua Wheaton? You'd never have tried something like this were Brendan here. Did you help my brother so I'd be at your mercy with him gone?"

Josh held on to his temper. Somehow. "Think what you want but you *will* marry me. You don't have enough money to go west. Your supplies were totally lost in the fire. You have nowhere to go here. Neither does your father. And lastly, Abby, no court in this state will let you keep Daniel if I petition to have him."

The fear that flared in her eyes nearly had him offering to pay her way west. *Nearly* but he couldn't let her go. He wasn't strong enough to stand on a platform and watch them leave.

"Abby, we'll have a good life. I know we will."

"That's what this is about. What you want your life to be. You know you can't take Daniel because he'd never stand for it. He'd fight you and you'd lose him."

"But you'll lose him, too, if you force me to be a father to him that way."

"I've no choice, do I? We'll go to Father Rafferty and see if he'll go along with this. But I'll tell you one place you won't have me. You'll sleep alone this and every night, Joshua Wheaton."

Did she think he didn't remember the way she'd just come alive in his arms? "I'm suppose to believe you don't want me as much as I want you? Every time I've kissed you, you've shown me you want me."

Color flamed in her cheeks. "A gentleman wouldn't have brought that up."

Josh arched an eyebrow. "I've found being a gentleman often loses a man more than it gains him. I will not have Harlan or the Henrys knowing my wife refuses to share my bed." When she opened her mouth to protest, he held up his hand and stood from his deceptively relaxed pose on the railing. "I'd never force you into anything you aren't ready for, Abby." He stepped close to her, glad to see she held her ground. Had she been fearful he would have backed down. He cupped her chin. Tipped her face up. Against her lips he whispered, "But know this. I will take every opportunity to tempt you into my arms."

Abby stepped back, fury burning in her gaze, but Josh continued in the same low seductive voice. "And judging from your past performances, it shouldn't take long till we both find a little piece of heaven on earth."

"It's *hell* you're buyin' this night, Joshua Wheaton. And it'll freeze over before I'll be givin' you anything resembling heaven."

Father Rafferty dashed Abby's last hope an hour later when he told Joshua it was about time he'd made an honest woman of her, then he'd happily waived the banns and woke his housekeeper for a second time that night to witness another marriage.

Josh had stopped by to pick up Michael, but there had been no help for her even from her da. Having saved Brendan from prison at best and a rope at worst, Josh was her father's hero. He'd refused to listen to Abby's protests, saying that things were now the way they should have been all along. He'd even agreed to live with them.

Abby watched as her father witnessed the cursed license Father Rafferty promised to file immediately. Come morning it looked like Daniel would be the only male in town she'd be speaking to.

"Now that the formalities are over with," Father Rafferty said as he turned to her and Joshua, who held her elbow in a death grip, "Joshua do you take this woman…"

Abby couldn't listen to the end of her westward dream. She looked up at the altar, tears flowing down her cheeks. She said "I do," only when Josh squeezed her arm and told her to "agree, dammit." At least *that* earned the great Joshua Wheaton a narrow-eyed glare from the good father.

As they left the church, torchlight lit up the western side of town nearly as bright as daybreak. The shouts of men, the screams of women and cries of children echoed in the night. "It's started," Josh said. "I don't think I'll ever forgive Harlan for what he's allowed to happen to this town tonight."

"We won't be solvin' the troubles of the world just now," Michael said. "We best be gettin' a move on, boyo. I don't think you'll be wanting to explain your activities this night to that mob."

Tight-lipped, Josh snapped the reins and the carriage sprang forward. He didn't say another word until they were in the house on the second floor. Abby started to turn into the room she'd been given days earlier. "Unless you want to explain our marriage to Daniel when he finds me in your bed in the morning, I suggest you accompany me down the hall to my room."

"I don't want to share your bed," Abby said through gritted teeth.

"Well, I don't much want to share a bed with a woman who had to be forced to marry me, then cried through the entire ceremony, but that's the way it is. Now decide which bed we share."

Hoping for at least one concession Abby pointed out, "Your parents didn't share a bedroom."

"And I won't have the kind of marriage they did. Pick."

"Your room," she snapped.

"Wise choice," Joshua said with an insolent grin. "It's far enough that sound won't carry to the other rooms."

Abby glared. "The only sounds they'd hear would be you shoutin' in pain if you so much as touch me."

He had the unbelievable nerve to chuckle as he pulled her along. Abby had had enough. She stopped dead in the hall and yanked her arm from his grasp. "I will not be pulled along like an errant child a second longer."

He smirked. That was the only way to describe the impudent expression on his face. It reminded her infuriatingly of Brendan's grin at Helena earlier that night in the church. Then, unbelievably, Josh scooped her up off the floor into his arms. Her face was inches from his and his gaze snared hers.

"You're right," he whispered, his voice low and sensual. "A bride deserves to be carried over the threshold on her wedding night. Not dragged. She deserves to be treated like a woman. Every inch of her body should be worshiped by her husband's lips. Remember the way my lips feel on your body, Abby? All over your body."

"Don't, Josh," she protested, but even to her own ears it sounded like the weakest of objections. Her breathing had become strained and she felt a delicious throbbing deep in her body.

Instead of heeding her weak demand, Josh continued in that same earthy tone that promised fulfillment as he walked toward his bedroom door, then inside, kicking the door shut behind him. "Oh, that's right. You don't want my lips on yours, my tongue caressing your nipples, or me inside you taking you to the stars. So—" abruptly he dropped her on the bed, his expression suddenly sharp and angry "—welcome to hell, Abby. Sleep tight." With that he turned, opened the door again and walked out, the door clicking quietly closed behind him before the sound of a lock cracked like a shot in the room.

He'd locked her in!

Abby sat up and stared at the door. The rotten, low-down snake in paradise. Sleep tight? She was strung so tight her muscles hurt. She wanted him. And worse. She still loved him. How could she love him and then hate him in the next thought?

Confused. Agitated. She bounded off the bed to pound on the door but stopped. No. She wouldn't give him the satisfaction and she didn't want him returning. If she could feel like this about him after he'd stomped all her dreams to dust, how much deeper would her feelings be if she shared herself with him as she once had? She had suffered enough when he'd left her behind and now he loved someone else. She would always wonder if he was thinking of Helena when he closed his eyes while buried inside her. Would he accidentally call out Helena's name in ecstasy as he'd once called her own?

Abby sank to the bed, tears flowing freely as she curled in a ball on top of the coverlet. Her body burned for him. Her heart craved his love and broke for the lack of it. He wanted her but he loved her brother's bride. Abby just didn't know how to survive giving all of herself to him when she'd be getting only half of him in return.

* * *

Josh stomped around the house at least a dozen times trying to sort out his thoughts and curb his temper—and his desire. It was a dangerous combination. He'd started out the ride home so angry over her tears during the ceremony he couldn't even think straight.

What was he? Some kind of ogre to have to force the woman he loved to wed him?

Then as the ride toward home had progressed he'd become thankful for Michael Kane's presence in the carriage because Abby's close proximity had ignited visions of what the night could bring. But, of course, she'd sworn to deny him.

He could have begged he supposed, but a man needed some pride. When a woman preferred living in poverty to living with him in luxury, and when she considered the love they'd shared in their youth a mistake…well, a man had to draw a line.

He wasn't sorry he'd married her, only that he'd had to apply pressure. He'd done it because he loved her and he knew that at least she desired him. He could build on that. At least now with them married, she couldn't go bolting across the continent in search of a better life. At least this way he still had a chance to show her he could provide that better life.

He was willing to risk everything because he still loved her more than life itself. So why was he outside in the middle of the night when he had a warm—if not willing—woman upstairs in his bed?

Josh shook his head in disgust. Half the time he wanted to throttle her. She claimed to want nothing from him but to be left alone. It was ironic that he would willingly give her the world but couldn't grant her that simple request.

He vaulted up the rear stairs and went to his room. Just inside the door he stopped as if he'd walked into a stone wall.

Abby lay curled in a self-protective ball in her faded blue dress. He hadn't even noticed what she'd been wearing at their wedding. He'd been too absorbed in his wants and in being angry over her tears. Guilt assailed him. She should at least have been wearing one of his mother's dresses. Instead she'd been wearing a threadbare cotton dress that had lost nearly all its color from years of wear.

He sat next to her on the bed and brushed her hair off her face—her tear-stained face. He'd brought her there, dumped her on the bed and without even letting her gather her night dress. "Ab. Abby," he called softly and shook her shoulder gently. "Come on, honey. Lets get you out of some of these things. You can't sleep in clothes that are wearing half the countryside."

Abby's eyelids never even flickered and Josh just didn't have the heart to wake her. Instead he went to the chest in the corner and took out a quilt to cover her. He looked at it in his hands. It wasn't just any quilt. It was the one Abby had made years earlier. It was supposed to have been for their bed. He'd taken it with him when he'd left Wheatonburg hoping she'd follow. For a long time, he'd wondered why he tortured himself by keeping it, but then he would climb in bed and settle down for the night feeling close to her and dream of times gone by.

With a sigh, he made at least part of his dream come true. He lay down beside his wife and pulled the quilt over them both.

Chapter Seventeen

In the predawn hours of the next day, Abby lay in that half-awake, half-slumberous state where reality and dreams seem to mesh just as they begin to fade away—the object of her desire just out of reach. It was the feel of Joshua's breath on the back of her neck that made her realize it really *was* his body nestled behind hers. This time it wasn't a dream. Her wishes and prayers had finally come true.

Then she remembered how it had come about and reality clashed with happily-ever-after. Though she was Joshua's wife, she'd awakened to find herself in the middle of a living nightmare, not a dream come true. Abby's mind spun with images of the night before. The wild kiss on the back porch that had gone too far. Josh telling her she had no choice but to marry him. His obvious anger after the ceremony that let her know she hadn't been the only one who'd felt forced. Joshua's lips on hers when he'd purposely aroused her, then her shock when he'd dumped her on the bed and locked her in the room.

She closed her eyes against the sudden burn of tears and listened to the sound of his breathing close at her back. It was a peaceful sound at odds with the wild beating of her heart and the anger that surged through her veins. She was now married to the man she loved and all he felt for her was lust and obligation.

It was worse than once again facing the town's scorn.

Bent on fleeing his bed, Abby grabbed at the quilt to throw it off but froze, staring at the soft material gripped in her fist.

The wedding ring quilt.

He still had the quilt her mother had helped her make for his birthday gift. Her throat ached and she fought more tears. It was to have been their wedding quilt.

And apparently it was.

But the wedding night had been far from the one they'd planned in that other lifetime of happiness and youth. "Why keep it all these years?" she whispered.

Behind her Joshua stirred and Abby, not wanting to deal with him when her thoughts and feelings were so stirred up and confused, crept out of bed to the door. She let out a pent-up breath when she found it unlocked.

Moving quickly, she raced down the hall, praying she wouldn't meet anyone and have to explain her rumpled appearance. Inside the room she'd been using until last night, Abby leaned back against the wall near the door. After a few minutes she pushed away from the smooth wooden panel and quickly washed. She hesitated when she reached for her good green dress. Next to it was Mrs. Wheaton's day gown. Today Joshua would announce their hasty marriage to Harlan Wheaton and Franklin Gowery. She needed to feel her best and this dress would do just that for her. It would give her confidence. Why not wear it?

In minutes Abby had dressed and was fussing with her hair. Disgusted, she tossed down her brush then picked it up again. Ruthlessly, she yanked it through her deep auburn hair until she had every tangle out and had tamed it into a high bun at the back of her head. She'd seen and admired Helena's hair when she'd worn it just this way. Tilting her head this way and that, Abby surveyed herself in the mirror. The style was a bit too severe, but then she noticed a few unruly strands loosening and springing back to frame her face with soft curls. She freed a few more strands, then stared at her reflection.

"So, you *can* make a silk purse of a sow's ear," she mused, then stiffened her shoulders. One thing she'd gained by this marriage—she'd never be relegated to the pigsty again. "Do your worst, Harlan Wheaton," she said to the woman in the mirror. "Abaigeal Kane *Wheaton* won't bow and scrape to the likes of you ever again."

She turned toward the door to the hall when someone knocked. "Come in," she called, bracing herself for a confrontation though she didn't know with whom.

"Abby?" Josh called quietly into the silence.

Immediately her composure fled as he entered and seemed to dwarf the room. "I needed to get dressed. Must I ask your permission from now on to leave a room?"

Josh grimaced. "You are never going to know how sorry I am for locking that door last night when I left. I was just so angry. I don't know how you make me do and say things I know I'll regret within minutes."

"How about because we hate each other? Did that ever occur to you before you condemned us to a life time of arguments?"

"I don't hate you, Ab."

"Well I hate—" She stopped. No. She wouldn't lie. She'd be spending an hour a week in Father Rafferty's confessional at this rate! "Damn you to hell, Joshua Wheaton! You make me say things I don't mean, as well. I hated you for years but now that I know you knew nothing of Daniel's birth, I just can't. But I'll never forgive you for not coming back for me anyway. Not for ten years did you darken my door and now you've come back, stolen my dreams and all but married me at gunpoint."

Josh smiled. "I thought two shotgun weddings in one night would overset even the unflappable Father Rafferty."

Abby stiffened and shot him her best narrow-eyed glare. "Don't you be tryin' to charm me. I won't have it. You wanted the wedding and you got your way, but you know what they say—be careful what you wish for. You planned the wedding, Joshua Wheaton. Now I'm going to plan the marriage. We'll be partners as we promised back when you tempted me to believe in fairy tales. But I've grown to be a woman since then. That foolish girl is gone. I'll do all the things I wanted to do to make this a good place to live and raise a family. You can carry on with your part of those plans but that's it. I'll tell you what I need and you'll supply it. If you keep me up-to-date on what you accomplish then I'll do the same."

Joshua crossed his arms and let his eyes feast on the fiery beauty who was his wife. Then he took a step toward her. Then another. And another. He noted again that she didn't give way, and loved her for it, though he did see worry flash across her expression.

"That takes care of the days," he said when they stood toe-to-toe. "But it leaves the nights." He took her chin and bent to touch his lips to hers. "And those, my darling, will be mine," he whispered, his lips brushing hers as he spoke. He reached out and grasped her arms, then pulled her to him and plundered her mouth. She responded as she always did and his body caught fire.

Why would she want to resist this? He couldn't. How did she think she could?

The most important answer to those questions was that neither of them could. And he intended to prove it to her, but not now. Hours with her wouldn't be enough time, so a few stolen moments before the house stirred would cheat them both.

He forced himself to slow and soften the kisses and turn them into a gentle promise. With one last butterfly kiss on each closed eyelid, he released her and stepped back. She turned away.

"I don't want this," she said, her voice quaking like a leaf in a windstorm.

Josh glanced in the cheval glass to see her biting her lip and fighting tears. He took her by the shoulders and turned her into his arms. "Yes, you do, Ab. We both do."

"Why is my mother crying?" a small, angry voice demanded from the nursery doorway. "What did you do to her?"

Josh held on to Abby, reluctant to let her go, but Abby pushed out of his arms. She looked at him and her expression ordered him to explain, but he had no answer for Daniel. He didn't understand her tears.

Abby shot him an annoyed look, took a deep breath, then she turned to face their son. "I'm crying because I'm so incredibly happy," Abby told Daniel. "Last night your father and I were wed by Father Rafferty."

Daniel's blue eyes seemed to catch fire. "You wouldn't have! He made you."

Seeing the anger flare in Abby's eyes through the looking glass, Josh put a hand on her back, hoping to gentle her mood but she shook off his touch. She marched over to Daniel and took him by the shoulders. "Now you listen to me, young man. No one, but no one makes me do anything I don't want to do. Is that understood?"

Daniel's chin quivered. "Yes, ma'am."

"Good. Now go put on your church clothes."

"Are we *all* going to church?" Daniel asked, all narrow-eyed and clearly skeptical, his eyes cutting toward Josh.

Abby's hands went to her hips. "And why wouldn't we be goin' together? We're a family now."

"'Cause he's a Baptist. If he comes into our church, God will strike him down dead. I thought you didn't want him dead."

Josh laughed. "I'm as Catholic as you, son. Have been since just after I went to Germany." He checked his watch. "Maybe you'd better do as your mother says. Early mass starts in less than an hour."

"Is there nothing you wouldn't do to make your father angry?" Abby asked after Daniel closed the door behind him.

"I told you how I came to feel about your church. I was all alone in Germany and I needed what I'd found at Saint Stephen's. I found it at a Catholic church there."

"I'm sorry. I shouldn't have accused you of that."

"No, you shouldn't," Josh said, then took a deep calming breath. "Abby, let's call a truce. We're going to encounter enough hostility over our marriage without being at each other's throats."

Josh held out his hand and Abby took it, accepting his cease-fire. Downstairs they received hearty congratulations from Mrs. Henry and polite felicitations from Mr. Henry. It was the last such reaction of the day.

Abby looked up the steps of Saint Stephen's to the doors that were usually open and ready to gather her close in comfort. Today they looked like a great yawning mouth ready to devour her. She stopped, unable to go farther. They'd be the center of attention when she walked in on Joshua's arm. After all the years she'd tried to fade into the woodwork, it would be horrible.

"Why are you so nervous?" Josh asked. "You've gotten married since last week. You didn't have a scarlet letter sewn onto your dress."

"That happened years ago," she muttered.

Josh sighed. "I'm sorry for my part in the way you've been treated, but now we've made it right. In a week they'll have something else to talk about. Besides, I'm sure the arrests last night will be far more news than our marriage."

Feeling better, she nodded. "I suppose you're right."

He should have been right. Twenty men had been jailed. But when the three of them stepped inside the sanctuary, a murmur moved through the congregation. It flowed like a wave toward the altar. Every head turned as they walked to the first open pew. Josh stopped and motioned her in. Abby nodded and genuflected before entering the pew after Daniel. Josh did the same as gracefully as if he'd been raised in the church.

Once seated, Abby glanced around then down at the dress she wore. When she'd picked the pretty peach dress she'd been thinking of the confidence it would give her when she faced Harlan and Franklin Gowery, but now she wondered if she'd done the right thing. Would her friends think she fancied herself above them now? Or would they understand that she had to dress to fit into the world of her new husband?

Husband.

Abby glanced at Joshua, who sat stiff as a board next to her. *He's as nervous as I am.* She hadn't known of his conversion because she hadn't seen Josh at church in the three months he'd been back. He'd said the church was a comfort to him. So why had he stayed away?

But she knew. He'd been accepted by few of the mining families and only those close to the Kanes. Since his return they'd shunned him as well because of what he'd done to one of their own. But he'd been just as much a victim as she had.

While Abby still felt betrayed that he'd never come back to Wheatonburg for her, she was sure nothing would have kept him away if he'd known about Daniel. He was an honorable man who'd realized he didn't love her.

And that was no one's business but theirs.

Abby linked her arm with his and smiled up at him, telling one and all that she had forgiven him. Josh blinked, shocked at first, then he smiled at her. That smile of his still enthralled her. The bell tinkling on the altar, announcing the beginning of mass, freed her of the power he had over her. In a blink it seemed mass was over and Father Rafferty stood at the back of the church, reaching out to take her hand. "And how is the new Mrs. Wheaton this lovely morning?"

"A little cranky, father," Josh replied unnecessarily when she growled.

Father Rafferty merely patted her hand. "Oh, now don't you be frettin' about our Abaigeal and her peppery disposition. Soon she'll be right as rain. You'll see," he promised then looked to the next person.

Josh cupped her elbow then and directed her to the carriage, where Daniel sat waiting. "Are you ready to beard the lion in his den?" Josh asked.

"I'm warnin' you, if Harlan calls me a whore again, I'll not be responsible for what I say to him."

They'd reached the carriage and Joshua stopped, turning to her and tilting her head up to his by her chin, his touch gentle. "If he does you won't need to say a word. You are my wife now and I'll blister his ears. And if Gowery says anything, I'll toss him out of the house."

"Thank you."

Josh's eyes hardened and he helped her into the carriage.

"Thanks are unnecessary. It's my duty, Abby. No one will ever be less than respectful to you and remain in Wheatonburg for long."

Abby fought tears. *Of course he doesn't want my thanks. I'm nothing but duty to him. Duty and a bed-warmer. She didn't want to be his duty and she was very afraid she wouldn't be able to resist warming his bed.*

The carriage ride back to Wheaton Manor was over too quickly. Josh turned the horse over to a groom and lifted her down from the seat. He kept his hands on her waist. "Relax," he said with a quick kiss. "The guillotine has not come to Pennsylvania."

Abby nodded and tried to do as he said, but all her efforts were for nothing as soon as they entered the foyer of the house. "Joshua, is that you? Franklin and I are in the library. We need to talk to you," Harlan Wheaton called out as he wheeled into the big double doorway at the rear off the large foyer. He did not look pleased.

"Ab, why don't you and Daniel go ask Mrs. Henry for a bite to eat while I take care of this."

Abby started to move away but stopped. "Daniel, you run along while your father and I speak with your grandfather."

Daniel looked unsure. "But—"

"Go. This is your house now and you have the full run of it but for your grandfather's room. Stay out of there."

Daniel shrugged and scampered toward the kitchen and Abby turned to Josh. "If you don't want folks to know you forced me into marriage, then you'd better stop acting guilty. If I'm your partner in revitalizing the town, I'd better start acting the part, as well."

Joshua weighed her words. "All right," he said slowly, "but don't say I didn't warn you."

"And don't forget *my* warning." Abby started toward the doorway her father-in-law had just vacated. "One nasty name pointed toward me or mine and I'm going to let him have it with both barrels."

"Fair enough," Josh agreed as they reached the library. He took her hand and tucked it into the crook of his arm. It was an oddly intimate gesture and she was honest enough with herself to admit she liked it.

Harlan looked up when they entered, his surprise and displeasure written on his face.

It was Franklin Gowery who spoke first. "Joshua, it was you we wanted to speak with."

Abby felt Joshua tense. "There is nothing you can't say in front of Abby. But first, I have an announcement. Last night Abby and I were married at St. Stephen's in town."

"Good God, Joshua," Harlan Wheaton gasped. "If you wanted the boy so badly why not just take him? You didn't have to marry her."

"I'd never take Daniel from Abby."

Abby thought something was odd about what Josh said, but, before she had the time to examine it, Gowery stood. "Sir, we had an agreement regarding Helena."

Josh nodded, acknowledging the truth of Gowery's point. "I am sorry to break my word but it couldn't be avoided."

"Helena will be utterly humiliated," Gowery shouted.

Abby coughed to hide a bubble of laughter and Josh said, "Had you not officially announced our engagement without our permission only a few people would have known of our agreement. I spoke with Helena about all of this yesterday morning. We were in complete agreement about our futures. We are still the best of friends. I have even promised to oversee her financial interests and will do so gladly until such time as she marries a man of her choosing."

Gowery's eyes flared and his face reddened. "That is not necessary. Her father left her in *my* care."

"Until she reached her majority. I now hold her power of attorney. You needn't trouble yourself further with her interests. I know she was a considerable burden."

"This is an utter outrage," Gowery shouted, his complexion nearly purple now. "You have her power of attorney? How can that be? She only came of age yesterday."

"And yesterday, Helena signed the power of attorney she asked my lawyer to have ready."

"Don't expect to hold it long. I'll convince her not to rely on someone who could break his word so easily. Especially someone who would marry a trollop because she gave him a quick roll in the hay and produced an ill-mannered by-blow!"

To Abby it didn't look as if Joshua even thought about his response. He just let go of her hand and let fly with a wonderfully executed left uppercut. Gowery dropped like a rock. "That is my wife and son you speak of, Gowery. Pick yourself up, and get out. I'll have Henry send your belongings to Philadelphia."

"That, sir, is just fine by me, but first I must speak to Helena," Gowery said as he got to his feet. Straightening his rumpled clothing, he looked like an outraged banty rooster. "There are things I must warn her about. That miner—" he pointed to Abby "—her brother, was one of the Workmen we were after, but he slipped our net last night. I must warn Helena that Kane killed her father. She wouldn't have a thing to do with him after learning that. I should never have waited so long to tell her."

"Are you talking about *Brendan* Kane?" Josh asked.

"One and the same."

"Brendan Kane is no more capable of cold-blooded murder than I am. I know the man. He stopped them from killing me. They blew up his house to punish him!"

"Don't be a fool, that was only to throw us off his trail or bring him to heel."

"Let me tell you something you don't know, Franklin," Joshua thundered. "Daniel was beaten up and threatened by a few young toughs under the influence of the AMU after Brendan and the Kanes took me in and cared for me. Abby was knocked down by the blast when they blew the Kanes' porch. Another few seconds and she'd have been dead. Brendan would never endanger his family or have stood for Daniel being frightened by anyone in AMU control if he had any influence with them whatsoever. And why would Helena need to know any of this?"

"Because it was Kane who took her innocence just to spoil her chance for happiness."

Though Josh was doing a fine job of defending her and her brother and acting as if what Gowery said was new to him, Abby could stay silent no longer. "I'd like to be knowin' how it is that Helena was so innocent when I was a trollop for doin' the same thing. You've a wicked double standard you live by, Mr. Gowery. Maybe if you stepped back and examined it and your conscience, you'd understand how a nasty bunch like the Workman got enough of a foothold in the AMU to take it over! It was an honorable idea at the outset.

"Joshua, I'm going to go move my things into your room. There's an odor in here that has more to do with hypocrisy than the dead animals hangin' about the walls!"

With pride, Josh watched Abby leave. "She has a point, Gowery," he said.

"None I'm interested in hearing. I insist on seeing Helena."

Josh made a great production of checking his watch, then putting it back in his pocket. He pursed his lips. "When we spoke last night, Helena never wanted to see you again. She said you've made her life a living hell since her father's death. I'll tell her you've gone and if she wishes, she will contact you."

"Harlan, are you just going to let your son treat a guest in this manner?"

"He has no say in my actions and has not for a decade."

On an oath Franklin Gowery turned and stalked out of the room. Not wanting to trust that he wouldn't charge straight to Helena's room, Josh followed.

But it wasn't necessary. Somehow Henry was at the bottom of the stairs holding Gowery's hat and overcoat. As he handed over the coat and hat, Henry took Gowery's arm and rushed him out the front door. Josh watched, amused, as the door closed behind them. He wished all his problems could be solved as easily. The squeak of Harlan's wheelchair drew Josh's attention.

"You're a fool," Harlan said.

Josh whirled to face his father. "Not. One. More. Word."

"Just tell me you at least planned to legitimize the boy and then divorce the mother and toss her out."

Joshua just stared for a long moment before he could speak. "*In…credible,*" he said. "How can you take something as holy and sacred as marriage and twist its meaning to something so ugly? There is one reason and only one reason I made Abby my wife. I love her and I cannot imagine life in this hellhole you call a town without her. It is probably the most selfish thing I've done in my entire life. They'd have been much happier without me." He paused and remembered one more fact he needed to impart to the man who'd fathered him. "Oh, you should also know I converted to Catholicism years ago, which is why I married Abby at St. Stephens. Catholic marriages are for life."

Chapter Eighteen

Josh looked up from his engineering journal. His dreams for this night were off-kilter with the reality of his first quiet evening as Abby's husband.

Across the parlor, she sat reading aloud to Daniel. Michael sat near them, listening and whittling. It should have been perfect. But something was wrong.

Harlan was in his own room. He'd taken his dinner there, so he wasn't the problem. But there was still an underlying air of tension in the room. With Abby his wife and Brendan safe, it should have dissipated, but the tension was still there. It gnawed at him. Taunted him. Abby stopped reading and looked up as if his gaze had called to her. And suddenly the air between them fairly sizzled.

"What does Jim do? What happens next Ma?" Daniel asked, drawing her attention back to him.

"That, my boy, is the next chapter. You'll find out tomorrow night. Right now it's bedtime."

Daniel's tone was filled with disgust when he said, "Why do I have to go to bed so early if I don't have to get up and do chores?"

"Now who was it who said you had no chores?" Michael asked. "I've decided to take on that caretaker's house ou' back and you are going to have to help me get it ready."

"Da, you promised to stay here," Abby protested.

"You know you're welcome here at the manor," Josh put in

"And if come winter 'tis too cold out there, I'll reconsider but for now, I think I best remove myself. You, Abby and Daniel need to settle in with each other without a second old man's nose in your business. And on that subject it will also be better to give Harlan time to get used to your marriage without me underfoot. By winter, Thomas'll have returned. can move back home with him. As long as you don't mind u' using the possession house, Joshua."

Josh knew that wouldn't work. Abby could never live i relative luxury while her brother and father lived in a posses sion house. He wouldn't be able to stand that, either. "Actually the cottage was built as a guest house. It only became known a the caretaker's cottage because of mother's pretensions. It' built as solidly as the manor and there's a fireplace in every room and has two bedchambers. I thought of moving out there mysel when I first returned, but I had to stay in the house to keep a eye on Gowery and Harlan for Brendan's sake. I'd appreciate i if you wouldn't think of worrying us by going back to your old home at all. Think of the guest house as your own. I'll have you furniture moved in and the place cleaned by some of the local women. I'm sure they'd appreciate the opportunity to earn cash.'

Michael nodded. "I'd be honored, son."

Josh felt tears burn at the back of his throat. He looked into Michael's steady green eyes and leaned forward on his chair "No, Michael, I'm honored. You were more a father to me than that bitter old man in there. I'll never forget or be able to repay you and your family for the way all of you took me to your hearts when I needed a real family. I hate that I disappointed you, and I appreciate more than I can say the chance you've given me to try making it right."

He looked pointedly at Abby then. "I think I'll take a stroll around the grounds before bed. If you'll all excuse me? If you see anything out there that will make it feel more like a home for your father and Thomas—new draperies or bedding— please order it."

Abby paced Josh's bedroom. Tonight would be very different from last night. What would she do when he came to her? What would he do?

Her stomach muscles tightened as images of his hands on her body and his mouth following the same path flooded her mind. She was instantly light-headed. He meant to seduce her. He'd told her he would. Sinking to the bed, she stared into the cheval glass across the room and admitted to the woman reflected there that she wanted him. But did wanting make it right? She didn't know anymore. Yesterday she would have said no. She'd learned passion's lesson all too well in the last ten years.

Tonight, though, her role in life was no longer that of the cast-aside lover and mother of his illegitimate son. He'd made her his wife and changed her world.

So what good would it do to deny herself the pleasure she could gain from this farce of a marriage? Could she love him more deeply than she already did?

Abby balled her hand into a fist. *He stole your dream of a life away from shame and disgrace.*

Did he? a quiet voice asked.

Abby didn't know who she was angrier at: Joshua or herself. He'd been bluffing about taking her son away. His anger at his father for even suggesting it had blown a hole in the threat a mile deep. He'd lied and she should have known.

With nothing else to do, she dressed for bed and went to

sit at the vanity. As she worked on taking her hair down, the door opened and Josh entered. Their eyes caught in the mirror. He tossed his jacket and vest onto a chair, his gaze never once breaking contact with hers. He unbuttoned the shirt then, walking silently toward her. Just as he stepped behind her, he pulled it off and dropped to one knee.

"You're awake."

Abby stared at his hard muscled chest with its sprinkling of golden hair. She cursed herself for yearning after him and sought to break his invisible hold on her. "Your prisoner finds sleep difficult," she replied sharply.

He winced a bit, but otherwise ignored the jibe and pushed her hands aside, taking over removing the pins. "I've dreamed of doing this for years. The one time we made love I forgot to. I've regretted it ever since. I know you're angry, sweetheart. And I understand. I know this ruined your plans, but I couldn't let you go. I asked for a truce this morning. Please let it continue. Don't make me feel as if I'm forcing you tonight, as well. Please."

Abby saw the anguish in his blue eyes. He'd never force her. If she'd have remembered that last night, she wouldn't be in this mess. She should have dared him to do his worst. Now if she could only understand why she hadn't.

"You'd never have taken Daniel from me."

His smile crooked, he moved her hair aside and kissed her neck. Fire shot through her veins and she stifled a gasp as he continued to feather kisses in a path to her cheek.

"I was desperate, Ab. Even though the threat got me what I wanted, it hurt that you knew me so little. Did *you* mean what you said to Daniel? Is it true that no one could ever force you to do something you didn't really want to do? Somewhere deep inside, did you want a life with me?"

He settled his hands on her waist, burning her wherever he

touched. A hot liquid warmth flooded her core even as her eyes filled with tears. His sultry breath on her neck, as he nipped at the sensitive lobe of her ear, made her shiver with burgeoning need.

"Is it true, Ab?" he asked, his voice whiskey-rough. "Did you want to be my wife? In your heart of hearts, don't you want this again? It's been so long, but I can still remember every second of that day in the meadow."

His mouth trailed downward to her shoulder. His lips and tongue and teeth set off a wildfire inside her. "Do you really not want what we can give each other? I've never felt this with anyone else, Ab. I've never needed like this. I've never wanted like this. Tell me you want this," he insisted.

Tears burned at the back of her eyes and she knew if she spoke, he'd hear the tears so she kept silent.

"Tell me to stop while I still can," Josh demanded, his voice husky and rough. His hands were roving her body. His hot breath on her conspired to send arrows of need and desire tearing through her.

"No. Don't stop," she managed to admit.

Josh stood, drawing her up and into his arms. He stared down at her with the most peculiar look on his face, then he groaned and took her lips in a long drugging kiss that went on and on. His tongue sought hers and the tart taste of tobacco and mint made her shudder in his arms.

He was all tenderness and fire.

Cupping her bottom, he pulled her fully against him. Strong and hard, the heat of him seared every nuance of him into her memory. He was the same and different from the boy he'd been that day in the meadow.

He groaned and rocked against her, igniting a blaze that set fire to her blood. He pulled her harder against him. It was as if he just couldn't get close enough.

Then he stepped back. His hands shaking, he fumbled with the ties of her gown and soon it slid off her shoulders to puddle at her feet. His blue eyes glowed like twin flames as his gaze moved over her.

"Beautiful," he murmured and swept her up into his arms.

Abby looped her arms around his strong neck, holding on for dear life as her world spun away from her and out of control. He followed her down onto the bed and took her mouth in a kiss so deep she felt it in the deepest part of her. She trembled as he covered her with his big hard body and she clung to him, her universe anchored solely by him. He was solid and good and his weight felt oh so perfect on her.

He broke the kiss and stared at her. "I wanted to take my time. I wanted this to take hours. But God help me I'm out of patience." His next kiss turned fierce.

She wanted to touch him. Wanted his hands on her but he swore suddenly and pushed to his feet. Bereft at first she smiled, noticing his hands were even more unsteady and he popped a couple of buttons as he tugged his breeches off. She had a few precious moments to admire the man he'd grown into, and to realize he had been little more than a boy when last they were together this way.

Broad shoulders and narrow hips, her eyes followed the arrow of hair from his navel downward. Fire and heat. He was all that and more. His skin glowed in the low lamplight and his muscles bunched and flexed with his every move. She needed him. And it was clear he was as on fire for her as she was for him.

"Come back to me," she whispered and held her arms out.

Josh surrendered to her plea and the need to be part of her. That need felt like a living thing clawing at him. Mindful of how long ago her last time had been, he tried to move carefully, hoping to be as gentle as possible. He was shaking with the effort to move into her slowly when she arched up to meet him.

His mind exploded in a conflagration of feelings and sensations that were beyond anything he'd ever felt. He surged inside her, his mind and body singed. Josh stiffened and held the scalding breath inside his chest when she started to quake in his arms—at the end of their lover's journey. And Josh knew he'd take her back there as many times as he could manage.

Sun streaming in the window woke Abby. She covered her eyes with her forearm then her pillow, but the harsh light put pay to the idea of going back to sleep. Then an unfamiliar ache reminded her she'd spent the night in Josh's arms.

He'd well and truly seduced her in seconds with his clever lips and hands and his husky, whiskey-rough voice. And after that first time, he'd been insatiable, returning to her arms time and again as the lamp burned lower and lower. Entwined in each others arms, they'd finally fallen into exhausted sleep as dawn broke.

She couldn't in all conscience even pretend she was sorry. If nothing else, Joshua was a very good lover. She had no basis for comparison, of course, but he'd made sure to satisfy her each time he'd come to her.

Abby glanced next to her and frowned. He was gone, a note tacked to his pillow. She stretched across the bed and lay on her stomach to read it. "Cave-in. Thank God Bren's safely out of there now. One less worry. JW." She sighed and traced the initials Brendan had designed for Joshua with her fingertip. "So you still use them, as well. If only you still loved me the way you did then."

Tears blurred the note. "But you don't," she whispered, her

voice breaking as the tears fell. She shook her head and ruthlessly scraped the moisture from her cheeks.

Partners. They were only supposed to be partners in the revitalization of Wheatonburg. That had been her condition for this marriage and he'd given every indication of accepting the limit on their relationship. But he'd warned her the night would be his. And he'd been right. It had been his. *She* had been his. He got everything he wanted and it had been embarrassingly easy to seduce her into surrendering. Maybe it was time Joshua found out life didn't always work out the way he wanted.

There had to be one battle she could win.

The bedroom was clearly the wrong place for her to make that point. She'd be foolish to deny herself the pleasure of his body and the chance for more children. She might have been forced to rethink her position—though thinking had had little to do with it.

But she *would* deny him something.

If they were to be together at night, then by God during the day they would *not* be. This time she wouldn't waver. This was a battle she would win. She would do as she'd once promised. She would make Wheatonburg a good place to live. And she would do it alone, just as she'd told Joshua she would. He could run the mines, make his improvements and she would make hers.

First, she would make sure Prescott lowered the prices in the company store. Then she would see that the school was moved to a better building. With lower prices in the company store and the higher wages Josh would pay once he got both the mines and factory up and running smoothly, the townspeople would be able live better lives. After that would come the possession houses. They would be repaired when they needed and rents would go toward purchase. This would become the workers' town. Not Harlan Wheaton's.

After a light meal, Abby had the stable boy hitch up the carriage and she headed for town. It was the first time she had worn her good green dress somewhere other than to a social or to mass. She felt like a new person as she entered the company store.

Mr. Prescott looked up from his credit book. "Mrs. Sullivan… er…Mrs. Wheaton," he corrected, looking uncomfortable. Oh, she'd bet that rankled. She was now the one *he* had to please.

"Good day to you, Mr. Prescott. I assume by your greeting that you've heard of our marriage."

"The whole town is buzzing about it. That and the arrests. Interesting that your brother managed to escape."

"Escape? Brendan left town to chase a dream, Mr. Prescott. He was gone hours before anyone was arrested and Joshua will eventually prove the charges brought against him are false."

"I saw the evidence against your brother with my own eyes."

"You saw the mark of what you consider another dirty Irish miner. You don't know one of the men from the others. If someone other than Brendan came in here and made his mark, you wouldn't know the difference. Would you?" She held up her hand to silence him when he looked up at her with a bewildered expression. She didn't want to listen to his small-minded lies. "No. Don't be denying it. We both know the truth. Now, I'd like to see your books."

He blinked. "Books? Oh. Yes. You read, don't you? I'm afraid I've nothing new since you were last in to clean."

Abby gritted her teeth and took a breath. Her mother had taught her to act like a lady and she wouldn't shame her by screaming like a fish wife.

"I'm talking about your *account* books. I want to see what

kind of profit margin the store has." She hesitated then forged ahead. "Joshua mentioned that he'd told you to cut it. You haven't. Now I will."

"Cut it? You can't do that!"

Abby arched one eyebrow. "Oh, but I can. And I will. Harlan turned the business over to Joshua and Josh turned the duties that pertain to the town over to me. This store is part of a town. You, Mr. Prescott, are under my jurisdiction."

And, oh, my, didn't saying that feel good!

Josh strained against the beam and it shifted upward just a little. "Come on, let's put our backs into it this time," he shouted. "On three. Pull him out when the beam's off him. One. Two. Three. Push!" He strained again and felt the wood move a good three inches. He gritted his teeth and strained harder, his shoulders and back aching. "Get him out of there! Come on!"

The trapped miner screamed as the broken bones in his legs shifted when his fellow workers pulled him free. One more life saved.

Josh took a deep breath and reached for another large rock that blocked the way to the two men still unaccounted for.

"Joshua," Helmut Faltsburg said as he put a hand on his shoulder. "You should rest."

"Rest? Are the wives of the two men in there going to be able to rest until they know? Do you think the two of them are resting in there or are they trying to claw their way out?"

"The other men are working in shifts. You haven't taken a break all day."

"I'll rest when my men aren't buried alive."

Helmut nodded. "All right. Then we dig. Let's go, men. Boss says we keep going."

Fifteen minutes later Josh pushed a rock aside and opened

up a small fissure to a chamber. The hand of Brian McAllister reached out and grasped his amidst the hoots and shouts of the other miners. He and the other man he'd been trapped with *had* been trying to dig from their side, but they had just about run out of air.

"Thank you. Thank you, Joshua," his old baseball teammate said when Josh pulled him through the hole they'd made larger together. While the other men pulled the second man free, Josh walked McAllister to the train car that would take them to the surface.

When he'd gained his breath, his old friend looked at Josh with serious eyes. "Grace gave me a son last night and we'd yet to decide on a name. Your son is named for my uncle because he died in a cave-in. I think it only fitting mine be named for you because I lived through one thanks to you. I think Brendan Kane said it all when he said you'd make a difference around here. Not once did your old man come to the fields when there was a cave-in. And here you are pulling my ass out of a pit yourself."

"Mining and making it safe is all I've wanted to do with my life since the day your uncle died down here."

McAllister shook his head. "It isn't my dream. I don't ever want to wait for death in a coal coffin again. I'd appreciate a chance at that furniture-making operation Brendan told me was coming."

Josh smiled and clapped McAllister on the back. "That's the least I can do for the father of my namesake. Why don't you show up there tomorrow. They're starting to clear some of the land and you can put your hand to blowing the stumps. Come on, let's get you up top so you can go see that pretty wife of yours, then I'll head home to my own."

But Josh didn't head home. What should have been the end of a long day turned out to be just the beginning. There was a problem with the railroad he knew had been caused by Gowery, part owner of the rail line.

He sent a telegram out explaining he owned stock as well and would sell it to a competitor if the problem wasn't solved immediately. That crisis averted, another took its place. The fan used to ventilate Lilybet stopped for no apparent reason. He and Helmut worked on it for the next two hours before Josh felt he could leave.

The manor was nearly dark when Josh reached home. It was hours past sunset and he was dead tired. He wondered how the day had been for Abby and Daniel. If Harlan had been his usual obnoxious self or if they had managed to steer clear of him.

"Good evening, Henry," he said when the older man opened the door before he could even reach for the knob.

"Evening, sir. Might I suggest a bath in the pantry? Mrs. Henry will have both our skins if you track up the stairs like that and you really shouldn't go to your new wife smelling quite so…"

Josh laughed. "Rank? Enough said, Henry," he said, looking down at his ruined clothes. "I suppose I should meet you around back."

Abby was sound asleep when he slid into bed about an hour later. In seconds she'd rolled into his arms and nestled her head beneath his chin. His heart swelled, wishing she would trust him as easily with her heart. A tear leaked from the corner of his eye. He loved her and he was very much afraid she hated him for destroying her dreams. He closed his eyes and sighed, falling into oblivion while holding his heart's desire in his aching arms.

"You think you're pretty smart don't you," Abby heard Harlan say when she neared the breakfast room a week later.

Daniel's voice carried just as well as her obnoxious father-in-law's. "I *know* I am. Mr. Marks told me so."

"What kind of fool would tell a whippersnapper like you he's smart? Soon you won't be going to school. We'll send to Philadelphia for a top-rate tutor to teach you in your own schoolroom upstairs. Then we'll see how smart you are."

"I'm not going back to my school?" Daniel asked.

"Not if I have any say in it."

Abby charged into the breakfast room loaded for bear. How dare Harlan Wheaton try to overrule her when her own father and brothers, who'd fed and clothed the boy, never had? "You have nothing to say about Daniel's education. It's none of your business."

Wheaton's face turned red with anger. "I won't have my grandson going to that school with the rabble."

"Funny, not a week ago you stuffed Daniel in the same category."

"They tease me, Ma," Daniel said. "I'd like a tutor. Really."

Abby couldn't believe her ears. Daniel loved and respected Mr. Marks. "The kind of schooling you get will be for me and your father to decide."

"Well, far as I can see it ain't none of his business, either. I want a tutor like Grandpa says I should have. I'm going out to play."

"Don't you dare take one step out that door."

"Oh, let the boy be, Abaigeal. He's high-spirited."

The moment Harlan spoke Daniel whirled away and was gone. Abby felt as if her head would explode. She took a long moment to pray for patience. But her patience with Harlan Wheaton had run out years ago.

"If you ever come between me and my son again, I'll tell him it was you who kept his parents from marrying all those years ago. And if you think he hates Joshua, just you wait and see how he'll feel about you."

Harlan called her a blackmailer then rolled away.

Abby stormed into Joshua's office half an hour later. It didn't matter that he had no control over him. Harlan was his father. "Your father," she shouted, "is a meddling, aggravating, agitating old bastard!"

"At the risk of sounding as childish as Daniel, please don't call him *my father.* I haven't thought of him that way since I found out what he did with our letters. And you left out sanctimonious, hypocritical, infuriating and several other adjectives that slip my mind just now."

Joshua smiled and rounded his desk, sauntering toward her and pulling her into his arms. "Has anyone ever told you how beautiful you are with your cheeks all red and your green eyes blazing?"

Abby stiffened and recited the Bill of Rights in her head. She had a right to her anger and would *not* let him charm her.

Josh let go and stepped back with a sigh. "What did he do that has you so riled?"

"He told Daniel he'd be having a tutor soon."

"To be honest, it isn't a bad idea. You said yourself Daniel is teased unmercifully at school."

"He's teased everywhere. What do you want to do? Lock him up all safe and sound in the manor to keep him from being hurt by the cruelty of others?"

"You make it sound as if he'd be a prisoner. I just want to keep him safe from their taunts."

"Then you should have let us go west!" she spat back and shot him a dark look. "Keep Harlan under control," she demanded and turned to leave.

Josh grasped her shoulder gently. It was the gentleness that stopped her in her tracks. "I'm sorry, Ab. I don't know what I can do to fix the mess I've made of things, but I'll try."

Abby nodded but didn't turn back to face him. All he had to do was touch her and she wanted him. This wouldn't do.

"I have things to see to," she said through tightly clamped teeth.

He let her go but trailed his fingers down her arm. "I wanted to tell you that Prescott came to complain about the price reductions. I sent him packing. I told him you're my wife and he should do as you say."

"Thank you." She glanced over her shoulder then, and was sorry she had. He looked exhausted and sad somehow. Abby stiffened her resolve and walked out. If things weren't falling into place as he'd thought they would, he had no one to blame but himself!

Josh sank into his desk chair and pressed the heels of his hands to his eyes. Things with Abby certainly weren't falling into place the way he'd thought they would. He didn't understand how the two of them could be so in tune in bed but so at odds with each other during every other minute of the day. Would he ever come to understand her?

A bold knock at the door dragged Josh out of his dark thoughts. He'd never get anything done at this rate. With a sigh he leaned back in his chair and called, "Come in."

Jamie Reynolds stepped in and Josh inclined his head in silent invitation toward a chair.

"I need to ask you some questions, Wheaton."

Josh had been waiting for this. A little amused, he leaned back farther and propped his elbows on the arms of his chair. He steepled his fingers and rested them against his lips. "And what would you want to question me about? Am I on your ridiculous list of suspects now?"

"I understand you don't agree with our findings regarding your…friend or brother-in-law as the case may be."

"The case is that he's both my friend and my brother-in-law. And as for your findings, Reynolds, I don't think you could *find* your ass with both hands. Brendan Kane is no more a Workman than I am."

Reynolds bristled. "That is for the courts to decide."

"Courts?" Josh laughed bitterly. "I know you aren't from this country but let me tell you something. Gowery's plans for those men have nothing to do with due process. He hired men to investigate and arrest them and now he's hiring the prosecutors. About the only thing those men will see of the real justice system in Pennsylvania is the judge and the court-room where Gowery plans to hold the trials. It's an utter disgrace."

"I am not a part of any of that. I volunteered to work with the Pinkertons for Helena's sake and I am here today to ask after her whereabouts. I went to see her a little while ago and was told she'd left. I know she didn't leave with Franklin or since then. I've had a man watching the train station."

Josh sighed. "Look, Reynolds, Helena hates you. Why don't you look for another bank account with an eligible female attached to rescue your failing fortunes? Leave Helena alone."

"Is that what you think my interest is in Helena? Is that what she thinks? I never wanted her for her money. I don't need it. Now she's out there all alone with no one to protect her. How could you let her do this?"

"I did nothing but set her free as she wished. I also helped her get away from people trying to decide her future for her. I booked passage for her to where she wanted to go."

Reynolds eyes lit. "Where? Where has she gone? I must find her. Is she with Kane?"

"Brendan only stayed here as long as he did to take care of Abby and Daniel. When I told him I planned to marry Abby, Brendan started making plans to leave. It's as much a coincidence that the AMU arrests took place on the night of

Helena's twenty-first birthday as it is that they both left town that same night."

Reynolds jumped to his feet. "Then they *are* together. Where has she gone? I have to save her from him."

Josh bit back a grin. *Well, isn't this perfect. He'll never find Amber before she sails. Perfect!* "I told you I booked her passage. She went to New York to take a clipper to California. Brendan wasn't with her."

"A clipper. Why a clipper? That's so dangerous. She could have ridden the train."

Jamie Reynolds's expression showed what looked like genuine concern. Josh wondered if perhaps he did feel something for Helena. "She may have wanted desperately to be on her own but she's also a bright girl. She is a lot safer from being accosted on a clipper than traveling alone on the transcontinental railroad. She knew Gowery would never catch her once she sailed and neither will you. All she has to do is stay hidden in New York until then."

"You don't understand how vulnerable and delicate she is. I have to try," he stated and was gone.

Josh shook his head and went back to his calculations, putting Gowery and Reynolds out of his mind. Helena and Brendan were safe now. And Amber wasn't in any danger from Reynolds. He smiled, remembering Abby's feisty lady friend. He almost wished the Irish Lord would catch up with Amber Dodd. It would serve him right.

Hours later Josh plodded home hoping for comfort and peace after a day straight from hell. An hour after Abby's morning visit and the subsequent one from Reynolds, three men had drowned when the river broke into River Fall and flooded it. There was no chance they would ever recover the bodies because they'd been hundreds of feet below the water level. To add to that heartache was a new danger to area residents. Acres of the surrounding land were in danger of developing hazardous sinkholes because the flooding could undermine the soil.

Then there'd been a fight between several miners when they learned Josh had changed the pay structure. They would now all be paid at the same rate regardless of ethnic origin. Whether other mine owners continued to pay the Irish a third less or not, Wheaton Mining would pay everyone equally.

After that crisis, Josh had gone back to his office, hoping for peace and quiet. Instead he found Sampson Parton, the state mine inspector, waiting for him there. The upshot of the man's visit was that thanks to Franklin Gowery's manipulations, Josh had four months to bring the mines up to standard or they would be closed by the state. Parton also warned if the men who'd been killed were found to have been endangered by any of the violations, Josh would be held criminally liable as current head of Wheaton Mining.

Josh had decided to go home after that, but only because he had nowhere else to go. He trudged up the front steps and entered the house to the sound of an argument piercing the air. It flooded out of the library, assaulting his already strained nerves. Tired to the bone, but spoiling for a fight, he stalked toward the sounds of discord. Michael and Harlan, both in wheelchairs, sat across the room from each other shouting derisive remarks at the top of their lungs.

"What the *hell* is going on in here?" Josh bellowed from the doorway. Blessed silence reigned.

Abby stepped into the room from behind him. "Welcome home to wedded bliss, my darlin'. They've been at it like that for hours. Apparently the in-laws haven't fallen in with your great master plan any more than Daniel and I have."

Josh narrowed his eyes, refusing to rise to the bait. "Then

let's separate them. Michael, did they bring your furniture up to the guest house?"

Michael nodded. "Late this afternoon. And the women you sent came in to clean. I just need me things from upstairs and I'll be well out of here." He glared at Harlan.

Josh walked to stand behind Michael. "I'll take you over home right now and see that you're settled in. Patrick McDade will be staying with you as your valet." He started pushing Michael across the room as he spoke. "He'll come here to pick up your meals and handle anything else you need help with. You are, of course, always welcome to take any meal you want with us. Just let us know when and Mrs. Henry will set an extra place for you."

"See here, I should have some say in who I eat dinner with," Harlan blustered.

At the door Josh stopped and turned back. "Of course you do. You are perfectly free to take dinner in your room anytime you wish." That said he left Harlan and Abby to battle each other or not. He really didn't care.

Abby watched Joshua push her father to the wide double doors at the back of the hallway then down the ramp into the darkness. Michael's voice floated back at her. "I'm sorry, Joshua. I hear from Daniel that you lost three carpenters in River Fall."

She hadn't said a word since she'd made her wry comment and now she thanked God she hadn't. She hadn't kept silent because she knew about what had happened. No. She'd just been appalled by how tired and drawn he looked. Now she understood why.

In the past week he'd come home after she went to bed most nights and usually found the energy to gather her close to make love to her. Some nights he was all fire and flash and others he was so slow and gentle with her it forced her to tear up when she remembered the nearly worshipful way he'd touched her. But she rarely saw him otherwise because she avoided him.

That morning when she'd stormed into his office at the mines she'd been too angry to notice how exhausted he looked at first. After she'd taken note of it, Abby had left, put it out of her mind and gotten on with her day.

He'd turned to her the last time he'd lost men, needing her comfort and support. But this time she'd made herself unavailable. Abby was suddenly ashamed of how she'd been treating him. The trouble was she had no idea how to change the pattern of their lives and still guard her heart. It was clear she had to find a way, though.

"He told me he dies a little every time a miner does," Daniel said, eyes narrowed and gazing at the door, a thoughtful expression on his face. "Do you really think he cares that much?"

"That's how I met him. He wanted to help save a young man but the men wouldn't take his help because of who his father was. I shamed them into letting him dig alongside them, but I've never been sure if I did him any favors."

"How come?" Daniel asked.

"Because he was only fifteen and it was him who dragged Danny McAllister's lifeless body out of there. And that day he swore he'd find a way to make mining safe. 'Tis an impossible task, but I don't think he'll ever give up trying no matter how much it takes out of him. Why do you ask?"

Daniel shrugged and walked away, leaving Abby to wonder what was going on in the boy's head. He never asked about Joshua. She watched as Daniel left the room and prayed her son had learned as much as she had that day.

Chapter Nineteen

Abby found Daniel in the library with Harlan about the same time the next day. The table was set for dinner and Josh was home early for a change, working in his study on some sort of engineering drawing.

"Are you joining us for dinner tonight, Harlan?" she asked.

"That depends," Harlan answered with a scowl. "Will I be Daniel's only grandfather in attendance?"

Abby crossed her arms in irritation. "Da's eating at home."

"Good," Harlan snapped then double-jumped Daniel's checkers in a way that wasn't allowed by any rule she'd ever heard. "King me!" he hooted like a nasty, victorious child.

Daniel gave him a slant-eyed scowled. "You can't do that. That's cheating."

"It is," Josh said from the doorway opposite where Abby stood.

Daniel scowled at Josh. Seeing that sour look directed at him, and not Harlan, sent an arrow piercing Abby's heart. She'd thought she'd seen a breakthrough yesterday. She didn't know how to reach her son where his father was concerned. Nor could she understand the camaraderie that had begun to spring up between her son and Harlan. It worried her because sooner or later he would show his true colors. She was very much afraid her son would be badly hurt.

"If I cheated," Harlan sneered, "none of you can prove it. My checker is where it is now and you can't prove where it was before I moved it. Let that be a lesson to you, my boy. Make sure all the witnesses are on your side before you make any moves in life, and if they are, you can do as you like."

"Or you could win fair and square," Joshua suggested. He stood negligently, his shoulder leaning against the doorjamb and his arms crossed. But Abby had begun to understand the steel beneath the surface of the man. He was tense and more than a little furious with his father.

Daniel looked from his grandfather to Josh then back again. He shrugged. "I'll remember that, Grandpa."

Josh cleared his throat. "Daniel, I wondered if you'd like to come out to the stable? There's something interesting out there I thought you'd enjoy."

"I'm playing checkers," Daniel answered and looked away.

"If your father wants to show you something, it would be polite to go as soon as you finish your game," Abby said, walking across the room. "And since your grandfather just ended the game by cheating, you're free now." She pushed all the remaining checkers into the pocket of the gaming table. "Go on with you. I'll put this to rights."

Daniel dragged himself to his feet and shuffled over to Josh. "So, what's so interesting?" he asked, his tone not at all to Abby's liking. Had he ever directed that tone at Brendan or her father he'd have gotten a good talking-to if not a flat hand applied to the seat of his pants. But Josh just took the abuse as if it were his due. It seemed the only time he disciplined Daniel was if the boy refused to do something for Abby or one of the Henrys. It was so typical of Joshua to defend everyone but himself.

* * *

With that thought in mind, Abby made short work of the table and followed them even though it violated her personal vow to avoid Joshua at all costs. The trouble with that vow was that her life had quickly become very lonely.

The few friends she'd had now treated her with uncomfortable deference—the kind you show toward someone whose charity you've taken. So Abby didn't feel comfortable talking to them about the new school or the addition to the hospital that would be started next. Loneliness seemed to stalk her these days and the only time she didn't feel alone was in Joshua's arms.

"Would you two please wait for a poor woman in long skirts?" she called out when she'd almost reached them.

Josh stopped and laughed, looking back. "I wondered if you still mourned the loss of short skirts. You've been complaining about it since the day we met."

"As if you wouldn't, were it you forced to wear them."

He let his gaze trail from her head to her toes. "Never having worn so pretty a dress, I couldn't say," Josh replied gallantly.

Abby felt her face color at the compliment. "It's another of your mother's that I took in."

He frowned. "You should have clothes of your own. And Daniel needs a whole new wardrobe, as well. I should have thought of this before. Suppose we plan to go into Philadelphia soon. There are all sorts of shops that sell store clothes for children. And we could visit a seamstress for you and then buy everything else you need in ladies' shops. And there's the World Exhibition for us to see, too."

Abby didn't know what to say but Daniel filled in the awkward moment for her. Unfortunately it was not done with any degree of gratitude or interest. "I like my clothes just fine," he grumbled.

But as usual Josh didn't let Daniel's attitude rattle him. "You can still wear them to play, but you need good clothes for church and the like. And going to the Exhibition is the chance of a lifetime. What do you say, Abby?"

"The Exhibition sounds interesting. I've read a few articles on it. I've never had things as nice as your mother's. They're just fine. Really. But I guess a new dress would be nice. Let's plan on it soon. Now, I'm dying of curiosity. What is this interesting surprise you have for Daniel?" she asked as they approached the stables.

"Look over here," he said, pointing to fenced-in pasture where a small chestnut mare stood placidly eating hay. "That is Ruby and she's all yours, Daniel."

Daniel had started climbing the fence but he froze. His eyes nearly popped out of his head as he stared at the beautiful animal. But he didn't say a word.

"You rode Dakota so well the day of the fire I thought you should have a horse of your own. Would you like to get closer?"

Abby could see the boy holding himself back. He almost smiled but it never happened. Instead when he climbed down, he turned away. "I don't want it! Give it to somebody who'll take your bribes." He ran then before either of them could stop him.

Josh smacked at the fence with the heel of his hand then stared out over the pasture, his jaw rock-hard.

"That boy," Abby said, her heart wrung by the hurt in Josh's eyes. "I'll tan his hide for that! Ungrateful. I'm ashamed to call him son right now. It's sorry I am that he acted that way, Joshua."

"No. Leave him alone. Let's face it, Ab. I was getting desperate. It *was* a bribe, so I guess I'm proud that he can stick to his guns like that. But I wish it wasn't over his hatred of me. He rebuffs every overture I make. Is it so much to ask that my son not hate me?"

She put a hand on his back. "No. No, it's not."

"You know what hurts? I'd have been a father to him all these years if it weren't for Harlan and he's the one Daniel's getting attached to. I'm jealous of that despicable old man. Can you believe that! It's infuriating."

"Mama use to say everything looks better on a full stomach and a good night's sleep. Let's go on up for dinner and make an early night of it."

Josh shook his head and leaned his arms on the top rail of the fence. "I've lost my appetite. I'll be along later."

Daniel looked out his window at the corral and the horse he was too ashamed to take. His father was still there and even from so far away, Daniel could see he was hurt. He felt real bad about that because Joshua Wheaton was a really nice man.

But Daniel also knew he didn't deserve his father's love. He'd ordered him killed back in November and the shame ate at him. He hadn't meant to but the result had almost been the same. Even though Sean Murphy wasn't a member, he'd still given Daniel's message to the Workmen and they'd tried to kill his father. Every time Daniel thought about those days when Joshua Wheaton had lain motionless after they'd beaten him so bad, he wanted to cry. Sometimes late at night he did.

Then when his father found out the way those big boys had ganged up on him, he'd made Uncle Brendan take him home though he wasn't ready. Daniel would never forget how pale and shaking with pain he'd been as they'd helped him into the carriage. All that agony just to keep *him* safe.

And now, try as he might, Daniel just couldn't seem to make his father hate him. He didn't know what else to do. He didn't think he could take the guilt anymore. Maybe he should just confess. Maybe that would make his father hate him without hurting him time and again.

Josh held Abby close as their breathing slowed. Glad he'd left a lamp glowing, he smiled as he brushed strands of her long hair off her face. "You're a wonderful lover. Do you know that?"

"You're complimenting yourself as you've taught me all I know of loving."

Josh stiffened, wishing he'd been her only teacher. At odd times the thought of her and Sullivan lying together haunted him. What had it been like for her with him? Had he hurt her? Had she liked being in his arms? She'd said she only felt this way with him but was that true? He didn't know what demon made him break his promise to himself but he did. "What was it like with Sullivan?"

"Joshua!" She sat up and looked down at him in shock. Her hair was all mussed and tousled and her lips were full and red from his kisses.

And he could have kicked himself for ruining one of their special moments. This was the only place he was happy these days. Abby had the ability to make him forget the mines and Daniel and even the standoffish way she treated him most days. "I'm sorry," he said quickly. "It's none of my business. I shouldn't have asked." He tried to pull her back into his arms, but he'd ruined the moment. Tears had flooded Abby's lovely emerald eyes. "I'm so sorry, Ab. Please don't cry."

"No," she said and shook her head. Josh felt his heart break right there and then. She hadn't refused his embrace in their bedroom since that first time he'd made love to her. This was all of her she would give him.

"I'm sorry," he said again not knowing how to fix what he'd destroyed with a careless comment.

"You've nothing to be sorry for! 'Tis I who am sorry. I'd forgotten you might not know. I even thought to have Brendan tell you but forgot what with the fire and, oh, just everything! Joshua, I married Liam Sullivan practically on his deathbed. I never shared anything with him but his name. He was dying of injuries from an accident at the mines. Doc Burke said it could take weeks and he needed care. Da struck a deal with him. We'd take care of him, if he married me to give my babe a name. It would have worked out fine for Daniel and me except Sullivan realized you had to be the father. He told anyone who came to see him, but swore them to silence until he was gone."

"That son of a bitch."

Abby smiled sadly. "I like to think of the good Lord extracting a bit of punishment each day for his tale carrying."

Josh shook his head and pulled her down onto his shoulder. She came unresisting this time and he sighed in relief. "I wasn't talking about Sullivan though he deserves the appellation, as well. I meant Harlan. He never told me. He just wrote that you'd married my enemy but he'd never told me the truth of why. And of course he never mentioned Sullivan's death."

Josh pushed up on his elbow and kissed her, running his hand from her knee to her shoulder and enjoying her gasp as he passed over her breast. *The hell with my pride. She needs to understand what she means to me.* "What you don't know, love," he said when he broke the kiss, "is why I never came home. I just couldn't live in the same town with you and Sullivan knowing you went to his bed every night."

"Oh, Joshua," she whispered and pulled him down for another heart-stopping kiss. "The only man who's ever touched me is you. You're the only one I ever wanted to. It's why I refused Sean Murphy's offer of marriage when I was so desperate. I couldn't stand the thought of being with him like this. But Sullivan was going to die. There was no doubt of it."

The need to brand her as his overcame him and there was no more time to sort out past or future. There was only time for need and desire and fulfillment as they both rushed toward an expression of something neither had the courage to name. Tomorrow there would be plenty of time for resolutions and words and private vows.

Josh woke before Abby as usual, but this morning when he opened his eyes, he got out of bed with purpose instead of lingering to watch Abby sleep. He intended to confront Harlan immediately. Learning what he had last night was the last straw. Harlan Wheaton would learn about the torment he'd put his son through for years.

Harlan was in the library, the game table already set up for checkers. He sat reading one of the thousands of books that had sat untouched for years. "Good morning, son."

"Actually, it *is* a good morning. I woke up today free for the first time in my life. You know what I'm free of? Guilt. Guilt for not feeling close to my own father. Guilt for despising my own father. Guilt for never wanting to see him again."

Harlan paled. "Joshua, what are you saying?"

"That as soon as I can build us another house, we'll be out of here. I'll see you're well cared for, but you won't be in my life, or in the lives of my wife and children. I just learned Sullivan was practically on his deathbed when Abby married him.

"Do you know the chief reason I stayed away all those years? I was in such incredible pain thinking she'd really married him. I knew I'd kill the son of a bitch if our paths crossed.

"Do you have any idea what you've cost me? I had to force the woman I love to marry me and she resents it. My son has been labeled a bastard from the day he was born because you had our letters to each other stolen."

Josh heard something break in the hall but kept on, unable to stop his tirade and not caring which of the help got an earfull. "And once I had them in my life you still couldn't come clean and tell me you'd lied about Sullivan. You are a twisted, bitter old man, and I can't wait till I never have to set eyes on you again!"

"You're my son," Harlan shouted. "You can't dismiss me from your life. I won't allow it."

"You know what Daniel always says to me? I'm not your son and you aren't my father." Josh didn't wait for a response. He no longer cared what lie his father would tell to get what he wanted. He would never trust a thing the man who'd fathered him said again. The truth had killed any feeling of respect or duty he'd had left.

Josh noticed a broken vase in the hall as he headed for the door. No doubt someone was off getting a broom to clean it up, but with Daniel tearing around the house leaving broken glass wasn't safe. He stopped to pick up the largest shards and detoured through the house.

After dumping the glass and mentioning the vase to Mrs. Henry, he rushed off to a meeting he'd scheduled with the men. He had work assignments to draw up, too, but after that, earning Abby and Daniel's love would be his main priority.

Abby tensed as Henry walked stiffly into the parlor at nearly half past noon. "We've searched the house and grounds. He's nowhere to be found, Miss Abby."

Mr. Marks frowned. "I really must be on my way. As I said,

when he didn't come to school this morning, I worried. With all the trouble over the Workmen being arrested, I thought I should check to make sure all was as it should be. Perhaps one of the children said something untoward to upset him. I'll question each of them and report if any of them knows anything."

Abby squeeze her temples. "When I got him up this morning, he wanted to play checkers with his grandfather before school."

Henry cleared his throat. "Miss Abby, I spoke with Mr. Wheaton. Young Daniel never came to see him this morning. Perhaps we best send for his father."

"Send for whose father?" Josh asked, entering the parlor. They all turned to stare at him, shocked expressions on each of their faces. "What? I came home for supper."

"Daniel never made it to school this morning," Abby explained. "I woke just as you left the room and went to get Daniel up for school. He wanted to play checkers with your father before he left."

"But he never went to see him," Henry said.

Joshua frowned. "You say you got him up just after I left the room?"

Abby felt her stomach flip. Josh looked worried, not angry that Daniel had played hooky. "He went down not five minutes after you. Why?"

Josh looked at Henry and gestured slightly with his head toward Mr. Marks.

"You mentioned needing to get back to the schoolhouse," Henry intoned in his best butler voice. "Allow me to see you to the door." Marks dutifully followed Henry out of the room.

Abby put a hand on Josh's shoulder and cupped his cheek. "You've turned five shades of pale. What is it?" she asked when the two men were gone.

"I had words with Harlan this morning about his lies about you and Sullivan. I think I mentioned that he'd had the letters we sent each other stolen to keep us apart. Has anyone checked Daniel's room?"

"Of course. He isn't there."

"Did anyone check to see if all of his things are still there?"

Abby felt the blood drain from her head. "You think he ran away? He's just a little boy. Where would he go?"

Josh clutched her to him, holding her as if he were afraid she'd be gone next. "If he did run away, I'll find him. I promise," he murmured against her hair.

"Do you understand what I want you to do, Danny?" Sean Murphy demanded.

Daniel understood. He understood a lot. He stared at Sean Murphy and knew he wasn't a friend as much as he was his father's enemy. And he wanted everything his enemy had—especially his wife.

That morning he'd also learned other truths. His father had always loved his mother and his grandfather had kept them apart. The grandfather he'd come to really like a lot was the cause of all his trouble.

"Well, do you?" Murphy asked again.

"S-sure," Daniel said, stalling. That morning, while sneaking away from the house, Daniel had run smack into Murphy. He'd pretended he had a perfect hiding place so Daniel could properly worry his parents and not have to go so far away. He'd gone along, afraid not to, because Murphy had been so persistent. He'd figured he'd just leave and be on his way once he was alone because he hadn't wanted to worry his parents at all. He'd just wanted to go away where he couldn't enjoy their love. Love he didn't deserve.

But Murphy had brought him into an old mine and hadn't

left. Daniel swallowed hard. "You want me to lure my father here so you can kill him."

"That's the plan. It'll look like an accident, then we'll both be well rid of him."

"I can't do it," Daniel said, calm suddenly and not frightened at all. He backed away, knowing what he had to do. "And I don't want to be rid of him. I love him and so does my mother."

He pivoted and ran but Murphy howled with rage and grabbed him, twisting his arm behind his back. Daniel cried out but his resolve didn't weaken. Murphy could kill him, but he'd never lure his father to his death. The day the Workmen had beaten Joshua, Daniel had kept him busy, giving the men time to get into position on Corker Road. It didn't matter that he hadn't known exactly why Sean told him to go over and talk to his father. He'd done it just the same.

Murphy grabbed Daniel by the throat, pressing him against his massive chest to choke off his air. "You'll do as I say!" he whispered in Daniel's ear.

"No!" Daniel gasped.

Murphy loosened his hand. "No, you won't, will you? You've fallen under his spell the way every one else has. No matter. I've another plan."

"What are you going to do?" Daniel asked as he felt a rope loop around his wrist. Daniel tried to wrench himself away, but Murphy pulled his other hand behind his back and bound his wrists together. He kicked the big man several times in the struggle. Murphy shoved him to the ground then put his knee in the middle of Daniel's back to keep him still. Though Daniel fought, his ankles were soon tied to his hands behind the back.

Trussed up like a Christmas turkey, Daniel was spitting mad. "When I get loose, you're going to be sorry," he snarled.

Murphy laughed. "Loose! Danny, you'll be dead in hours. I'm going to leave you here and lure your father with a promise to help find you," Murphy continued. "Then I'm going to blow this mine sky-high and the two of you with it. With both of you gone, there won't be even a little reminder of him for Abby. She'll finally be able to love me."

"No!" Daniel screamed as he struggled against the bonds.

"Scream all you want. No one's going to hear you." He carried Daniel into a small adjacent chamber. "And no one's going to find you in here. You should've cooperated, Danny. We were supposed to be friends," he said as he dumped Daniel on the floor then shoved him head first into a crevice.

All Daniel could hear echoing off the walls as he struggled for air in the pitch blackness was Sean Murphy's scary laugh and water dripping close by. Daniel tried moving. He wasn't really stuck! He had to get out of the crevice, then get free somehow. He had to warn his da. He had to.

Josh had looked everywhere, unmindful of the rain that had twice thundered down in torrential spurts of fury. He couldn't think of anywhere he'd missed and still he hadn't turned up even one sign of Daniel or of anyone who'd seen him. No trains had gone through town today, so he couldn't have hidden in a boxcar to get out of town. He seemed to have vanished off the face of the earth.

There was an even more frightening worry that had occurred to him and had been haunting him for hours. Someone could have kidnapped Daniel knowing the blow would strike at the heart of Wheaton Mining. *His* heart.

He'd been so selfish, Josh thought. He should have sent both Abby and Daniel west where they wanted to go. But he'd kept them there, thinking of himself, not them. Now it was too late. Now Daniel was gone.

"No luck, sir?" Henry asked, opening the door before Josh reached the third step.

Josh shook his head and saw Abby follow Henry outside.

"I just came home to change clothes. I'll go out again as soon as I have," he assured her. "I have Constable Addison and several of the remaining Pinkerton agents looking, as well. No one's seen him, but we'll keep looking."

Except there's virtually nowhere else to look.

Abby's lower lip quivered. "It's getting dark. Where could he be?"

"Joshua Wheaton," a voice called and Josh turned back toward the road.

Sean Murphy came running up the path. "I heard Danny's missing. I don't know if it's anything, but I saw a man I didn't recognize hefting a bag on his back and carrying it into one of the old closed tunnels. I'm thinkin' it would have been just the right shape to hold a boy Danny's size."

Joshua turned back to Abby. "I'll be back, sweetheart. And I'll bring him home safe. I promise."

"Be careful," she urged, reaching a hand out to him.

"Always." He promised and smiled. Taking her hand, he gave it a gentle squeeze. As he turned away from her and jogged down the steps, he nodded to Sean. "Thanks, Murphy."

"I thought you might like a hand. Danny's a great little boy. I may not have a chance to be his father the way I've always hoped, but I still care about him."

Josh shrugged. "Sure. I might need the help. Now which tunnel was it you saw him go into?"

Abby watched Josh pull Sean up behind him to ride pillion and then Sean turned and looked at her. His smile sent a shiver up Abby's spine. She watched as they rode out of sight, and tried to understand her reaction to the often annoyingly persistent Sean Murphy. Then it hit her.

A scene from a day long past flooded her mind. She'd been cleaning in the back of the store when she'd heard Ethan Prescott greet someone as Kane. She'd gone to the front of the store expecting Thomas or Brendan. But it had been Sean standing there.

Since then she'd often noticed Prescott mix up Sean and Brendan, though to her they looked nothing alike. She tried to remember if he'd ever really mixed up any other men as she'd accused that day she'd demanded to see the books. She realized he hadn't. He'd only confused Sean and Brendan.

Did that mean it was Sean Murphy who'd helped frame Brendan? Would Sean turn against a friend? She remembered the day long past when Sean and Brendan had argued about her. Sean had offered to wed her and give Daniel a name but Brendan and her father had already secured Liam Sullivan's cooperation. Sean had been so furious he and Brendan had even come to blows.

Had Joshua just ridden off with an enemy to guard his back?

"Henry, we have to find those Pinkertons Josh has looking for Daniel. What if it was Sean who took Daniel in the first place?"

Chapter Twenty

Josh felt so stupid he wanted to scream. They'd just ridden out of sight of the house when Murphy shoved a gun in his ribs and began to outline his diabolical plans.

Now as they trudged sharply downhill into the bowels of the earth, Josh felt sweat coat his skin in spite of his wet clothing. And it wasn't caused by the gun at his back. The walls were closing in on him. It had happened a few times before when the timbers creaked so much he knew a cave-in was imminent. But these timbers were silent for the most part.

His panic came from fear for Daniel. Josh stopped. "Where's Daniel?"

Murphy poked him hard in the back. "Somewhere deep in the mine. He's trussed up good and proper in a crevice only I know about. It was me who made it, you see, on the last day we worked this mine two years ago. So don't get any ideas. If you jump me, you'll never find him."

The barrel of the shotgun was so close at that moment Josh knew he'd have a fair chance to disarm Murphy. But Daniel was in trouble, tied up somewhere. But he had no idea in what part of the mine.

One thing he did know was that pockets of gas could collect in small crevices and suffocate a man in minutes. He didn't want to think how long it would take to kill a boy.

"Just take me to him," Josh growled through gritted teeth, "and he'd better be alive or you'll have more trouble on your hands than you know what to do with."

Murphy laughed. "And weren't you and Brendan always two peas in a pod? He was supposed to be my friend but he refused to press my suit with Abby. It's her right to decide, he'd always say, but then you came back and soon he was saving your ass from men I'd sent after you."

"You?"

He lifted the lamp higher and stared at Josh. "I want to see your face. I'm the one the AMU listens to. I'm not so much a joke anymore, am I? And just to put a topper on the whole plan, I helped framed Brendan for Destiny."

"You who signed Brendan's initials to that December explosives order?" Josh asked, trying not to show any surprise that the bumbling Sean Murphy had been able to pull off so elaborate a plan of revenge.

"I had to pay him back. He could've helped me with Abby. He had to pay. Just like Daniel had to pay for not luring you here today. What kind of son would he have made for me, I ask you? Disobeying this way. He had to be punished. Now move. It's time to meet your maker, too."

Too? Josh's heart nearly stopped. "Is my son still alive, Murphy?" he demanded.

"Well, of course he is. I couldn't kill Danny."

"But you said you plan to."

"I said I was going to bring the mountain down on the two of you. It'll be doing the killing. Not me."

Josh stared at the man. He was unhinged! And a man with a damaged mind was dangerous.

Murphy kept the gun trained on Josh at all times as they went deeper. He hadn't lied about how far into the old mine he'd hidden Daniel. He shoved Josh and purposely tripped him a few times, laughing with an edge of insanity each time Josh fell in the darkness.

But Josh held his temper for Daniel's sake, and he didn't lose his direction, either. He knew exactly where he needed to go to get back to the main shaft.

"Stop here. Put your hands behind your back."

Instead Josh turned to face Murphy. "Not a chance. You want this all to play out your way, but I draw the line here. You give me Daniel unharmed and untied or you're going to have to shoot me to tie me. And that, *boyo,* won't look like an accident when they find my body," he added in a mocking Irish lilt.

In the muted darkness left by the Davy safety lamp Murphy had set on the floor, Josh never saw the blow from the butt of the shotgun coming. One second he was standing, and what seemed like the next, he woke lying on his side with his hands and feet tied.

"Da, you've got to wake up," he heard Daniel whisper from somewhere near. "Murphy's setting charges."

His eyes filled with emotion, Josh looked into Daniel's worried face. "You called me Da."

"I shouldn't. I haven't the right but I wanted to, at least once."

Josh wondered if the blow to the head had more than just scrambled his brain. "Why shouldn't you? I *am* your da."

"But you deserve better. Not a son who gets you beat up and nearly killed."

"Son, you didn't plan this. Murphy did."

"The other time on Corker Road," Daniel said, tears suddenly flowing. "He told me to talk to you to keep you late.

But I didn't know he told those men to hurt you. He was supposed to make you go away and leave us alone. I didn't ask for dead. I didn't! I wasn't sure it was my fault till those boys grabbed me. They said it was me who ordered you killed. I didn't mean it. You yelled at Ma and I was mad."

Josh blinked. "Let me get this straight. The day Sean took you out of the company store to calm you down, he told you what?"

"I said I wanted you gone. He said he had some friends who could make you go away for good. He said he loved Ma but she'd only ever loved you. He said if you were gone he'd be my da. It sounded like a good idea, because I thought you never wanted me."

"So the boys who grabbed you made you think you were an accomplice. Dan, no AMU leader sends men to kill a mine owner on the say-so of a nine-year-old boy."

Daniel sniffled. "You should hate me. I tried to make you hate me, but you just wouldn't no matter how hard I tried. I'm sorry. I really liked Ruby. I wish I took the chance to ride her."

"You will ride her. I promise. Now listen to me. Can you scoot around and get your feet up here near my hands where I can work on those knots?"

"Sure, that's how I got out of that crack and got this far."

So Murphy thought Daniel was still where he put him. Good.

"Da." Daniel's voice was but a whisper some minutes later. "I wish just once I'd have let you hug me."

"Me, too," Josh said. He wanted to reassure Daniel that there would be plenty of time later for hugs, but he couldn't bring himself to lie by promising something he didn't think he'd be able to deliver. His chances of getting both of them free were slim to none. But he'd be damned if he'd let Daniel die in the same mines that had destroyed his own life.

It took him several minutes but he finally loosened the knot and had Daniel's feet free. "Okay now, Dan," he said, shimmying along the ground while he gathered the extra rope in a coil. "Now take the rope and get to your feet. Hold it tight, son, and don't drop it. It could snag on something. I want you to run for the shaft and get to the surface. It's a long, tough incline to the top, but you can make it. I know you can."

"But what about you?"

"I'll try to be along, Dan. But you have to get going, so you can tell everyone what's going on down here. Always take the left-hand tunnel and you'll get to the shaft. Watch out for Murphy. If he's ahead of you, hide in a breast till he passes you on his way back here. He'll have to come back to untie me if he's going to make this look like an accident. Go on now and tell your ma I love her."

Daniel hesitated.

"Go!" Josh urged.

Daniel scurried into the darkness, and Josh scooted along the floor till he was back in the position Murphy had left him in. It wasn't long till Murphy returned.

Josh pretended unconsciousness, and, as he'd thought, Murphy untied him. Josh kicked hard with both feet just as Murphy stood. The big miner tripped and fell backward.

Josh scrabbled toward him but Murphy was faster than Josh thought he'd be. The gun was in Murphy's hand and he cackled, sounding anything but sane.

"Do you think I'm stupid, Wheaton? You aren't getting out of here alive. I've planned well. You and your bastard will be dead, and I'll be there to comfort and help Abby when your father tosses her and Michael out on the street and no one will be the wiser."

Daniel was free so what did he have to lose? Josh grinned, hoping to make Murphy angry enough that he'd make a mistake. "Are you sure? After all *you* set the charges. I hear you're as clumsy with explosives as you are at dancing and Abby had plenty to say about the agonies of dancing with you."

Murphy bellowed and fired at him. Josh was ready and dove to the side but the bullet caught him in the shoulder and spun him around. Stunned momentarily he saw Murphy pivot and run into the tunnel.

Josh stood and reached for the Davy lamp when somewhere in the tunnel an explosion rocked the mountain. Josh dropped and rolled against the wall as rubble fell and Murphy's scream reverberated down the tunnel toward him. Josh covered his head as shock after shock shook the earth. Rocks and dirt rained down but the wall at his back stayed intact as did most of the chamber where he was. He coughed as he pushed himself to his feet cradling his arm. He moved cautiously toward the main shaft only to encounter a wall of coal and rock. He swallowed hard.

Murphy had surely been caught in his own trap, but so had he. He might very well be as much a dead man as Murphy probably already was.

Daniel scrabbled up the last of the old track. The light ahead was almost blinding. His da had been right about the incline being hard going, but he pushed on knowing he needed to get help. He was sure his father had sent him to safety thinking he wouldn't live by the way he'd said to tell Ma, *"I love you."* Daniel just couldn't let that happen.

His legs shaking, he stumbled out of the tunnel just as his mother and a bunch of Pinkerton men came running toward him. He looked up into her tear-filled eyes as she hugged him.

His mother took his face in her hands. "Oh, you're all dirty and scratched up but thank the Lord you're safe. Have you seen your father?" she asked as someone untied his hands.

"Back in there," he answered. "Da got my feet untied and sent me out. We got to get him help. Sean Murphy's crazy, Ma. He's going to kill him." Daniel burst into tears and wrapped his arms around her waist.

And then Abby's heart tore in two as a huge chain of explosions rocked the earth and spewed up dust from the old tunnel.

"Joshua!" she screamed and let go of Daniel to run toward the yawning entrance, calling his name over and over. Someone grabbed her around the waist and pulled her back. She stared at the mine as it continued to belch black dust.

An odd thought crossed her mind that was frightening in its possible prophecy. This was the same mine where a cave-in years ago first brought Joshua into her life. A man/boy wanting to fill his father's soiled shoes by helping dig for a man he'd never met but whose life he'd felt responsible for. Had that same mine taken him out of her life now?

Abby felt a hand settle on her shoulder. She whirled to face Brian McAllister. He gently dried her tears with a dingy handkerchief and only then did she realize she was crying.

"Abaigeal, he didn't give up on me and though I swore to never enter another tunnel, I'm here to tell you I won't rest till he's out of there. Joshua Wheaton knows mines. If anyone could find a safe pocket, he could."

He turned. "Let's get to it, men," he shouted to the miners the explosions had drawn, "that's our boss down there."

With picks and shovels and lanterns the Irish workers from the first shift moved toward the entrance. The Welshmen talked softly amongst themselves then followed as did the German and the English after them.

She prayed he'd live to see that one of his dreams had been realized. Ethnic origin had ceased to be a consideration in Wheatonburg. They all worked together, shoulder-to-shoulder, because they all respected Josh.

And she loved him.

But she'd never told him.

She'd refused to trust him, though none of the strife that had torn their young lives apart had been his fault. She'd guarded her pride, lest she let him know of her love because he felt only obligation to her. She'd hidden her love behind closed doors and under the covers of their bed like some guilty secret.

Now, without him, her life would once again be no life at all.

"Ma," Daniel said, tugging on her skirt to get her attention. "He said to tell you he loves you. Is he dead?"

Abby thought if ever words could kill, Joshua's message would have dealt her a death blow. But she couldn't lie down and die of her breaking heart. She'd failed him enough in the last weeks. She straightened her shoulders.

"No. No, he isn't. And we're going to dig 'round the clock to get him out of there."

Brian McAllister came out of the tunnel and walked back to her then, shaking his head. "Murphy brought it down good and proper. We need more men, Abby. Cars back on these tracks. Mules to pull them out once we've fill them with rubble. And lumber for temporary shoring."

"I'll send Daniel for Helmut Faltsburg. You'll have anything you need. Just get him out of there," she begged.

Brian McAllister helped Helmut organize rescue operations and kept her abreast of their progress. But each time he approached her, he looked less and less hopeful. It was near dawn when she saw his silhouette moving toward her in the shadow of the torches that lit the area outside the shaft.

The young miner dropped to a log next to her. "We're running out of time, Abaigeal. We just aren't making the kind of progress we need to if he was at the back of the mine where Daniel says he left him. We want to try something. Helmut just got back from talkin' to Harlan Wheaton. He's not for our idea but that's because he's not…not—"

"Not what, Brian?" she demanded.

McAllister looked at the ground. "He's thinking this is a recovery not a rescue." Her silence had him looking up at her. "He thinks we're after a body. Not Joshua. He's given up and doesn't want to waste more resources. A lot of the men are giving up, as well."

"It's only been twelve hours!" She would not accept that. "I'd know. I'd *know* if he were gone. What is it you're wanting to do?"

"Helmut and I want to use explosives."

Abby stared at the man. No wonder Harlan hadn't agreed. "But—"

"Listen to me. We don't have a lot of time. He's got to be running out of air. I've been playing with dynamite and nitro all my life. Helmut knows these tunnels and where they go. I'm talking about a controlled explosion. We want to try reaching him from another tunnel. Helmut says Josh was working on a plan to use this old tunnel to vent Lilybet. We can't find his drawings but—"

That perked up Abby's spirits. "Drawings? He was working on something at home. He left drawings in the study!"

"Can you get them?"

"Let Harlan Wheaton try to stop me!"

Brian gave her a sharp nod. "Then I'll start readying the charges."

* * *

Abby looked up at the moon. The second night of Joshua's interment in the old mine was just about at an end. She'd given Helmut the plans Josh had left in the study nearly twenty-four hours earlier. She hadn't been able to sleep more than a few hours through the night. Drawn to be as close to Josh as she could be, she'd returned to sit huddled near the fire where the men warmed up before going back inside Lilybet to remove the debris from Brian's small, controlled explosions.

Someone laid a blanket over her shoulders and she looked up, nodding a thank-you to one of the coal-covered men who was trying to save Joshua's life. The men had sent ton after ton of rubble out to the slag heap and still Brian blasted. And they dug. And they hauled. They'd all had as little sleep as her.

Josh dropped back down and closed his eyes. He couldn't work any longer. He was using up what oxygen there was left on a futile effort. They had probably given up hope already and he wasn't going to dig himself out. Especially when he couldn't even see his own progress. He closed his eyes and fought tears. All he'd ever wanted was to keep this from happening to other men. Now he'd die the way countless miners had gone before him, and the way countless more would follow.

In the long dark hours since the explosions had walled him in, he'd faced a tough truth. He'd wasted his life. Mining would never be safe. Men were still going to die wresting a living from the bowels of the earth in a hundred years from then. He'd been a fool to spend his life fighting the inevitable.

The worst part was he'd had a second chance for happiness and he'd thrown it away. He'd been handed his fondest wish. He'd been granted the second chance with Abby he'd always wanted, and he'd made the same mistakes again. He'd wanted their lives to follow *his* plan just like last time. He hadn't listened to what Abby wanted from life. Once before he had ignored her wishes and he'd lost her. And now he had lost again.

Had he taken the time to woo her? Had he promised to grant *her* fondest wish by taking her west where their pasts would no longer haunt her or their son?

No.

He'd blackmailed her into marriage then entombed her in Wheatonburg the way he was now entombed in one of its mines. It was the height of irony that this was the same damned mine that had started his life on the wrong path.

What a fitting end.

He put his head back against the cold rock and wished for Abby's soft breast to cushion his last sleep.

Abby listened to yet another explosion echo from Lilybet. It was high noon and the sun was strong, warming the workers who milled about. She looked around and realized most of the people in the town had drifted to the mine fields. Several women came up to her to pay their respects and Abby wanted to tell them to go away—that she was not the Widow Wheaton yet. But she held her tongue. They, like her, wanted something to do and trying to offer comfort was all they could think to do.

Abby was not so lucky. Daniel leaned against her side. He was like a little ghost, shadowing her, seldom taking his eyes off Lilybet's entrance.

"Ma," he whispered, his voice quivering as he pointed to an ore car being pulled from the mine. Abby held her breath as miners flooded from the tunnel. Her heart stopped. There was a stretcher atop the oar car. Brian McAllister walked next to it.

Daniel started to pull her that way and Abby's steps faltered. She stumbled and the blood rushed in her ears. She couldn't hear if the men were jubilant or mourning. All she knew was that a blanket covered Joshua, even his face.

When she reached the edge of the crowd it parted for her and Daniel. Her tears rained down. Why did they always have to bring the bodies out on the ore cars? It was like being thrust into the middle of a funeral cortege when you hadn't yet been told the deceased was gone.

"Joshua," she whispered as she reached for the blanket covering his beloved face.

Brian grabbed her hand. "He's been underground for two days."

"I need to see him," she sobbed. She wouldn't believe he was gone until she looked at him. Cold. Still. Lifeless.

"Let us get him in the shade of the ore car. He needs time to get used to the light."

"He's alive?" she asked, her voice choked with tears.

"Now didn't I promise to get him out of there for you? Murphy shot him but it doesn't look too bad. He's unconscious, though. The air had gotten pretty thin in there but luckily there was scarcely any firedamp. We sent for Doc Burke."

She noticed Daniel crying softly then and took his face in her hands. "Do you hear that? Your da is alive." Then she hugged her son fiercely as they lifted the stretcher to the ground and into the shade of the ore car.

Abby dropped to her knees at Josh's side and pulled the blanket away. His face was covered with coal dust and his blond hair was dulled by it, but to her he looked beautiful. Someone brought a bucket of water with a ladle and handed her a towel. She spilled some water on the towel and wiped away the worst of the dirt. He had a nasty cut on his temple, too. He winced and moaned when she touched it with the cloth.

With Brian's help, she pillowed Josh's face against her breasts and tried to get him to drink. More of it spilled down her front than went between his lips, but his tongue came out to capture some of the liquid and his eyelids flickered. He squinted and his eyes opened to look at her.

"Am I alive or is heaven our last wish being granted into eternity?"

"Oh, and didn't he kiss the Blarney stone when he visited the old sod," Brian joked and stood. He must have given some sort of sign, because a great cheer went up across the coal field.

But Abby had eyes only for Joshua.

"Is Daniel okay?" he asked, his voice husky, his throat clearly raw.

"Right as rain now that his da is safe." Abby glanced up at their son. "Isn't that right, Daniel?"

Daniel sniffled and wiped his eyes on his shirt sleeve before stepping to where Josh could see him. "You okay, Da?"

Josh nodded. "Fine," he tried to say, but it came out like a croak.

"Here. Have some more water," Abby said and helped him drink. "Is there anything else you want?"

"Just hold me," he whispered.

Abby looked around and noticed all eyes were upon them still. There were friends there, but there were also people who'd treated her like a leper for years. And it was those people who had made her ashamed of her feelings for him.

"I love you," she told him boldly for all to hear. "I've loved you from the day we met. I've never stopped loving you. Not for one minute of the last ten years, and I won't stop for the next hundred and ten, either."

Josh smiled, his eyes suddenly bright. "And I love you, Ab. We're leaving here. You, me and Daniel. If your father wants to come along, he's welcome. We're going west the way you wanted. I'll find something to do out there. I don't care what. I'm sorry I threatened you to get what I wanted, and that I didn't listen to what you need. I promise I'll make it up to you."

"Oh, but you already have. You saved Daniel and you came out alive. That's all I care about."

"And all I care about is you and Daniel," he said. Josh smiled and held his good arm up to Daniel, who sank into his father's embrace for the first of a lifetime of hugs. Then, with his blue eyes shining in the sunlight, Josh pulled her close, too.

They were a family at last.

* * * * *

Celebrate 60 years of
pure reading pleasure with Harlequin®!
Silhouette® Romantic Suspense
is celebrating with the glamour-filled,
adrenaline-charged series
LOVE IN 60 SECONDS
starting in April 2009.
Six stories that promise to bring the glitz
of Las Vegas, the danger of revenge, the mystery
of a missing diamond, family scandals
and ripped-from-the-headlines intrigue.
Get your heart racing
as love happens in sixty seconds!

Enjoy a sneak peek of
USA TODAY bestselling author
Marie Ferrarella's
THE HEIRESS'S 2-WEEK AFFAIR
Available April 2009
from Silhouette® Romantic Suspense.

Eight years ago Matt Shaffer had vanished out of Natalie Rothchild's life, leaving behind a one-line note tucked under a pillow that had grown cold: *I'm sorry, but this just isn't going to work.*

That was it. No explanation, no real indication of remorse. The note had been as clinical and compassionless as an eviction notice, which, in effect, it had been, Natalie thought as she navigated through the morning traffic. Matt had written the note to evict her from his life.

She'd spent the next two weeks crying, breaking down without warning as she walked down the street, or as she sat staring at a meal she couldn't bring herself to eat.

Candace, she remembered with a bittersweet pang, had tried to get her to go clubbing in order to get her to forget about Matt.

She'd turned her twin down, but she did get her act together. If Matt didn't think enough of their relationship to try to contact her, to try to make her understand why he'd changed so radically from lover to stranger, then to hell with him. He was dead to her, she resolved. And he'd remained that way.

Until twenty minutes ago.

The adrenaline in her veins kept mounting.

Natalie focused on her driving. Vegas in the daylight wasn't nearly as alluring, as magical and glitzy as it was after dark. Like an aging woman best seen in soft lighting, Vegas's imperfections were all visible in the daylight. Natalie supposed that was why people like her sister didn't like to get up until noon. They lived for the night.

Except that Candace could no longer do that.

The thought brought a fresh, sharp ache with it.

"Damn it, Candy, what a waste," Natalie murmured under her breath.

She pulled up before the Janus casino. One of the three valets currently on duty came to life and made a beeline for her vehicle.

"Welcome to the Janus," the young attendant said cheerfully as he opened her door with a flourish.

"We'll see," she replied solemnly.

As he pulled away with her car, Natalie looked up at the casino's logo. Janus was the Roman god with two faces, one pointed toward the past, the other facing the future. It struck her as rather ironic, given what she was doing here, seeking out someone from her past in order to get answers so that the future could be settled.

The moment she entered the casino, the Vegas phenomena took hold. It was like stepping into a world where time did not matter or even make an appearance. There was only a sense of "now."

Because in Natalie's experience she'd discovered that bartenders knew the inner workings of any establishment they worked for better than anyone else, she made her way to the first bar she saw within the casino.

The bartender in attendance was a gregarious man in his early forties. He had a quick, sexy smile, which was probably one of the main reasons he'd been hired. His name tag identified him as Kevin.

Moving to her end of the bar, Kevin asked, "What'll it be, pretty lady?"

"Information." She saw a dubious look cross his brow. To counter that, she took out her badge. Granted she wasn't here in an official capacity, but Kevin didn't need to know that. "Were you on duty last night?"

Kevin began to wipe the gleaming black surface of the bar. "You mean during the gala?"

"Yes."

The smile gracing his lips was a satisfied one. Last night had obviously been profitable for him, she judged. "I caught an extra shift."

She took out Candace's photograph and carefully placed it on the bar. "Did you happen to see this woman there?"

The bartender glanced at the picture. Mild interest turned to recognition. "You mean Candace Rothchild? Yeah, she was here, loud and brassy as always. But not for long," he added, looking rather disappointed. There was always a circus when Candace was around, Natalie thought. "She and the boss had at it and then he had our head of security escort her out."

She latched onto the first part of his statement. "They argued? About what?"

He shook his head. "Couldn't tell you. Too far away for anything but body language," he confessed.

"And the head of security?" she asked.

"He got her to leave."

She leaned in over the bar. "Tell me about him."

"Don't know much," the bartender admitted. "Just that his name's Matt Shaffer. Boss flew him in from L.A., where he was head of security for Montgomery Enterprises."

There was no avoiding it, she thought darkly. She was going to have to talk to Matt. The thought left her cold. "Do you know where I can find him right now?"

Kevin glanced at his watch. "He should be in his office. On the second floor, toward the rear." He gave her the numbers of the rooms where the monitors that kept watch over the casino guests as they tried their luck against the house were located.

Taking out a twenty, she placed it on the bar. "Thanks for your help."

Kevin slipped the bill into his vest pocket. "Anytime, lovely lady," he called after her. "Anytime."

She debated going up the stairs, then decided on the elevator. The car that took her up to the second floor was empty. Natalie stepped out of the elevator, looked around to get her bearings and then walked toward the rear of the floor.

"Into the Valley of Death rode the six hundred," she silently recited, digging deep for a line from a poem by Tennyson. Wrapping her hand around a brass handle, she opened one of the glass doors and walked in.

The woman whose desk was closest to the door looked up. "You can't come in here. This is a restricted area."

Natalie already had her ID in her hand and held it up. "I'm looking for Matt Shaffer," she told the woman.

God, even saying his name made her mouth go dry. She was supposed to be over him, to have moved on with her life. What happened?

The woman began to answer her. "He's—"

"Right here."

The deep voice came from behind her. Natalie felt every single nerve ending go on tactical alert at the same moment that all the hairs at the back of her neck stood up. Eight years had passed, but she would have recognized his voice anywhere.

* * * * *

*Why did Matt Shaffer leave
heiress-turned-cop Natalie Rothchild?
What does he know about
the death of Natalie's twin sister?
Come and meet these two reunited lovers
and learn the secrets of the Rothchild family in*
THE HEIRESS'S 2-WEEK AFFAIR
by USA TODAY *bestselling author
Marie Ferrarella.
The first book in Silhouette® Romantic Suspense's
wildly romantic new continuity,*
LOVE IN 60 SECONDS!
Available April 2009.

You're invited to join our Tell Harlequin Reader Panel!

By joining our new reader panel you will:

- Receive Harlequin® books—they are FREE and yours to keep with no obligation to purchase anything!
- Participate in fun online surveys
- Exchange opinions and ideas with women just like you
- Have a say in our new book ideas and help us publish the best in women's fiction

In addition, you will have a chance to win great prizes and receive special gifts!
See Web site for details. Some conditions apply.
Space is limited.

To join, visit us at
www.TellHarlequin.com.

REQUEST YOUR FREE BOOKS!

Harlequin® Historical
Historical Romantic Adventure!

2 FREE NOVELS PLUS 2 FREE GIFTS!

YES! Please send me 2 FREE Harlequin® Historical novels and my 2 FREE gifts (gifts are worth about $10). After receiving them, if I don't wish to receive any more books, I can return the shipping statement marked "cancel". If I don't cancel, I will receive 6 brand-new novels every month and be billed just $4.94 per book in the U.S. or $5.49 per book in Canada, plus 25¢ shipping and handling per book and applicable taxes, if any*. That's a savings of 20% off the cover price! I understand that accepting the 2 free books and gifts places me under no obligation to buy anything. I can always return a shipment and cancel at any time. Even if I never buy another book, the two free books and gifts are mine to keep forever.

246 HDN ERUM 349 HDN ERUA

Name	(PLEASE PRINT)
Address	Apt. #
City	State/Prov. Zip/Postal Code

Signature (if under 18, a parent or guardian must sign)

Mail to the Harlequin Reader Service:
IN U.S.A.: P.O. Box 1867, Buffalo, NY 14240-1867
IN CANADA: P.O. Box 609, Fort Erie, Ontario L2A 5X3

Not valid to current subscribers of Harlequin Historical books.

Want to try two free books from another line?
Call 1-800-873-8635 or visit www.morefreebooks.com.

* Terms and prices subject to change without notice. N.Y. residents add applicable sales tax. Canadian residents will be charged applicable provincial taxes and GST. Offer not valid in Quebec. This offer is limited to one order per household. All orders subject to approval. Credit or debit balances in a customer's account(s) may be offset by any other outstanding balance owed by or to the customer. Please allow 4 to 6 weeks for delivery. Offer available while quantities last.

Your Privacy: Harlequin Books is committed to protecting your privacy. Our Privacy Policy is available online at www.eHarlequin.com or upon request from the Reader Service. From time to time we make our lists of customers available to reputable third parties who may have a product or service of interest to you. If you would prefer we not share your name and address, please check here. ☐

HH08R

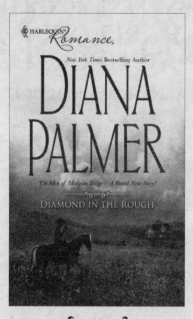

DIAMOND IN THE ROUGH

John Callister is a millionaire rancher, yet when he meets lovely Sassy Peale and she thinks he's a cowboy, he goes along with her misconception. He's had enough of gold diggers, and this is a chance to be valued for himself, not his money. But when Sassy finds out the truth, she feels John was merely playing with her. John will have to convince her that he's truly the man she fell in love with—a diamond in the rough.

THE MEN OF MEDICINE RIDGE—a brand-new miniseries set in the wilds of Montana!

Available April 2009 wherever you buy books.

www.eHarlequin.com

HRI7577